CRADLE TO GRAVE

A DETECTIVE KAY HUNTER MURDER MYSTERY

RACHEL AMPHLETT

SAXON
PUBLISHING

Copyright © 2019 by Rachel Amphlett

All rights reserved.

No part of this book may be reproduced, stored in a retrieval system, or transmitted by any means, electronic, mechanical, photocopying or otherwise, without the prior written permission of the author.

This is a work of fiction. While the locations in this book are a mixture of real and imagined, the characters are totally fictitious. Any resemblance to actual people living or dead is entirely coincidental.

ONE

Michael Cornish placed his hand on his young son's shoulder as they crossed the footbridge over the River Medway, mindful of the hidden dangers from the dark waters below.

The seven-year-old hadn't stopped talking since they'd left their house in Loose half an hour earlier. At first he'd been sleepy, grumbling about being woken at six o'clock in the morning. Then, as Michael had checked in his rear-view mirror that the boy had fastened his seat belt properly, Daniel's face had broken into a wide grin, his sheer joy and excitement at the prospect of spending the day fishing with his dad evident by the questions peppered from the back seat as the car had woven through the roads towards the river.

Michael knew it wouldn't last.

It was this fear that now kept Michael's attention on

the narrow stone-covered path that snaked away from the blue railings of the bridge and along a public byway at the water's edge. He couldn't shake the thought that he only had a few more years left before Daniel decided that hanging out with his dad on a Saturday morning was the last thing he wanted to do.

Fear turned to sadness; a pre-emptive grief.

'Dad, look!'

Michael turned his attention to the heron that rose into the sky.

'We scared him, right?'

'He'll be back, don't worry. I've seen him here before. Mind your step.'

He tightened his grip as Daniel stumbled, then righted himself.

As they walked, Michael turned his gaze to three boats on the far side of the riverbank, varying sizes of cabin cruiser that bobbed on a gentle current, colourful hulls offset by white decking. In all but the first one, the curtains were closed, the owners away – or enjoying a lie-in.

A lone figure sat on the back deck of the first cruiser, an older man who wore a baseball cap as he polished a brass trombone, the metalwork gleaming in the sunlight. He raised his hand in greeting as they passed.

Daniel waved back, grinning. 'Do you think he's going to play that, Dad?'

'I hope not. I don't think his neighbours would thank him for it this time of the morning. Maybe he was playing in a band last night, or getting ready for tonight.'

'Could we hire a boat one day?'

'Of course. We'll have to check with your mum first.'

'She could come, too. She'd like it.'

'You're right, I think she would.'

'Will I catch anything?' Unperturbed by the terrain, the boy swatted his bamboo pole fishing net at a patch of stinging nettles they passed.

'Maybe some small stuff. Remember what I said, though – you need to be quiet and keep still, otherwise you'll scare them away.'

'Okay.' Daniel lifted the bright-red net to his face and pushed his glasses up his nose, frowning. 'Hope I catch more than just tadpoles this time.'

'Wrong time of year, mate. Don't worry. You'll get something, I'm sure.'

His son's enthusiasm took him back to his time growing up in Tovil, fishing with his own father at this very spot and trying to land something bigger than a minnow.

Not a pike, though.

Something special.

Then he'd gotten older, and for years the river hadn't factored into his life at all. It wasn't until he and

Michelle had Daniel that he'd remembered what it was like to be that age – and what he missed about it. He might work all hours in his role as a mobile mechanic, but he spent time with Daniel whenever he could, knowing Michelle relished the few hours of peace and quiet their Saturday outings afforded her.

Michael's attention was taken by a sudden rumble to his right, moments before a three-car passenger train roared past, its wheels swooshing along the line towards Paddock Wood. As it disappeared between the trees, a calmness returned to the riverbank.

A soft *plop* reached him, and he paused, crouching next to his son.

'Keep still. See that log poking out from the bank?'

'Yeah.'

'The water's rippling, see?'

'Why? What is it?'

'Either a water vole, or an otter. Quiet now.'

Holding his breath, Michael pointed at movement on the water's surface as a sleek brown streak of fur burst from the water and scampered up the opposite bank.

'Otter! We saw an otter!' Daniel spun around and grinned at him. 'That was so cool.'

'Did you like that?'

'Yeah – wait until I tell them at school next week.' He slipped his hand into Michael's and tugged. 'Let's fish, Dad.'

'Okay. There's a good spot along here, over by that

tree. Your granddad used to bring me here when I was your age. Let's go.'

Moments later, Michael cast off his line and dug his boots into the soft undergrowth, his shoulders relaxing.

Daniel crouched at the water's edge, his brow furrowed as he swept his net back and forth in the shallows, and Michael smiled at the boy's expression of sheer concentration. A light breeze ruffled his strawberry-blond hair that was darkening every year, another reminder that his childhood was passing too fast for his father's liking.

Michael craned his neck to see further up the riverbank, but saw no-one else. They had the place to themselves. Not that he was overly surprised – with the summer drawing to its inevitable end, most people were making the most of the weather and spending Friday nights having barbecues or sitting outside in pub gardens until darkness set in. It was only because it was his turn to be designated driver last night that he was here, and Michelle was having a lie-in.

'What do you think, shall we buy some cakes on the way home? Do you think your mum would like that?'

'Yes!' Daniel grinned up at him, then went back to inspecting his net. 'Haven't caught anything yet, Dad.'

'Patience, kiddo. Waiting is half the fun.'

Michael's gaze turned back to the river, and he blinked as he caught sight of some *thing* further upstream.

For a moment, he couldn't understand what he was

seeing. The spread-eagled form floated along on the gentle current, brushing against the reeds that clumped against the bank only a few metres away, then spun around on an eddy and drew closer.

A chill crept across Michael's shoulders, goosebumps rising on his arms. He swallowed, gagging as the form became something more tangible, more terrifying.

It drew closer, water lapping over the dark material covering the lower half, the upper end covered in dark matted hair that seemed to—

'Daniel? Grab your net. We're going.'

'But, Dad—'

'Now, please.'

He reached out and steered Daniel away from the riverbank so he was facing the train line instead, all the while fighting down a rising panic.

Pulling out his mobile phone, he peered at the screen.

No signal.

Heart racing, he wound in his line, cursing under his breath as it snagged and tangled around the reel. He snipped the trailing hook and dropped that and the broken line into the tackle box, wrapped his fingers around the handle, and then grabbed Daniel's wrist.

'Come on. Back to the car.'

'What's wrong, Daddy?'

'Nothing. I just remembered I promised your mum I'd have you home by now.'

'But we only just got here.'

'I know. We'll do this another day, though. Promise.'

Michael bit back the lie, knowing he would never fish on this stretch of the river again.

Maybe never fish again.

Ever.

As they approached the footbridge, he glanced over his shoulder to the waterway. The trombone player had disappeared inside the cabin on his boat, the others were still deserted.

Beyond, by the tree he'd been standing under with his son only moments ago, the body continued its gruesome journey.

He placed the tackle box on the ground and looked at his phone again. Two bars of signal, thank God.

'What is your emergency, please?'

'Police.'

'Putting you through.'

'Daddy?' Daniel's voice hit a higher note, and he stepped closer to Michael, dropping his fishing net next to the tackle box. His bottom lip quivered. 'What's going on?'

He gave Daniel a gentle shove. 'Go and wait by the car. I'll be there in a second.'

Michael's son trudged onwards, not asking why, and not turning back. His heart gave a lurch; his son would never understand, because he'd never tell him what he'd seen.

'Hello? What is your emergency, please?'

Michael took a deep breath, realising at that moment his life would never be the same. He closed his eyes, and tried to keep his voice steady.

'There's a dead man floating down the River Medway near Tovil Bridge.'

TWO

Detective Inspector Kay Hunter slammed shut the door of the mud-streaked silver pool car and hurried after her detective sergeant.

Ian Barnes, late forties, greyer around the temples this past year, held up the crime scene tape draped between two ornamental posts, and pointed at the river running beneath their feet.

'This is the outer cordon,' he said. 'The body got tangled up under one of the pylons of the bridge after the call came in. Uniform organised the underwater search team and forensics.'

'Witness?' said Kay.

'Got sent home after his initial statement was taken. You heard he had his seven-year-old son with him?'

'Christ. Did the boy see it?'

'No. I figured uniform did the right thing in the circumstances.'

'Sounds good.'

They paused in the middle of the bridge and Kay peered over the railings, hooking a tendril of blonde hair behind her ear.

Below, the pathway alongside the River Medway was teeming with white-suited forensic specialists and their accumulated equipment.

A team of three divers stood up to their knees in the shallows, their attention taken by activities underneath the steel and concrete construction. A fourth diver emerged from the middle of the water to Kay's left, his neoprene suit glistening as he raised his hand and gestured to his colleagues.

'All clear there, then,' said Barnes.

A group of six people were milling about on a concrete pier beside the boats. Two uniformed officers stood close by with their notebooks out, one holding a radio to his mouth.

'What about the boat owners?' Kay pointed to the three cabin cruisers further upstream on the opposite bank. She spotted two women amongst the men, and all seemed to be middle-aged or older. 'What do we know about them?'

'Locals. One couple – the pair nearest that boat at the end – are from Thanet. Apparently, they come down here every other weekend for a break. The ones who own the middle boat are from Yalding and stopped here overnight on their way up to the estuary later today. All bar one of them were asleep,' said Barnes. 'The nearest boat is owned by a local jazz musician. He saw our witness this morning as he was making his way up the riverbank towards a popular fishing spot. You can see it up there, by that beech tree.'

Kay shielded her eyes against the morning sunlight.

The riverbank curved away from Tovil, its path mirrored by the railway line to the right beyond a line of trees. A wide grassy bank sloped gently from the railway line to the Medway Footpath that stretched onwards towards East Farleigh and beyond. Wild flowers flourished, and a pair of swans graced the water's edge. The whole vista was one of Kentish idyll.

Except for the body underneath the bridge where she stood.

She slapped her hands on the railing and turned. 'Let's go. Who's in charge down there?'

'Harry Davis. He was out on patrol with Parker when the call came in. They were first on scene.'

Kay followed Barnes down the other side of the footbridge and raised her hand at the older police sergeant who hovered on the footpath.

'Morning, Harry. Good work getting this organised.'

He handed a clipboard to her. 'Thanks, guv. Morning, Ian.'

Kay signed the crime scene log, then paused at the blue and white tape that fluttered in the breeze off the waterway and cast her gaze towards the group of divers now conversing with the CSIs on the path a few metres away.

'What's the current status?'

Harry turned and gestured towards a form that lay amongst a tangle of reeds beside one of the divers. He wrinkled his nose. 'They've managed to retrieve the body from the bridge pylon about ten minutes ago. Harriet is here. Lucas is around somewhere – he's already confirmed the bloke is dead.'

Kay sought out the Home Office pathologist and spotted him further up the riverbank, the tops of office buildings in Maidstone visible through the line of trees beyond his position.

Lucas Anderson held his mobile phone to his ear while he gesticulated in the air. He saw her, pointed to his watch, then returned to his phone call.

Kay's eyes moved to the shortest of the three CSIs cloaked in white suits as the CSI lead, Harriet Baker, started to move towards them.

'Morning, you two,' she said. She tugged at the mask that covered her mouth and nose, then jerked her gloved thumb over her shoulder. 'You're going to have one hell of a job identifying him.'

Kay's heart fell. 'Has he been in the water too long?'

'No – he hasn't got a face.'

A stunned silence followed Harriet's words.

'You what?' said Barnes eventually.

'Yes, I know. God knows who he pissed off but he didn't fall in the Medway by accident, that much is certain,' said the CSI lead.

'Bloody hell,' said Kay. She glanced over her shoulder as Lucas approached. 'Morning.'

'Kay.' He shook hands with her, then Barnes, and tucked his phone into his pocket.

'Busy morning?' said Barnes, raising an eyebrow.

'I've got two technicians on holiday,' said Lucas. 'And now, this.'

'All right,' said Kay. 'Fill us in, you two – what have you managed to ascertain so far?'

Lucas scratched his chin. 'Obviously I'll confirm once the post mortem is complete, but Harriet's probably told you our man is missing most of his face. Initial examination seems to point to a gunshot wound to the back of the head, with the exit wound causing the damage to the front.'

'How long has he been in there, do you think?' said Kay.

'Not long. There isn't a lot of bloating to his body, so assuming he fell – or was pushed – face down, I don't think he ingested much water, and I doubt there's enough in his lungs to suggest he drowned. Again, I'll confirm once we do the PM.'

'Was he killed along this stretch?' Kay turned away from the pathologist and watched the group of CSIs who were working, heads down, under a copse of trees that lined the riverbank further upstream.

'I don't believe so,' said Harriet. 'My team are processing that scene further up to rule it out – it's where the witness said he first saw the body in the water.'

'So he floated here?' said Barnes.

'That's what we think, reading the witness statement and talking to the divers, yes.'

Kay shielded her eyes and squinted at the river as it curved away to the left and out of sight a quarter of a mile from where she stood.

'Then where the bloody hell did he come from?'

THREE

By the time Kay and Barnes retreated over the footbridge to their car, three more patrol cars and a coroner's van had joined the throng of vehicles parked in the dead-end street.

An inquisitive crowd had gathered at a third cordon behind two patrol vehicles near the T-junction with the main road, their necks craned as they tried to find out what was going on.

Kay glared up at the sky at the beat of a helicopter's blades, then back towards the river. 'Bloody hell, Ian. The vultures are circling.'

Barnes raised his hand to one of the coroner's team and gestured towards the footbridge. 'Can you work as quickly as possible to get the body away?' he said. 'Before that lot get any footage for tonight's news. It'll only be a matter of time before we have more reporters down here at this rate.'

The man's brow furrowed. 'Has the pathologist been?'

'He's down there with the CSIs, so you'll be able to get clearance from him to move the victim.'

'Okay. Leave it with us.'

Kay watched the man make his way over the footbridge, and then tapped Barnes on the arm and pointed at the car.

'Back to the station. We need to get the team up to date with what's going on down here, and then take a look at where our victim might have hit the water.'

She scrolled through her text messages as Barnes drove, delegating tasks from her existing caseload as much as possible so that she could concentrate on the major inquiry that would follow the discovery of the body in the river.

Raising her head as the car slowed, she was surprised to find they were already at the security gate to the town centre station.

'How fast were you going?'

'It's early. The traffic's light. You would've noticed, but you haven't looked up from that screen since we left Tovil,' said Barnes, and winked.

He led the way through the lower levels of the police station and up a flight of stairs, turned right at the end and pushed open the door into a large office space.

Sunlight streamed through the windows at the front of the room, the sound of passing traffic on Palace Avenue filtering through the thick glass.

Kay paused at the threshold and let Barnes go ahead of her, then took a deep breath.

A new investigation, and with it all the complexities and problems that would no doubt test her skills to the limit.

She exhaled as a familiar lanky form weaved between the desks towards her, followed closely by a woman in her early thirties with short jet black hair who was struggling to keep up with him.

Gavin Piper nodded to Barnes at his desk as he drew closer. 'We got here as soon as we could.'

Kay narrowed her eyes at him. The detective constable's blond hair stuck up in spikes despite his efforts to tame it, and she shook her head at his tanned skin.

'It's not fair, Piper. You were only away for five days.'

He snorted. 'And some welcome back this is, guv. Do we know who he is?'

'No – and it's not going to be easy, either. Lucas said the victim's face was shot away.'

Detective Constable Carys Miles winced, then hissed through her teeth. 'Bloody hell. I wonder who he pissed off? Any identification?'

Kay shook her head. 'Nothing at all, not according to Harriet. Let's move over there, and I'll update you.'

She brushed past Gavin and crossed to where he had set up a freshly wiped whiteboard. Next to it, he'd cleared all the usual social notices from a cork board and had pinned a map of the River Medway along the top of it, the location of the victim's body already highlighted.

Glancing over her shoulder at a gaggle of uniformed and suited junior personnel who hovered at the periphery of the small group, she snatched up a thick marker pen and turned to them.

'Good start with this, Piper.' She paused as Carys thrust a mug of coffee at her. 'Thanks. Right, actions – Gavin, I need you to organise setting up the rest of this incident room as soon as possible. Liaise with Theresa in admin and see if you can get personnel to assign Debbie West to the team for the duration of the investigation. She's familiar with everyone, and I'd like to have her on board as office manager.'

Gavin scribbled in his notebook as she spoke. 'Got that, guv. What about IT?'

'Get them to help you – we'll need as many desks set up as possible before lunchtime today. I have a feeling this one is going to take most of our resources this week. Carys – can you make sure this map is complete? Find out how far up this stretch of water goes before it meets a lock or weir. Phone the local office of the Environment Agency as well to see if they'll provide an idea of flow rates on this stretch of the river. We need to find out where that body could've travelled from before the search teams get down there, so we can narrow down a scope of work for them.'

The detective constable looked up from her

notetaking. 'Do you want search teams starting at the possible point of origin as well as from where the body was found at Tovil?'

'Definitely,' said Kay. 'We need to explore the possibility that whoever did this to him may have walked part of the Medway Footpath to make their escape, and having a second search team start from where he might have entered the water, we'll halve the time. We need results on this today. Ian, I need you to work the missing persons angle from here this morning. Find out if what we know about our victim so far – height, average weight, hair colour – ties in with any reports on file.'

'Will do, guv.'

Kay finished writing her notes on the board, then re-capped the pen and faced her team once more. 'Carys – as soon as you've finished talking with the Environment Agency I want you down at the river coordinating with Harriet's lot and the uniformed search team. I'll need a running report about anything they find so I can keep the team at this end up to date.'

The detective constable nodded. 'What about media, guv?'

On cue, the clatter of a helicopter reverberated through the windows, and Kay raised an eyebrow.

'Leave that with me. I'll speak with DCI Sharp about a coordinated statement before that lot start the rumour mill circulating. Dismissed.'

FOUR

Carys took a map from Harry Davis and narrowed her eyes against the glare off the River Medway.

The police divers had dispersed half an hour ago, satisfied that the waterway held no further clues to the victim's identity, and now a group of uniformed police officers and forensic specialists hovered on the towpath, waiting for her instructions.

Her mobile phone vibrated in the vest she'd slipped over her jacket. Her heart missed a beat when she saw the phone number displayed on the screen.

'DC Carys Miles.'

'Detective, it's Ray Annerley from the Environment Agency. I've got the information you were after.'

'Thanks for getting back to me so quickly. What can you tell me?'

'Based on the time of year and the fact we haven't had a flood event in recent days, we reckon that your man could've entered the water anywhere from East Farleigh lock onwards before reaching Tovil.'

Carys bit back a sigh. 'That's nearly two miles.'

'It's the best we can do, I'm afraid. The first lock from your position is at East Farleigh – I don't think he would've passed through that without someone noticing.'

'How long do you think he was in the water for?'

'From there? A day at most.'

Carys thanked him, and ended the call. At least the Environment Agency's timings matched the pathologist's initial findings.

'Okay, everyone. Gather around, please. Have you all got a copy of the map showing the Medway Path from Harry?'

A murmur rumbled through the group in response.

'I've had the Environment Agency on the phone, and they've just confirmed that our search area should start at East Farleigh lock. Given flow rates and current weather conditions, they concur with Lucas Anderson's opinion that our victim was in the water for no more than a day. Bearing that in mind, we'll split up into two groups – one to continue from here, and the other starting at East Farleigh lock.'

Pausing, she checked her notes. A bead of sweat trickled between her shoulder blades, and she forced herself to relax. She had conducted many searches before, but had never been responsible for leading one.

The burst of pride that had surged through her at

Kay's instructions to carry out the task threatened to turn to anxiety as the sheer scale of what lay ahead became apparent. It didn't help that there hadn't been time to engage the Police Search Advisor to assist in the task – the person responsible was stuck in traffic outside Folkestone and wouldn't reach Maidstone for another two hours.

Kay hadn't been prepared to wait, so in the meantime had instructed the allocated Lost Person Search Manager – Sergeant Harry Davis – to coordinate the initial parameters.

Carys cleared her throat. 'Our search objective is to find any evidence that might be related to our victim, or the perpetrator of the crime. At the present time, we don't know where the victim entered the water, so you'll need to include signs of a struggle, blood spatter from a gunshot wound, or other indicators. We also need to bear in mind that his killer may have escaped along the Medway Path after shooting him.'

Turning over the map, she indicated the satellite photograph that had been printed on the back. 'If you take a look at this, you'll see that between here and East Farleigh there are several egress routes the killer could have taken. We have another uniform team conducting house-to-house enquiries in streets that border the river, but you'll need to check all footpaths leading off the main Medway Path as well.'

She cast her gaze around the gathered throng. 'I realise this is a massive undertaking, but we've got almost eleven hours of daylight available to us. DI Hunter is seeking further assistance from Headquarters to bring in additional personnel later today to continue the search. Any questions?'

When no-one raised their hand, she turned to the older police sergeant next to her.

'Harry, can you lead the first group from here?'

Davis nodded, then began to bark orders at his colleagues.

Carys watched the group move up the towpath away from the footbridge, and turned to the remaining personnel.

'Let's go.'

BATTING a dancing crowd of midges away from her face, Carys pulled down her navy baseball cap and cursed under her breath as she stood on the medieval bridge that crossed the River Medway at East Farleigh.

A steady stream of traffic flowed behind her.

She hadn't dared to suggest the bridge be closed, given the assertions by the Environment Agency that the victim had entered the water after the lock to the left of the structure.

The busy thoroughfare was a popular route into the southern suburbs of Maidstone, with the narrow road managed by sets of traffic lights that allowed a few cars through at a time.

If she closed off access without sufficient evidence to give her cause to do so, she'd never hear the end of it from her colleagues in Traffic.

Her lips narrowed as she ran her eyes over the weir to the right of the lock, a concrete quay separating the two, enabling boat owners to progress along the river and the local authority to manage the flow of water.

Leaning her arms on the ragstone-constructed arch, she watched as the group of uniformed officers made their way along the path in a short line.

She'd elected to split them up – one line of five officers taking the lead, a second group behind them. Three forensic specialists hovered at the rear, ready to take any findings into evidence for processing and elimination.

Carys took a deep breath, then waited for a break in the traffic and jogged across the road.

An old converted red-brick pumping station stood to her left, floor-to-ceiling blinds across the windows to offset the bright sunshine – or the sight of so many uniformed police officers crawling over the landscape.

She slowed as she reached the car park beyond the pumping station, squeezed between two patrol cars, and hurried back along the path and under the bridge towards her colleagues.

Brushing past the CSIs, she caught up with PC Aaron Stewart in the second search group.

He paused, his large frame casting a shadow over Carys.

Shielding her eyes, she jutted her chin towards the two teams. 'Anything yet?'

'No. No signs of blood spatter on the sides of the lock on the downstream edges, and we've checked the other side nearest the weir, too.'

Carys pulled out her mobile phone. 'I've got full signal down here, so I'll join you.'

'Sounds good.'

They fell into line, and she lowered her gaze to the ground. Each officer worked methodically, sweeping their eyes across the rough stone and dirt path or, in the case of the two officers over to her far left, the thick vegetation that grew between the Medway Path and the fence erected beside the railway.

Pulling up her collar to ward off the sun, Carys looked up at a call from the group ahead of theirs.

To the right, jutting out into the water, was a concrete jetty and she held her breath as three officers spread out and began combing the rough surface for clues. She recognised PC Dave Morrison as he crouched on all fours and leaned over the edge, before easing back to a sitting position and pointing his thumb downwards.

'No bloodstains or anything there, either,' said Stewart.

Carys unfolded her map. 'Where's the first spur in this path?'

'There's a property about half a mile up, with access

to Barming. If you look at the satellite image, it seems it's a popular spot for narrowboats to moor.'

She flipped over the page, then frowned. 'With a house and that many boats nearby, you'd have thought someone would've reported a gunshot.'

'Maybe. There are fields all around them, though so they might have written it off as a crow scarer or something. If they're not used to hearing it, a gunshot can sound like a car backfiring, too.'

Carys bit her lip, then craned her neck to see how the first group were progressing. She tucked the map back into her pocket, and ploughed onwards, trying to ignore the sense of unease that was turning her stomach.

What if the man had been shot elsewhere, and his body then dumped in the river? She shook her head, muttering under her breath. No, because someone would have had to have carried his body – too hard across the fields and a busy railway line, and too risky to cross the bridge with the amount of traffic that used it day and night.

She shuddered as a train flew past, its horn blaring. The stretch of track held too many memories for her – memories that kept her awake some nights, when her mind turned to what could have been if it wasn't for—

'They've got something.'

Stewart's voice crashed into her thoughts, and her head snapped up.

'Where?'

The police constable pointed to a female officer at

the right of the first team, who had raised her hand in the air, bringing her group to a standstill.

Carys watched, her fists clenched, as the woman moved towards a brightly coloured cabin cruiser moored next to the path, her movements methodical as she checked the thick grass on the riverbank.

Satisfied the way was clear, a male colleague helped her over the gunwale. She rapped her knuckles on the cabin door, and then peeked through a round window.

A split second later, she spun on her heel and beckoned.

'Wait here,' said Carys. 'I think this is it.'

FIVE

Reaching the boat, Carys ran her eyes over the blue-striped chine and found a name – *Lucky Lady* – splashed across the paintwork nearest the bow. At the stern, a registration number had been stamped in white paint, bold and clear.

A single window stretched the length of the cabin along the left-hand side, and as she wandered up to the bow, she noticed that it and the two forward-facing windows had curtains pulled across them.

PC Laura Hanway called out to her before introducing herself, and then pointed to the cabin door. 'It's locked, ma'am. But there's blood spatter over here on the deck, as well as the right-hand side of the cockpit and cabin.'

Carys wandered back to the stern. She reached up for the female officer's outstretched hand, and hoisted herself onto the fibreglass deck of the cabin cruiser.

Similar to the other vessels she'd seen moored at Tovil, the cockpit was open to the elements, a grey tarpaulin rolled up and stowed at the far end of the cramped space.

The female police officer stepped back to give Carys more room, her light-brown hair pulled back into a tidy bun at the nape of her neck. She gestured to the window with a gloved hand.

'The door's locked, but it looks like there was a struggle.'

'Okay, off you get. Let's get the CSIs over here and ready to start taking samples,' said Carys. 'After you've done that, run the registration number past the Environment Agency – as soon as they have any information, get them to phone it through to the incident room. Ask Aaron to join me, would you?'

'Ma'am.'

Carys turned her attention to the waiting search team. 'Continue the grid search, and I want three of you concentrating on the riverbank alongside this vessel. This could be the place where our victim went in.'

Moments later, Aaron Stewart climbed aboard and raised an eyebrow. 'What've you got?'

'Stay close to the cabin door,' said Carys. 'I don't want us contaminating evidence any more than we might've done already.'

'Okay.'

'Laura's right. The place is a tip inside, and – look – there are bloodstains. The door's locked, and I haven't found a spare key out here. Do you reckon you could break it down?'

'Probable cause, ma'am?'

'One dead man, signs of a struggle, and perhaps someone else in there in need of medical attention.'

'Stand back.'

Carys moved away from the cabin window, and hovered behind Stewart. As he took a step forward, she ran her gaze over the bloodstains.

This had to be the place. No fisherman in his right mind would leave his boat in such a state.

Stewart lashed out with his boot, splintering the thin wooden door under the flimsy lock, and pulled his telescopic nightstick from his utility belt. 'With all due respect, stay here.'

'Got that.' Carys pulled out her nightstick and hovered at the threshold while the police officer ducked his head under the low frame and stepped down into the cabin.

She wrinkled her nose at a faint tang to the air that escaped the living quarters of the boat, and stooped to peer through the broken pieces of door that now clung to the hinges.

Muted sunlight shone through the curtains at the windows, creating a gloom that hung in the air, malevolent and foreboding. Stewart moved through the space with care, his tall frame stooped as he swung left and right, his nightstick held in a tight grip.

'Police! Anyone here?' he said. 'If you're injured, call out.'

Carys held her breath.

The boat remained silent.

'There's a door through to the forward cabin,' said Stewart. 'I'm going through.'

The sound of his knuckles against wood reached her, and then he pulled the door.

He swore under his breath.

'What's up?'

'It's clear. There's no-one here, but you'd better come and look at this.'

Carys placed her gloved hand on the door frame and climbed down the four steps that led into the cabin, before making her way to where Stewart stood at the far end.

She thrust her arms out for balance as the boat moved in the water, her eyes sweeping the opened drawers, the contents strewn across the cabin seats. In the galley, a refrigerator had been opened, remnants of food smeared up the walls and trampled underfoot.

The police constable stepped to one side as she approached, his face troubled. 'Look.'

Peering through the door, Carys's breath caught in her throat. She swallowed to batten down the fear.

She had to concentrate.

She had to do her job.

A child's clothing had been pulled from an old

sports bag that lay open on the bed – blue dungarees, white cotton vest tops, a pair of brown sandals. Amongst the tiny pairs of jeans and jumpers tossed aside, two picture books lay open, their pages creased. A toy car lay abandoned on the floor of the cabin, and a colourful plastic cup lay on its side on a three-drawer dresser.

'Oh, no.' Carys took a step forward, and crouched. She lifted the rumpled blankets from the side of the bed, then looked underneath. 'Not hiding anywhere?'

'I've checked the head as well. No-one in there.'

Carys straightened, and beckoned to Stewart to follow her outside.

'I'll get forensics in here. I want you to stay posted by the main door, okay?'

'Will do.'

'Give me a hand.' Carys called to one of the police constables on the river path, and climbed off the boat before pulling out her mobile phone.

She hit the speed dial, her hands shaking, and began to hurry back to her car.

'Guv? We've found an abandoned boat that shows signs of a struggle. There are bloodstains on the gunwale, and the contents of the cabin have been ransacked. We're waiting for the Environment Agency to tell us who the boat is registered to.'

'All right,' said Kay. 'Get yourself back here. Well done.'

'Wait.' Carys held the phone tighter to her ear, and started running. 'Don't hang up.'

'What's wrong?'

'I think we've got a missing child as well.'

SIX

DCI Devon Sharp looked up from the HOLMES2 report in his right hand as Kay burst through the door into his office, and raised an eyebrow.

'Have we got a breakthrough?'

Kay took a deep breath, forcing herself to calm down. The tension in Carys's voice had been evident, and it was all Kay could do not to emulate it at the news her detective constable had shared.

'Carys and the search team have located a cabin cruiser abandoned on the River Medway west of East Farleigh. There are bloodstains on the gunwales, signs of a struggle – and it appears that we might have a missing child as well.'

Sharp rose from his chair, tossed the report to one side, and gestured towards the incident room, his grey eyes troubled.

'Do we have an identity for the victim yet? Have you got any idea who the child might be?'

'Nothing yet. They're still searching the boat,' said Kay as she hurried after his imposing figure. 'Carys had a police constable get in touch with the Environment Agency again, with a note of the boat's registration number. We want to know if they can corroborate the location of the body this morning with the boat to see if the river flow would've carried him from that location. I don't want to call off the other search team until we have that information.'

'Good thinking. Where is Carys?'

'She's on her way back here now.'

Barnes crossed the room to where they stood by the whiteboard, his face pale at the new development. 'I've spoken to Harriet and she'll liaise with the underwater search team to have them dive the river and look for a weapon or shell casings while her lot are processing the boat. I'll call Hazel Aldridge and get her on standby as well. We're going to need her by the sound of things.'

Kay nodded. The formally trained Family Liaison Officer would be the main point of contact for any next of kin, once the victim's identity was known, and would provide valuable information to assist in the investigation as the family divulged any details about what might have occurred prior to the man's death while the search for the missing child continued.

'Where's Alistair? Has he got back from Folkestone yet?' said Sharp.

'He's on his way,' said Barnes. 'Hughes on the front desk called me to say he just saw his car pull in.'

'Good – the last thing we need is to try and coordinate a search operation like this is turning out to be, without our Police Search Advisor.'

The door to the incident crashed open, and Carys appeared. She tapped Gavin on the shoulder and hurried to where Kay stood, closely followed by a man in his late fifties with a shock of white hair that was almost as spiky as Gavin's.

He rolled up his shirt sleeves as he approached, nodded to Sharp, and then shook hands with the rest of the detectives gathered at the front of the room.

Kay felt a surge of adrenalin. The addition of the local PolSA, Alistair Matthews, would add an element to the search that was desperately needed, and she welcomed his expertise.

'Harry's still there, coordinating the rest of the search,' said Carys. 'I got here as soon as I could. The traffic is bloody horrendous now.'

'It's the last week of summer,' said Alistair, 'and it's going to hamper our efforts if we're not careful.'

Kay gave her detective constable a few seconds to get her breath back, and then gestured to the whiteboard. 'Download any photographs you've got on your phone, Carys, and get them filed on HOLMES2 straight away. Gavin – can you get those printed out and the best ones put on here, so everyone can familiarise themselves with the crime scene?'

'Will do, guv.'

'What can you tell us about the cabin cruiser?' said Sharp, his arms crossed over his chest. 'And what makes you think there's a missing child involved?'

'The cabin cruiser was in reasonable condition,' said Carys. 'Not new – perhaps six or seven years old, I'm guessing. The paintwork has held up well, but hasn't been applied recently. PC Laura Hanway was amongst the first group in the search team, and found bloodstains on the starboard side of the boat – nearest the water. She called out to me, and by the time I climbed on board and joined her, she was peering through the window between the deck and the cabin. It was clear there had been a struggle at some point – the place was trashed, and so I asked PC Aaron Stewart to break down the door in case someone was lying injured.'

'Was there anyone on board?' said Kay.

'No, but when Aaron moved through to the forward cabin, that's when he found children's clothing and toys tossed everywhere.'

'What sort of clothing?' said Alistair, and pulled out his notebook.

'I saw T-shirts – green, blue, and a couple with TV characters on the front – a dinosaur was on one of them. Striped socks, a pair of jeans, and some red dungarees. There was a pair of brown sandals, too.'

Kay swallowed as she listened to the list of items being reeled off by Carys. The thought that somewhere out there, a small child was lost and frightened – or worse – brought the threat of bile to her throat. She clenched her fists, digging her nails into the palms of her hands.

'What size clothing? Age?' said Alistair. 'Girl or boy?'

Carys blinked. 'I'm – I'm not sure. Um, maybe three or four. I thought maybe a boy – there were action heroes on the other T-shirts, and a couple of toy cars on the bed.'

'What about forensics?'

'There's a team of four at the scene now. They were with our search team, and they can request support from the other team working eastwards from Tovil if they need it.'

'Great work, Carys,' said Kay. She narrowed her eyes at the PolSA, who had opened his mouth once more.

Carys had faltered under his questioning, and Kay was determined to keep her young protégée's confidence levels high. If she began to doubt her decisions out in the field, she would never recover. She saw reflections of herself at the same age in Carys, and knew she would need to watch the younger woman carefully over the ensuing days so that she didn't become overwhelmed by the level of responsibility she surely felt.

Amongst the bedlam of the incident room teeming with investigators and people calling to each other, Kay heard another mobile phone start ringing, and spun around to face Barnes.

The detective sergeant held up a finger, murmuring into the phone.

'Put it on speaker phone, Ian,' barked Sharp, and signalled to the rest of the team to join them.

'This is Detective Chief Inspector Devon Sharp. Who is this?'

'It's PC Laura Hanway, guv. I'm at the boat.'

'What have you got for us? Anything?'

'I've heard back from the Environment Agency. The boat is registered to a hire company called Toppings based at Tonbridge. I've called them, and they've confirmed the abandoned boat – *Lucky Lady* – was rented by someone called Greg Victor. The owner also said that he had a little girl with him.'

SEVEN

'Can they confirm if the girl is Greg Victor's daughter?' said Kay.

'No, guv and they don't know her name – he didn't introduce her to them. Apparently, Greg's car is still parked outside their office.'

'Registration number?' said Gavin as he took a spare seat next to a computer, his fingers tapping a computer keyboard.

Laura recited it.

'He hasn't got previous, and there's nothing else on HOLMES2 relating to that name,' said Gavin. 'Nothing for the vehicle, either.'

'Did the hire company give you an address for him?' said Kay.

'A post office box number only,' said Laura.

'Give it to Barnes so he can get on to the Royal Mail.'

CRADLE TO GRAVE 41

'Pass them to me if they drag their feet,' said Sharp.

'Will do, guv,' said Barnes. 'Any photographs of the girl, Laura?'

'None.' She paused, and they could hear her moving through the boat's cabin. 'There's no identification for either of them, but Patrick and the other CSIs are confident this is where the victim was shot. The blood spatter is consistent with a gunshot wound.'

'All right, Laura – thank you,' said Kay. 'Keep us posted on anything else you find.'

She signalled to Gavin. 'Get on to the media relations team and have them ready to issue an alert for a missing child as soon as we manage to find an address and next of kin for Greg Victor. We need urgent clarification of who this little girl is as well – whether she's his daughter or not, and then we need to figure out why she's been taken.'

'Will do, guv.'

'Update the underwater search team, too. She might not have been taken – she might have run away, or fallen over the side of the boat when he was attacked. Keep the search teams there until we can eliminate either of those possibilities.'

'What about revised search parameters?' said Alistair.

'We'll start at the boat and spread out wider if we don't find anything. It's the best course of action with the little information we've got to work with.' Fighting down her terror at the thought of a small child being thrown into the river or wandering off on her own along a towpath in the dark, Kay turned back to the map of the River Medway and rested her hands on her hips. 'Okay, so our victim is shot where he's moored next to the Medway Path just past East Farleigh. On to our third scenario. What's the nearest point of escape for anyone with a small child in tow?'

Barnes placed his reading glasses onto his nose and moved closer. 'Nearest point is the bridge at East Farleigh. There are a couple of footpaths off the Medway Path between where the boat was found and Fant, too.'

'East Farleigh would've been a risk with a kid,' said Kay. 'Too much attention if she was upset, maybe.'

'Not if she knew the person or persons who took her.'

'After seeing someone get shot dead?'

'Maybe they shot him after they took her off the boat.'

'All right. Good point.'

'If not that way, the footpaths, then – past this small-holding here. There's a track that winds its way up to the Tonbridge Road. If they were on foot and had a car parked further up the track, the residents might not have heard them.'

'I think that's our best bet. It's a route that would attract less attention. What do you think, Alistair?'

The PolSA wandered over to where they stood, and then nodded. 'I'd agree. I'll head over to East Farleigh to split up the search team working there, and we'll get a group to follow up those two leads.'

'Thanks,' said Kay.

'Guv, I'll try to find some CCTV or private security film footage from the properties around the lock at East Farleigh so we can rule that out,' said Barnes.

'Agreed, thanks, Ian. It's best to be sure.' Kay turned to the rest of the team who were hovering in the background. 'Back to work everyone. Standing around isn't going to find her.'

She turned to Sharp and Alistair as the other detectives hurried back to their desks. 'Is there anything else you need from me, Alistair?'

'No – but phone me as you get updating information, please. We'll focus our search on those two footpaths for now, but I'll keep you informed on any developments from that end with regard to the dive team as well.'

With that, he turned on his heel and hurried from the incident room, his mobile phone already to his ear.

Kay exhaled, and ran her gaze over the heads of her team as they worked.

'I'll make some phone calls, see if the Chief Super can allocate more staff to us,' said Sharp. 'We need to coordinate the shifts, too. We're going to do this little girl no favours at all if we're all tired, so I'd suggest I'll take the night shift and you can get some rest.'

'I'll have Carys head off now,' said Kay. 'That way,

she can come back tonight and give you the support you need.'

He nodded, his face grim. 'I don't like this, Kay. We've never had an incident like it here. What are your first thoughts?'

Kay ran her hand through her hair. 'We've received no communications about a possible ransom for the return of this girl, and if the information from the Environment Agency is right, then she was taken late yesterday afternoon – perhaps early evening. But why was she there in the first place with Greg Victor? If she was kidnapped, why would they take her from there? Why all that risk in shooting Greg?'

'Do you think the kidnappers panicked?'

'Maybe.' Kay rolled her shoulders, trying to ease out the tension that was already giving her a headache at the base of her skull. 'Or they were sending a message to someone.'

'Hell of a message.'

'Mmm.' She raised her hand and beckoned to Carys.

'What is it, guv?'

'DCI Sharp is going to run the investigation through the night so we've got twenty-four-hour coverage until we find this missing girl. Get yourself off home now – I want you to come back at eight o'clock tonight to support him. I'll sort out the paperwork tomorrow.'

'No problem. Will you phone me if you find her before I get back?'

'Of course. I'll leave you a message if you don't pick up.'

'Thanks.'

'Guv.' Barnes replaced his desk phone in its cradle and pushed his way past two uniformed officers as Carys headed out the door. He held up a piece of paper. 'The Royal Mail depot at Parkwood just called. We've got an address for Greg Victor, just outside Tonbridge.'

'Anything on the system related to the address?'

'Nothing. It's clear. No issues.'

Kay was already moving towards her desk. 'Get on to Tonbridge station, and ask if two of their officers can meet us there,' she said. 'I'm coming with you.'

'Guv? Before you go…' said Gavin, craning his neck from where he sat at his computer.

'Yes?'

'There is another possibility. The people who took the missing child, I mean. If they didn't use one of those footpaths to escape with her.'

'Spit it out, Piper,' said Barnes.

Kay raised her hand to silence him. 'What is it, Gav?'

'What if they made their escape by boat, not on foot?'

Kay took a step back, her insides twisting as if someone had punched her in the stomach.

'Bloody hell, Gav. You could be right.'

'I've got this,' said Sharp. 'You two head over to Tonbridge. Gavin – start looking at what other boats have been hired on the River Medway this past week. I'll get some more officers to help with the house-to-house enquiries and update them to start asking whether any other boats have been seen on the river with a little girl on board.'

'Ask if anyone's hired a boat in the name of Greg Victor as well, Gavin,' said Kay, 'just in case they're posing as him to escape.'

She waited until Barnes had returned to his desk and began stuffing his pockets with car keys, mobile phone and a notebook, then turned back to Sharp. 'I'll be back as soon as I can. You need to get some rest if you're working tonight.'

He waved her out the door. 'I can always rely on coffee later if I need it. Go.'

EIGHT

Kay flipped down the sun visor over the windscreen and squinted against the late afternoon glare.

A haze cloaked the fields to her left as Barnes guided the pool car past a stream of traffic on the dual carriageway past the large hop farm outside Paddock Wood, and as she watched families play in the landscaped recreation area on the opposite side of the road, she wondered at the sense of normality in the world around her.

Somewhere out there was a frightened child, who had no idea what was happening to her.

She swallowed, and turned her attention back to the road while her detective sergeant sped past a roundabout, the car surging forward as soon as he had space to overtake the vehicle in front of them.

Kay resisted the urge to check her watch – Barnes

was doing the best he could with the late-season tourist traffic.

Finally, they reached the outskirts of Tonbridge and he slowed the car to a standstill on a tree-lined avenue. A large four-bedroom house was partly hidden behind a tall privet hedge and a pair of fir trees, the driveway bereft of any vehicles.

A little further up the street, a liveried patrol car had been parked next to two wheelie bins, its occupants elsewhere.

'This is the place,' he said. 'Looks like uniform got here first.'

Kay led the way up the driveway and rang the doorbell, her shoulders relaxing when PC Ben Allen answered.

'Afternoon, guv. We got here about ten minutes ago. Mrs Victor is in the living room. Nigel's broken the news to her.'

'Thanks, Ben.'

Both Ben and his colleague, Nigel Best, were Tonbridge-based police constables who Kay had worked with before, and she was grateful that the two experienced officers were on hand.

'Before you go in, guv – there's something you should know.'

Kay paused, her hand on the door handle. 'What?'

'Greg Victor was her brother-in-law,' said Ben. 'Annette's husband, Robert Victor, is Greg's older brother. Alice – the kid who's gone missing – is their only child.'

'What else do we know about Greg?'

'His ex-wife and daughter live in Nottingham. We've asked our colleagues up there to liaise with the family and keep us updated with any developments from that angle.'

'Okay, good work. Thanks, Ben.'

Kay's first impression of Annette Victor when she walked through the door was that the woman appeared to be almost translucent.

A slim form rose from a sofa next to the window, pale-green eyes peering out from a long fringe of golden hair that brushed across the woman's shoulders. Her alabaster skin was a striking contrast against the black short-sleeved top she wore over skinny jeans, worry lines ageing her beyond the mid-thirties Kay guessed her to be.

Her hand shook as she held it out. 'You must be Detective Kay Hunter.'

'Mrs Victor. This is my colleague, Detective Sergeant Ian Barnes.' Kay nodded to Nigel Best. 'I'm sorry if my questions are going to seem a little harsh and to the point, but it's a process we have to follow in the circumstances. I understand my colleagues have let you know that we have reason to believe that a man by the name of Greg Victor was the victim of a murder late last night. Please can you confirm he was your brother-in-law?'

'Yes, that's right. Where's Alice? She was with him. He said he'd look after her.'

'We don't have the answer to that at the moment, Mrs Victor. We—'

'It's Annette. Call me Annette.'

'Thank you. We've only identified Greg through the boat hire company within the past hour, and we're moving as fast as we can on the information. When was the last time you saw your daughter?'

'Yesterday morning.'

'Why was she with Greg yesterday?'

'She's been going on and on all summer about a boat trip with him after she heard him talking about it at a barbecue we had earlier in the summer. He's taken her fishing down by the river here before. They're very close, and so when he suggested an overnight trip, we agreed. He babysits for us when we have the occasional night out in London or whatever, so there were no problems.' A sob escaped her lips. 'He bought her a life jacket and everything. I thought she'd be safe. I-I can't believe he's dead. Who would do this?'

'We're doing everything we can to find that out. Does Alice have any medical issues we should be aware of? Any allergies?'

'No. She's a very healthy child.' Annette reached out for a box of tissues, and gently blew her nose. 'I can't believe this is happening.'

'I have to ask – have you received any ransom demands for Alice's return?'

The woman paled further. 'I— No, no I haven't. Oh my God. Do you think— Why would someone kidnap her?'

'That's what we're trying to ascertain, Annette. It may be that she left the boat of her own accord. It was located near East Farleigh lock – on the Medway Path heading towards Tovil. Does Alice know anyone along that route?'

'No. No – she's never been along that part of the river. She's only five years old, and I've only ever walked her along the towpath near the park here. We sometimes stop to feed the ducks.'

'Did your brother-in-law live here with you?'

Annette dabbed at her eyes. 'Greg was staying here for a while, so he could find his feet. He moved down from Nottingham a few months ago after his marriage broke up – he's been looking for work. He has an eight-year-old daughter, Sadie, and I know he misses her dreadfully so he's been spoiling Alice rotten since he's been with us.'

'How old is he?' said Kay.

'Thirty-four last month. He's a bit younger than my husband, Robert.'

'Where is Robert at the moment?'

'France – he had a business meeting in Orléans on Tuesday and then another meeting somewhere near Chartres on Wednesday morning, so he left on Monday. He was planning to stay there tonight as well on his way back from some other meetings.'

'Have you spoken to him?'

'Not since the police arrived here, no. And I couldn't get a signal for him earlier. That sometimes happens.'

'What does he do for a living?'

'He's a wine merchant, specialising in boutique vineyards on the Continent. That's why I can't always reach him on the phone – he's often traipsing around in the middle of a field somewhere.'

'How did he get there – did he fly?'

'Yes, from Gatwick. He hires a car at the other end – Paris.'

'And you, Annette – do you work?'

'I did before Alice was born. I'm waiting until she's settled into her new school before I take on anything again.'

'Were you close to his brother Greg?'

Annette shrugged. 'I suppose so. I mean, obviously it's been a bit strained around here with him living here and all that.'

'In what way?'

'Well, when I first offered, I imagined it'd be for a couple of weeks. Not four months.'

'What sort of work does he do?'

'To be honest, I'm not sure. He was applying for work in warehousing, forklift truck driving, that sort of thing. Anything, I guess, to get a foothold down here.'

'Why did he leave Nottingham?' said Barnes.

'I don't think the marriage split was amicable. I overheard him tell Robert that his wife cheated on him, and he couldn't bear to be near her.'

'Did he give you any indication he might have had any other problems there? Through work, I mean, or other people he knew?'

'Why? Do you think that might be why Alice has been taken?' Annette's eyes opened wide. 'Oh my God. I don't know.'

'What did he do in Nottingham, work-wise?' said Kay.

'I think he was working in an abattoir,' said Annette. 'Part-time only, mind, and I know he hated the work. Couldn't wait to get out of there.'

'Have any friends or ex-work colleagues been in touch from that time?'

'Not to my knowledge. Although, we don't have a landline, so if they did, they would have phoned his mobile.'

'May I take a look at his room, Mrs Victor?' said Barnes.

'Why would you want to do that?'

'It helps us get an idea of what Greg was like, and he might have left something behind that will help us locate your daughter,' said Kay.

'Oh. All right.' Annette waited until Barnes had left the room. 'What are you doing about finding Alice?'

'We've currently got four search teams working

between East Farleigh, where Greg's boat was found, and Tovil. Until we were able to identify your brother's body, though, we couldn't expand the search. Do you have a photograph of Alice you could give to me? We're going to have a media conference as soon as I get back to the station, and we'll put out an alert for her.'

'Is that it? Just a press conference?'

'No, it's not,' said Kay. 'While that's taking place, my team and I will be working around the clock until we find her. As we speak, those search team members are coordinating with my colleagues back at the police station, and we have another team of officers monitoring CCTV cameras around the area to see if we can locate her.'

'I want to help with the search. I should be out there, looking for her.'

'It's better if you're here, in case she finds her way home,' said Kay. 'We have trained specialists doing the house-to-house enquiries and area searches, and they're liaising closely with my investigation team on a regular basis.'

She paused at the sound of the doorbell.

Moments later, Nigel opened the living room door and ushered in a petite brunette officer.

Hazel Aldridge was a police constable with West Division and specialised in family liaison duties when required. Right now, she was dressed in a smart trouser suit, her hair tied back in a loose ponytail.

Kay made the introductions, and indicated to Hazel

to sit in the armchair facing them. 'Annette, Hazel is going to be your point of contact throughout this investigation, so if you have any questions about what we're doing, she can be on hand to help you.'

'Okay.' Annette had paled further, the reality of her situation beginning to sink in. Her hands shook as she eased herself from the sofa and scrutinised the contents of a bookshelf at the far end of the room, before returning with a silver-framed photograph. 'This is the most recent one I have of Alice. It was taken at her fifth birthday party in June.'

Kay swallowed as she looked at the girl in the picture.

Blue eyes stared out at her, a face of innocence framed with blonde hair in pigtails. Alice wore a cute smile and with a button nose that sat perfectly in the middle of her face, it was all Kay could do to batten down the emotions that were tearing through her.

'It confused our team for a while – they found toy cars and things like that on the boat.'

Annette sniffed, and folded her arms across her chest. A faint smile passed over her lips. 'She wants to be a racing driver when she grows up.'

'Can I take this?'

'Yes.'

Kay slipped the photograph from the frame, and tucked it carefully into her bag. 'Hazel will stay with you this evening, if that's okay? Or would you prefer that we find her a hotel nearby?'

'Please, stay here,' said Annette, turning to the family liaison officer. 'I'd rather know the moment you have any news. You can have the guest room at the back of the house. At least then, you can help me explain to Robert what's going on when he gets back.'

'Thank you,' said Hazel. 'That'll be just fine. If you could let us have a note of Robert's mobile number and travel itinerary, we'll work to get in touch with him for you.'

'I haven't got his itinerary, but I can give you his mobile number.'

Hearing footsteps on the stairs, Kay rose from her chair and held out her hand to Annette. 'We'll head back to the station now and get the media conference on the way. As soon as we have any news, I'll be in touch. In the meantime, if you hear from anyone – anyone at all – about the whereabouts of Alice, please tell Hazel.'

'I will. Thank you.'

Kay left the living room, and found Barnes in the hallway talking to Ben. 'Anything?'

He shook his head, and opened the front door for her.

'Ben, ask Robert Victor to phone me the moment he gets back from France tomorrow, just in case we miss him at the airport.'

'Will do, guv.'

'Okay, let's go.'

'There was no mobile phone, no wallet, and no laptop computer in his room. Harriet's team didn't find them on the boat, either,' said Barnes as they walked back to the car. He paused, tossing the keys from one hand to the other as he stared over the car roof towards the house. 'I don't like this, Kay. I don't like this one at all.'

NINE

Kay tied her hair back into a bun and checked her face in the rear-view mirror before pursing her lips.

Dark circles had formed under her eyes since the morning, and she fished in her handbag for her emergency supplies of make-up.

That done, she scowled at her reflection, then stuck out her tongue.

She didn't care what the waiting cameras thought of her looks. She needed them to focus on the fact they had a missing five-year-old, and she had precisely ten minutes to get to the media conference room before the appeal went out live.

Snatching her bag from the passenger seat, she climbed out and aimed her key fob over her shoulder at the car.

The car park was already full of vans and cars emblazoned with the familiar logos of the local television, radio and newspaper companies, while a lone cameraman paced back and forth next to a black four-wheel drive vehicle, a cigarette in his hand as he spoke loudly into a mobile phone.

Kay stalked towards the front doors of the red-brick building that housed Kent Police headquarters, and jogged up the steps.

Sharp met her at the entrance to the conference room as she was clipping her credentials to her lapel, and steered her through the throng of journalists that cluttered the space.

'The Chief Superintendent can't make this one,' he called over the noise. 'She's in the middle of a budget meeting with the Commissioner, and trying to find us some more people to help us.'

Kay nodded in response, but said nothing.

Reaching a long table draped in a blue cloth at the end of the room, Sharp pulled out a chair for her facing the cameras and gestured to a woman who hovered at a door to his right.

Joanne Fletcher, the administrative assistant who worked for media relations, turned to the throng of journalists and camera operators and raised her voice.

'Ladies and gentlemen, that's five minutes until we go live. Five minutes, please.'

Kay took a briefing folder from Joanne and flipped it open, scanning the text of the press release within.

'We've kept it focused on Alice at the moment,' said Joanne, her voice low. 'Until we have more information about how Greg Victor died and we have a positive identification, we felt it would have overshadowed the fact that his niece has been missing for almost twenty-four hours.'

'This reads fine to me,' said Sharp. He tossed the folder onto the table in front of his seat and surveyed the room as reporters began to take their seats.

Kay watched him, taking her cue from her senior officer. Buttoning up her jacket, she rested her hands on the table and focused on what was to come.

'Two minutes,' called Joanne.

As the press officer took her seat in the front row, Sharp lowered himself into the chair to Kay's left.

He reached out and filled two glasses with water from a jug that had been placed on the table between them and passed one to her.

'All set?' he said.

'Ready when you are. Looks like we've got some familiar faces.'

She ran her gaze over the people in the first three rows, instantly picking out Jonathan Aspley from the *Kentish Times*. She looked away before he could catch her eye, and instead found Suzi Chambers from the local television channel staring at her.

'The vulture is here, too,' said Sharp under his breath. 'We'll have to watch that one.'

'Agreed,' said Kay.

A media conference for a missing child was a delicate balance – they had to get the word out that

Alice was missing in order to rally members of the public to be vigilant and to keep watch for the little girl, but they also had to be careful that the reporters didn't sensationalise the story in any way.

Only a few miles away, a distraught mother was counting on their every action, and Kay was determined that she wouldn't let down Annette Victor.

'Any news on whether Robert Victor is home?' she said.

'No.'

Kay swallowed, thankful that at least Annette had the support of Hazel Aldridge while the televised appeal went out.

'Here we go,' said Sharp, and took a sip of water.

The ceiling lights dimmed at the back of the room, turning everyone's attention to the Kent Police logo behind Kay and Sharp.

A silence filled the space.

The DCI took his cue from Joanne, who counted in the seconds to the live broadcast, and then began to speak.

'My name is Detective Chief Inspector Devon Sharp, and I'm joined today by Detective Inspector Kay Hunter.' Introductions made, he launched into the prepared press release.

As Kay listened, she kept her eyes on the crowd, peering through the flashes of cameras and phones at the hushed throng of media professionals.

Despite a healthy animosity towards some of them,

she recognised they would do all they could to spread the word about Alice, even if their end goal was different to hers.

For some of the reporters, the little girl's disappearance would be viewed as a godsend to the end of what had been a quiet news week.

For others, especially those with children of their own at home, it would serve as a harsh reminder that danger could lurk within any community, and that they would do anything to find the girl.

'Any questions?'

Sharp's voice cut through her thoughts, and Kay dug her fingernails into her palms.

'Why was Alice on the boat?' said a male voice from the back of the room.

'It was a family outing,' said Sharp. 'Alice was accompanied by her uncle, Greg Victor. At some point late yesterday, Mr Victor was attacked, and we believe Alice was either taken, or left behind on the boat before she wandered off on her own.'

A cacophony of voices bounced off the ceiling tiles, and Sharp pointed at Jonathan Aspley for the next question.

'What can you tell us about Greg Victor?'

'Nothing at the present time,' said Sharp. 'That is a separate investigation. Our focus is to find Alice. She's five years old, alone, and scared. I'd ask all of you to keep your questions in relation to her, please.'

'Have any ransom demands been made?' said a female voice to the left of Kay.

'We haven't been informed by the family of any ransom demands,' said Sharp, 'but kidnapping is a line of enquiry we are pursuing until we have information that lends itself otherwise.'

'What can people do to help?'

Kay breathed a sigh of relief at the question from a male reporter she recognised from the *Kent Messenger*.

'Thank you, Mark,' said Sharp. 'We urge all residents who live near the River Medway between Tonbridge and Maidstone to check their properties for any signs of Alice. She may be wandering, trying to find her way home, or confused and lost. Check your outbuildings, garden sheds, garages, for any sign of her as soon as you can. If you have a boat on the river, go and check that, too. It's not cold at this time of year, but we don't know what clothing she had on when she went missing, and she certainly hasn't eaten for twenty-four hours.'

Kay watched as Sharp directed his eyes at the nearest camera before speaking again.

'Alice will be a very scared little girl, and we need to bring her home to her mother and father as quickly as possible.'

TEN

Kay yawned as she turned off the A20, and smiled at a patrol car that shot past in the opposite direction as she recognised the two occupants.

Her eyes caught the clock on the dashboard display – half past eight.

She was due back to the incident room at seven in the morning to relieve Sharp, but doubted she'd sleep. Having left Headquarters only fifteen minutes ago, she'd already glanced at her mobile phone on the passenger seat twice while stopped at traffic lights, willing a call to come through that would tell her Alice had been found safe.

Bleary-eyed, she weaved her way along a side street and then indicated left, savouring the warmth that blew through the open window and fluttered her hair.

Nearly twelve hours had passed since her phone had shrilled from its position on the bedside table, jostling her awake and delivering the news that a body had been found in the river.

She exhaled as the car crackled over the gravel driveway outside the house and braked to a standstill behind Adam's new four-wheel drive, the back window emblazoned with the name and phone number for his veterinary surgery.

Easing herself from behind the wheel, she staggered across to the front door.

It swung open before she had a chance to insert her key in the lock and her partner, Adam, enveloped her in a hug.

He held her for a moment, neither of them speaking.

She inhaled the musky scent of his soap, burying her face against the soft cotton white T-shirt he wore over faded jeans, and curled her fingers into the thick wavy black hair at the nape of his neck.

Adam pulled away with a sigh, before leading her into the hallway and closing the door.

'I saw the press conference,' he said. 'No news?'

'Not yet.' She reached out and squeezed his hand. 'I have to find her.'

'I know.'

Three years ago, Kay had suffered a miscarriage after a wrongful allegation had been made against her at work, and the stress had torn her apart. Finding out she would never have children had been the final cruel blow, and if it wasn't for Adam at her side, she knew she would have never recovered physically.

The emotional scars remained for both of them.

'Come on through to the kitchen,' he said. 'I figured you wouldn't want to eat much in the circumstances, so I've made soup. You can take the leftovers to work in the morning.'

Kay's shoulders began to relax as she followed him through to the back of the house, the blue and purple hues of a late summer sunset glowing through the kitchen window above the sink.

She frowned.

A large cage had been placed in the middle of the lawn. A box-like structure took up one side of it, and a long low trough had been set down next to a large ceramic bowl.

'Rescue chickens,' said Adam, before she could ask. 'Three of them. The farmer went broke, and abandoned the whole lot. A neighbour raised the alarm late yesterday. I'm just keeping an eye on them before they get rehomed by a family over at Barming.'

'What's wrong with them?'

'Dehydration, mostly, which is why they're hiding in the shelter, I expect. They'll be fine now that they're out of the place they were being kept in. I'll monitor them over the next week or so to make sure they haven't picked up any avian diseases, and then they'll be good to go.'

Kay noticed his top lip curl. 'How many were rescued in total?'

'Forty. The others didn't make it.'

She ran her hand over his back. 'But some did.'

'Yes.' He managed a smile.

'Will they lay eggs?'

'I doubt it. Not after what they've been through. They're all being kept as pets, as far as I know. There were a lot of regulars at the surgery who wanted to help when they heard the battery farm had gone out of business.'

Kay moved to one of the bar stools next to the central worktop and shoved her bag to the far end as Adam placed a glass of wine in front of her before returning to the stove.

An aroma of a rich vegetable broth hung in the air, and her stomach rumbled despite the anxiety that gripped her.

'What time are you out in the morning?' he said.

'Sharp needs me there by seven at the latest,' she said. 'He and Carys are working overnight.'

She watched as he reached into a drawer for a ladle and filled two large bowls with soup before setting one down in front of her, and passed her a spoon.

'Thanks,' she said, tearing a slice of bread in half and dunking the crust in the hot liquid. 'This smells great.'

Although Adam had been right about her stomach flip-flopping with nerves over the investigation, she relished the opportunity to spend some quiet time with him, to take a moment from the onslaught of the amount of information she was having to process, and to recharge before returning to the incident room.

She scraped the last of the soup off her bowl with her spoon, and sat back on the stool.

'That was fabulous, thanks.'

'There's more if you want it?' Adam raised an eyebrow.

'I'd better not. I won't sleep if I'm stuffed.'

She smiled, not wanting him to worry, and pulled her phone out of her bag.

There were no new messages.

'You're not going to sleep anyway, are you?'

She shook her head. 'I don't think so.'

Adam pushed the empty bowls away, and took her hand. 'At least rest.'

'I'll try.' Kay ran a hand through her hair and tried to blink away the tiredness that seized her.

In her mind, the image of Alice's face haunted her thoughts, and she bit back the fear. She had a job to do, and she would do all she could to reunite the little girl with her mother.

Whatever it took.

ELEVEN

Gavin Piper slurped the second large cappuccino he'd ordered since six o'clock that morning, and stared at his computer screen.

Half an hour ago, he'd handed a steaming takeaway cup of hot chocolate to Carys before sending her home. His colleague had looked exhausted, her tiredness exacerbated by the lack of progress in locating Alice overnight.

After leaving the incident room the previous evening, he'd headed straight for the gym around the corner from his flat, taking out his frustration with a brutal boxing session that had left him exhausted.

He still hadn't slept, and his appetite had disappeared.

He hit the refresh icon at the top of the email provider's website URL for the seventeenth time in the past fifteen minutes, his other hand hovering over the speed dial on his desk phone while his foot tapped the floor.

He scowled as a soft stress ball hit the back of his head and then landed next to the keyboard.

'If you don't stop tapping your foot, the next object to hit your head will be the cricket ball Sharp keeps in his office,' said Barnes.

'Sorry. Can't help it.' Gavin turned away from the screen to find the older detective glaring at him. 'I just want to find her.'

Barnes's eyes softened. 'We all do, Piper. We all do. I take it there's no news from the boat hire companies?'

'Not yet. I'm waiting to hear back from a family-run business at Yalding. They should be in by now. Their website says they're open on Sundays.'

Barnes checked his watch. 'It's six forty-five. What time do they open?'

'Eight.'

'Give it another half an hour and call them again. And maybe give the caffeine a miss for a few hours.'

'Okay.'

'What about the other side of Maidstone? Wasn't there a boat hire company there?'

'There's a small operator just past Allington lock. They're not in until tomorrow, but I've left messages on the mobile number on their site.' Gavin held up a folder. 'Carys did a search and found their details on the Companies House website, so if I don't get an answer from them by nine o'clock, I was going to go over to the address listed to see if I can find someone to talk to.'

'All right. Sounds like you've got it under control,' said Barnes. 'Well done.'

Gavin swivelled in his chair as the door to the incident room opened and Kay strode in, mobile phone in hand and her hair tied back in a no-nonsense bun.

'Morning. Any news?' she said as she reached Barnes's desk.

'Nothing yet,' said the detective sergeant. 'Sharp is in his office. I tried to get him to leave an hour ago, but he wouldn't hear of it.'

The DI's lips pursed, and in that moment, Gavin saw the strain she was under.

'Guv, I'm waiting for a phone call back from the boat hire companies but do you want me to grab you a croissant or something for breakfast?' he said.

'Thanks – but don't worry.' Kay raised a thermos flask she'd been carrying. 'Adam's determined I won't pass out from starvation today, so I've got enough soup in here to feed the five thousand. And you wouldn't believe the size of the breakfast I've just had.'

She managed a smile, and put her bags on her desk before knocking on Sharp's office door.

Gavin turned away as his desk phone began to ring, and cleared his throat before answering. 'DC Piper.'

'Gav, it's Harriet. I've just heard back from the underwater search team.'

He beckoned to Barnes before putting the CSI lead on speakerphone. 'What've they found?'

'Well, I suppose it's a bit of good news – there's no sign of Alice in the River Medway. They've worked their way between Teston Bridge and Tovil since yesterday morning, including the weirs and lock. They took a break between ten o'clock last night and four o'clock this morning, but along with what we've managed to ascertain from our searches along the Medway Path, there's nothing to suggest that she wandered off on her own. Neither did she fall or get pushed into the river. There's no sign of her.'

'So, she was taken by someone,' said Barnes, running a hand over his chin.

'That's what I'm thinking,' said Harriet. 'But I'll leave that to you to investigate.'

'What about forensics from the boat?' said Gavin.

'Still working through them. We got traces of fibres in the decking – it might be old and unrelated to our victim or his killer, but I'll confirm that once we've taken a closer look. As for fingerprints and other trace evidence, it's going to be a day or so before we're able to give you the full picture. We'll update you piecemeal as we find anything of use.'

'What about the weapon?' said Barnes. 'Has that been found?'

'No – not on the boat, or in the water. The divers are packing up now.' Harriet covered her phone and spoke to someone in the background before returning to them. 'Have you heard from Lucas this morning?'

'Not yet,' said Gavin. 'He was hoping to get a chance to do the post mortem this afternoon so we'll let you know what transpires from that.'

'Okay, thanks. I'll call you as soon as I have anything new to report once we've assessed our findings.'

His mobile phone began to vibrate on the desk as he replaced the desk phone in its cradle, and he snatched it up.

'Hello? It's Frank Hutchins from Nettlestead boat hire near Yalding. Is that Detective Piper?'

'Yes, yes it is.' Gavin shoved his keyboard out of the way, flipped open his notebook to a new page, and checked his watch before recording the time and date and underlining it. 'I'm hoping you can help me.'

'Does this have anything to do with the missing girl?'

'It could have a bearing on that investigation, yes.'

'In that case, what can I do to help?'

The man's voice was cheerful, and Gavin sensed an underlying eagerness to answer his questions.

'I have to ask that what we discuss is treated as confidential,' he said, in an attempt to rein in Hutchins' clear penchant for gossip.

'Of course, of course.' The boat yard's owner sounded suitably chastened. 'Mum's the word.'

'Thanks. Do you have any bookings for boats in the name of Greg Victor? I'm interested in dates between the beginning of last week and the end of next in particular.'

'Hang on. I'll check the calendar. My daughter usually deals with this side of the business – it's all done electronically through our website, so it takes me a while to find my way around.'

Gavin muted the phone as Kay emerged from Sharp's office and headed towards his desk.

'What's happening?' she said.

'Just got a call back from one of the boat hire companies,' he said. 'And Harriet called.'

He started to tap his foot as the seconds dragged out, then stopped as Barnes glared at him.

The detective sergeant began talking to Kay in low tones, bringing her up to date with Harriet's assertion that the missing girl hadn't toppled into the water.

'Hello?'

Gavin's attention snapped back to the caller. 'I'm here.'

'I've got nothing in the diary in the name of Greg Victor.'

'Okay. What about any boats that were hired last week, but weren't collected? Did you have any bookings where customers didn't turn up?'

'Let's have a look.'

Barnes raised an eyebrow.

'He's looking,' said Gavin.

'At this rate, it'd be quicker if I took a car over there and looked myself,' the DS growled.

Gavin shook his head to silence him as Hutchins came back on the line.

'No, all our boats were picked up as planned. And they all came back, too.'

'Any missing from the yard that weren't booked?'

'No, all accounted for. We have security gates on the lane that leads to the yard, and CCTV cameras along the river side.'

'Could we get a copy of that CCTV footage to help us eliminate any activities through that stretch of water?'

'Of course. I'll pass on your phone number to my daughter and ask her to liaise with you to get the footage over.'

'All right. Thanks for your help.'

Gavin's shoulders sagged as he ended the call and turned to face Kay.

Sharp hovered at her side, his expression grim.

'Nothing?' he said.

'Not there, guv. I'm waiting for someone to call me back from the boat hire place at Allington. There were three there – two came back clear, but I need to speak to the last one.'

'Where are we with the CCTV from the borough council, guv?' said Barnes. 'Did anything come in overnight?'

Sharp shook his head. 'Nothing yet. Andy Grey is

over at headquarters and will chase up his contact there this morning. He's on standby for the digital forensics once we find Greg Victor's laptop and mobile phone, too. If we find them. Carys got a phone call from Hazel earlier this morning. There's no word from Robert Victor yet. Both she and Annette have tried to call him repeatedly, but his phone isn't connecting.'

'Guv, you should head off and get some rest,' said Kay. 'I'll call you as soon as we have a viable lead on Alice's whereabouts.'

The detective chief inspector checked his watch. 'Did any of you sleep last night?'

Barnes looked sheepish, and Gavin shook his head.

'Not much,' said Kay.

'I thought so. I'll be back at six o'clock,' said Sharp. 'I'll speak with the Chief Superintendent about getting more resources in from tomorrow via uniform. Now that the summer festivals are over, we might be able to get extra help from Tonbridge, too.'

'Thanks, guv,' said Kay.

Gavin watched the detective chief inspector leave, and then pushed his chair back.

'Where are you going?' said Barnes.

He shoved his mobile phone in his pocket. 'I can't sit here doing nothing, waiting for them to call, Ian. I'm going over to that address at Allington.'

TWELVE

A fresh breeze nipped at Gavin's neck as he locked the car, the early morning sunlight casting dappled shadows through the trees beside him.

He flipped up his collar and crossed the gravel car park that abutted the motel and pub next door to it, his mood darkened by the reality that Alice had been missing for over thirty-six hours, and there was still no sign of her.

It was as if the child had vanished into thin air, and he couldn't imagine how traumatised her parents must be.

He shook his head to clear the thought and turned his focus to a narrow twisting lane that led from the car park to the water's edge.

To his right, the pub's decking sprawled alongside the towpath. Rows of picnic tables had been set up for the patrons so they could sit and admire the scenery and the boats passing by.

Gavin noted that the brightly coloured brewery umbrellas had been taken indoors for safekeeping overnight and propped up against the floor-to-ceiling patio doors. No doubt if the manager hadn't done so, the same umbrellas would be cropping up that morning for sale at some of the less salubrious car boot sales in the county, to be bought by locals for their own gardens.

Two ducks waddled between the table legs, stopping now and then to peck at morsels stuck between the cracks in the decking before moving on in search of other culinary treasures.

Gavin turned his attention to the river.

An array of boats lined both sides of the banks on the Maidstone side, and a peacefulness enveloped the scene. The soft lap of water against hulls carried across the water as two cyclists shot past on mountain bikes, raising their hands in thanks as Gavin stepped back to let them pass.

He watched them recede into the distance, then turned his attention to a concrete slipway on the opposite side of the river. Next to it, a large pontoon had been piled high with equipment, and he spotted a line of boats in the yard beyond. Spotting the name of the company next to it, he turned away.

He'd already spoken to the helpful owners, and knew Greg Victor hadn't been in touch with them.

He set a brisk pace along the Medway Path towards

the steel and concrete structure of the lock, and took in the narrowboats and cabin cruisers moored either side of it. Talking to the boat yard owners across the other side, he'd ascertained that the lock provided a staging post between the tidal waters of the upper Medway and the calmer currents that flowed south through Maidstone and beyond into the Kentish countryside.

An idea had started to form as he'd tossed and turned last night, but he couldn't quite lay his finger on it yet. It nibbled away at the edges of his thoughts, fretting and worrying at the periphery.

He kicked a stone at the side of the path in frustration, and felt a little better as it flew into the water with a satisfying *plop*.

A little way past the lock, he found the small boat yard owned by Markus Tiverton.

Unlike the two larger companies he'd already spoken to, Tiverton's Hire appeared to be struggling.

Two scruffy cabin cruisers bobbed on the current, their fenders scraping against the concrete kerbing that had been constructed to reinforce the path beside the yard. Faded lettering along the sides proclaimed names for the boats, both ending in cheerful exclamation marks that were a stark contrast to the tattered curtains hanging at the windows and torn canvas awnings.

A sense of dereliction surrounded both vessels, which served as depressing examples of changing times within the hire trade on the Medway.

Compared to the brightly painted hire boats nearer

the pub and motel, Tiverton's vessels looked as if they'd sink at the first bow wave from a passing narrowboat, and Gavin wondered if either of them were safe.

A low-slung porta cabin served as the hire company's office, the cream-coloured walls worn in places. A gutter pipe hung off the right-hand side, a damp patch creating an indentation in the ground below it giving an indication as to how long it had been since anyone had thought to fix it.

He pulled out his mobile phone and dialled the landline number for the company again as he hovered at the step.

He could hear the phone ringing on the other side of the door, but there was no movement inside. No-one in.

Frustrated, he tried the mobile phone number he'd spotted on the side of one of the hire boats and then cursed as that went through to a lazy voicemail message as well.

'Can I help you?'

He spun around at the voice to see a squat man in his sixties storming towards him, his brow furrowed.

Gavin held out his warrant card as the man drew closer, and noticed his shoulders sag a little.

'I thought you looked too well dressed to be a burglar,' he said. 'What do you want?'

'Sorry, and you are?'

'Alan Evershall. I own the narrowboat over there, the *Daisy Lee*.'

'Do you know where Markus Tiverton is?'

'Down the coast, I reckon. He and Evelyn left early yesterday morning.' Evershall shrugged. 'It's not busy this weekend, so I suppose they thought they'd have a short break.'

'They went by boat?'

Evershall gave him a withering look. 'Well, they didn't drive. No – Markus has a four-berth cabin cruiser. They use it with friends for holidays and stuff.'

'When's he due back?'

'Well, he mentioned when I saw him on Friday that they were just going around the coast to Hastings for the weekend, so I'd imagine he'll be back late tonight or early tomorrow morning. Needs to be, see? In case of any bookings.'

Gavin ran his gaze over the dilapidated temporary office building and hire boats, and raised an eyebrow.

Evershall shrugged. 'I know, but it's still a business that needs to be run.'

'Then you'd think he'd be answering his mobile phone.' Gavin shook his head. 'How long have you known them?'

'I moved down this way about three years ago, so I suppose it must be about two months after that – after I bought *Daisy*. I saw Markus most mornings when I was around and about, and we got talking. Us boat people tend to look out for each other.'

'Are you likely to see him when he gets back?'

'Depends what time,' said Evershall. 'If he's back

late tonight, I probably won't see him until mid-morning. I've got family visiting later today.'

Gavin rummaged in his pocket and withdrew a business card. 'I've been trying to phone his mobile number for the past twenty-four hours. When you see him, could you ask him to call me if he hasn't spoken to me by then?'

Evershall turned the card in his fingers. 'This about the girl that's gone missing?'

'Yes. Do you know anything that could have a bearing on the case?'

'Wish I did, poor mite. I've got two granddaughters about the same age. Dreadful business, that.'

'Will you pass that on for me?'

'Of course.'

'Thanks.'

Gavin made his way back to the car, his shoes scuffing on the path as he mulled over his conversation with Evershall.

He scowled at a fisherman who tipped his hat as he passed him in the car park and called a cheery good morning, and then threw himself into the driver's seat and banged his fist against the steering wheel.

It galled him to think that there were people leading ordinary lives, enjoying themselves while a family waited for news about their missing daughter.

News he didn't have.

THIRTEEN

Barnes eyed the sign on the wall opposite the stairwell and curled his lip.

A few metres away, Kay paced the tiled corridor of the second level of Darent Valley Hospital, one hand over her ear to mitigate the voices carrying along from the pharmacy.

He checked his watch.

Lucas had brought forward the time for the post mortem on their victim. He'd phoned the incident room an hour ago as Barnes had been chewing a ham sandwich that had grown warm in its plastic wrapping while he'd been scrolling through reports on his computer screen. At the sound of the Home Office pathologist's voice, his appetite had waned and upon being summoned to the mortuary, he'd thrown the rest of the sandwich away.

With Gavin out following up leads, it had fallen to him to accompany the DI to the hospital.

He didn't say anything to Kay, but he would much rather have spent the afternoon focusing his efforts on leading the search for Alice.

Out of all his colleagues, he was the one who could most closely relate to what Annette Victor was going through. Only three years ago, his daughter had been kidnapped by a serial killer hell-bent on wreaking his revenge on Barnes and the police. It had been a miracle she had survived.

He clenched his fists and forced himself to do the job in hand as Kay finished her call and hurried back to where he waited.

'That was Gavin. No luck at the boat hire place – he spoke to someone moored close by who told him the owners are away until late tonight or tomorrow morning. In the meantime, there's a group of locals who want to help the search team. I said we'd pop over to see them when we've finished here to make sure they're coordinating with our people.'

'It's taking too long to find her,' he said. 'We should have something by now, but there's been no sighting.'

He clamped his mouth shut, hearing the tremble in his voice.

'I know, Ian. I know.' Kay jutted her chin at the sign pointing the way to the mortuary. 'Shall we get this over and done with?'

'Shouldn't take long,' said Barnes as he followed her. 'Cause of death, gunshot wound to head.'

'Don't let Lucas hear you say that.'

Fifteen minutes later, he'd swapped his suit for a set of plastic overalls that he'd pulled over his shirt and trousers, and tugged disposable bootees over his shoes. He scuffed along the polished tiled floor towards the double doors into the morgue, and held one open for Kay.

Immediately, the stench hit him.

He might tease Gavin about his dread at attending post mortems, but right now Barnes would rather be anywhere else than here.

The remnants of his ham sandwich tumbled in his stomach, and he suppressed a sickly belch in his throat as they approached the gurney in the middle of the room.

Lucas paused in his work and nodded when they drew closer, then placed the electric saw he'd been wielding to one side.

'How's it going?' said Kay. She kept away from the victim's head – or what was left of it – and positioned herself at the feet.

Barnes joined her, cleared his throat, and forced himself to concentrate on what the Home Office pathologist was saying.

'Our victim didn't stand a chance,' said Lucas.

'Harriet's team recovered the bullet yesterday,' said Barnes. 'She reckons it came from a nine millimetre.'

'I'm surprised there was much left of it after that journey,' said Lucas, gesturing to the victim's head.

'Point blank range?'

'I would say so. I've examined the cranial cavity, and whoever shot him pointed the gun within inches of the base of his skull. The bullet exited through the bridge of his nose, taking most of his brain and face with it.'

'So any clothing on the shooter would have gun residue on it,' said Kay.

'If he hasn't already dumped his clothes,' said Barnes. 'And it sounds like the killer could've been shorter than Greg if the bullet travelled at that angle.'

'It's worth considering,' said Lucas.

Kay took a step back and assessed the pitiful form laid out on the gurney. 'Any other injuries?'

The pathologist stepped away from the victim's head and gently lifted the man's hand. 'He has a broken wrist, probably caused when he went over the side of the boat – I've spoken to Carys's chap at the Environment Agency and he confirms there were no weirs or other obstacles that he could have collided with enough force to do that on his way downstream, not the way the current flows there. There's an old knee injury – probably ten years old or so. It looks like the sort of injury you'd expect to see in someone who played a lot of sport when they were younger. Apart from that, he was a healthy individual.'

'All right, thanks, Lucas,' said Kay.

Barnes could hear the disappointment in her voice. 'Will you get the fingerprint details over to us as soon as you can?' he said to Lucas. 'I'll have someone run them through the system again to corroborate the evidence we've got to date.'

'Will do,' said Lucas. 'We'll also get the other samples over to Harriet and her team so they can test them against what they took from the boat.'

'Sounds good. We'll get out of your way. Thanks.'

'Any news about the little girl?'

Kay pursed her lips. 'Not yet.'

She turned away, and Barnes nodded to Lucas before hurrying to catch up with her, catching the door as it swung shut. She paused outside, and leaned against the wall, the back of her coveralls squashing the contents of a staff bulletin board.

'She's out there, somewhere,' said Barnes, his voice strained.

Her eyes met his, and she rubbed her arms to ease the goosebumps that prickled her skin.

'I hope so, Ian. I don't know what I'm going to do if we're too late.'

FOURTEEN

Kay rolled up her sleeves as Police Sergeant Harry Davis strode across the recreation area towards her, a man and woman at his side.

A throng of people crowded next to a marquee that had been erected next to the entrance a few metres away, gathering around a group of uniformed police officers who worked in pairs handing out leaflets.

At the far end of the park, a swing set, roundabout and slide stood abandoned. Not a single child could be seen across the expanse of green that stretched from the back of the community hall to the primary school playing field.

Kay turned away from the sorry sight.

'Detective Inspector, this is Reverend Maureen McCaffery of the local All Saints' church and Peter Johnson, headmaster of the primary school here,' said Harry, and waited while Kay and Barnes introduced themselves. 'Maureen gave the incident room a call after the media appeal went out last night and between them they've organised this group of volunteers to help. They're providing food and drink for the officers conducting the search.'

'That's brilliant,' said Kay as she watched the groups manning barbecues under the shade of gazebos. 'Thank you very much.'

'We had to do something,' said Peter, shaking his head. 'I've got a daughter about the same age at home. I can't imagine what her parents are going through.'

'What's your plan of action, Harry?' said Barnes as the two local community members wandered off and joined a large group that were heading in the direction of a footpath that led across a field of barley.

'The teams have finished the house-to-house enquiries for properties abutting the railway and the Medway Path,' said the police sergeant. 'We've concluded that there's no trace of Alice on the towpath between East Farleigh and Tovil, so after speaking with Alistair Matthews I've moved my officers forward to the stretch beyond Tovil and into Maidstone.'

He held up a map and tapped the page. 'I've arranged to work with personnel here to start searching the wider area north of the riverbank and railway, to eliminate the possibility that Alice might have wandered further afield, or that whoever took her cut through the footpaths and woodland that borders the boundary along here.'

Kay frowned. 'And there's been absolutely no sighting of her by property owners next to the river?'

'Nothing, I'm afraid.'

'I suppose it was a long shot, given the time of night we think Greg Victor was killed,' said Barnes. 'Even if it's still light until nearly ten o'clock in the evening, most people would have been indoors watching television or something rather than sitting outside.'

'I'm inclined to agree,' said Harry. 'But at least this way we can door knock a few more residents and ask them to check any outbuildings. Not everyone will have seen the appeal last night, or the papers this morning with Alice's photograph inside.'

'You'll stay here until they're finished?' said Kay.

'Yes. I'd rather be on hand in case something is found.'

'How many officers have you got working with you?'

The police sergeant snorted. 'Not enough. As usual.'

Kay turned to watch a second group of officers cross the lane and head east towards Maidstone, and took a step back in surprise as a group of teenagers handed out bottles of water to them as they passed. 'There are teenagers helping, too.'

Harry smiled. 'Not all of them are stuck indoors playing computer games. It seems that when Peter rang around to ask some of the parents to help, the older siblings decided to come too. They've taken it upon themselves to set up a social media group and deliver leaflets around the housing estates in that direction.'

'There's hope yet,' said Barnes. 'Is there anything we can do?'

Shaking his head, Harry tugged on his cap and folded the map. 'No, but thanks. It's all under control. I'll give you a call if I have anything to report. I'd imagine we'll be here for a few hours yet by the time we've worked our way through this grid pattern.'

'I'll call you if we find out anything that might help you,' said Kay.

He raised his hand in farewell, then jogged away across to where two of his officers stood talking to Maureen and Peter.

Kay turned to Barnes, who wore a haunted expression as he watched the last of the search groups leave the recreation area.

She had no words of comfort to give him – the little girl had been missing too long already without news of her whereabouts or a sighting. She wondered how many parents had volunteered out of a sense of duty, and how many had signed up out of a sense of fear because someone in their midst had brutally slain a man before taking a child and disappearing without a trace.

Kay frowned. 'Ian? We've been assuming that whoever shot Greg Victor panicked. What if all this was premeditated?'

'Annette said she hadn't received any ransom demands.'

'What if it's not about kidnapping? What if whoever took Alice has no intention of giving her back?'

Barnes's eyes darkened. 'You mean—'

Kay gestured towards the car. 'Phone the incident room while I drive us back there. Have them go through the sex offenders register again to see who's closest to this location or the Victors' home in Tonbridge as a start. After you've done that, get on to Hazel. Find out what social media accounts Annette and her husband have, and whether they've ever posted photographs of Alice outside of their group of friends.'

Her detective sergeant had his phone to his ear by the time she'd thrown the car into gear and was bumping it over the rough surface of the car park behind the school.

As she listened to him speak, she recalled another conversation and shoved the car into a lower gear.

The car surged forwards as she overtook a slow-moving camper van with her foot flat to the floor.

The conversation beside her ended, and she clenched her jaw.

'Kay? What's wrong?' said Barnes.

'What if Gavin's right, Ian? What if whoever took Alice escaped with her by boat?'

Barnes ran a hand over his eyes before he answered.

'She could be anywhere, guv. They could have taken her out of the country by now.'

FIFTEEN

Four hours later, Kay gathered together the notes she'd spread across her desk as Sharp walked through the door to the incident room, and pushed back her chair.

'Front of the room, everyone. Let's get the briefing underway,' she said. 'I know some of you have been here a while today so the sooner we can get through this, you can head home and get some rest.'

'How're you doing?' Sharp murmured as he joined her at the front of the room.

Kay ran a hand over tired eyes, and fought down a yawn. 'All right, in the circumstances. We've got a lot of information coming in after yesterday's press conference. Debbie and her team have started getting statements and other details from the searches and house-to-house enquiries into HOLMES2.'

She turned her attention to the team of police officers who had corralled themselves at the end of the room closest to the whiteboard. It never ceased to amaze her how many people could be involved in a major investigation, and she saw that many of her colleagues were having to stand – all the chairs and available desk space was taken.

'We're going to need a bigger room,' she said to Sharp.

'I spoke to the Chief Super on the way over here,' he said. 'We're going to move the investigation next door over to headquarters so you can use that space as well. I'd have preferred to move you lot over to HQ, but she's of the opinion that you're more centralised here so if any members of the public want to drop in with information to help, then they can. You're a bit more accessible to the town centre for anyone who doesn't drive.'

'Okay, thanks, guv.' She cleared her throat, and then turned to Barnes. 'Ian, could you start and give us an update on your conversations with Hazel this afternoon?'

The detective sergeant loosened his tie, and flipped through the pages of his notebook. 'Annette Victor confirms that she's never posted photographs of Alice on social media. Annette only has a couple of accounts and hasn't used those much. Said she doesn't have time, and that it's not her sort of thing. She doesn't think her husband, Robert, has ever had a social media account.'

Kay frowned. 'What about Greg Victor?'

'We had a bit more luck there,' said Barnes. 'He's

got a social media account but hasn't posted anything to his timeline since leaving Nottingham. Not that what's on there is of much use anyway – it's mostly reposted jokes, videos, things like that. No photos of Alice, and no mention of him moving down this way. His personal details still show his location as being Nottingham.'

'Has Robert Victor been in touch yet?' said Sharp.

'No-one's heard from him, guv.'

'Wasn't he due back last night?' said Kay.

Barnes shrugged. 'Annette told Hazel that sometimes he gets delayed – or another meeting gets added on to the end of his trip at the last minute. She doesn't have an alternative phone number for him, either.'

'What about the hire car he was driving? Can you get those details from his office as well? They must have booked that for him before he flew out, so we might be able to trace him that way.'

'I've got a note to do that.'

'Thanks, Ian. Okay – who's looking into the sex offenders register and previous convictions for assault in relation to local names?' said Kay.

'Me, guv.' Debbie West raised her hand, then moved to the front of the room so everyone could see her. A police constable with considerable experience and an uncanny way with the HOLMES2 database, she was always someone Kay could rely upon.

'Right,' she said. 'There were fifteen names on the sex offenders register, and we coordinated with uniform to interview those over the course of this afternoon. We've also spoken to anyone with previous assault convictions as well as those on warrant and awaiting sentencing. Long story short, none of them have been in contact with the Victor family, nor have they been anywhere near that stretch of the River Medway. Two of the men on warrant are away from home at the moment – one is visiting his mother in Cardiff, and the other is at his brother's house in Penzance. Local forces spoke with them, and confirm that they haven't been in the Kent area for the past two weeks.'

'Dead end, then,' said Barnes, his voice glum.

Kay wasn't sure whether to feel relieved or frustrated. 'Thanks, Debbie. Good work. Who was looking through the Tonbridge side of things?'

'Over here.' PC Phillip Parker raised his hand. 'I've spoken to the head of the kindergarten where Alice has been continuing to attend twice a week until she starts school next month. It's quite an exclusive place, with a limited number of children there over the summer holidays. She can't recall her staff reporting anyone hanging around outside the gates or acting suspicious in recent weeks. There haven't been any incidents or upsets amongst the parents or kids, and she isn't aware of any threats to Alice or any of the other children. We've been working through the list of friends and acquaintances that Hazel got from Annette, and we haven't come across anything untoward from that angle. I've made a start adding statements from their neighbours into HOLMES2, and I'll finish that before I leave tonight.'

'Thanks, Phillip,' said Sharp. He raised his chin as the door opened, and Alistair pushed his way through the gathered officers. 'Any news?'

The PolSA shook his head, his brow furrowed.

'The last group from the search teams got back twenty minutes ago and are being debriefed by Harry at the recreation area,' he said, 'but we've got nothing. There've been no sightings of Alice. The residents out that way have been fantastic, checking their sheds again and putting up posters, but—'

He broke off with a helpless shrug.

Kay turned to Gavin. 'Piper, get on to that boat hire company in Allington first thing in the morning. We have to refocus our search on the possibility that Alice was kidnapped and taken somewhere by boat now that the land-based searches haven't turned up anything conclusive.'

'Will do, guv.'

'Has anyone got an update from Harriet?' said Kay. 'What's the latest from the team down at East Farleigh?'

'The divers have completed their search of the river and the lock,' said Debbie. 'No sign of a discarded weapon. They've been working on Greg Victor's car this afternoon. Harriet's assistant, Patrick, spoke with the boat hire company at Tonbridge and they've confirmed no-one's been back to try to collect the car since he left it with them on Friday morning. Patrick's report will be emailed over first thing tomorrow morning, but he confirms they found blonde hair on the material covering a child seat, and there were toys in the footwell.'

'Did the divers or Harriet's team find anything to suggest what might have happened to Alice?' said Kay.

'Nothing,' said Debbie. 'Nothing at all.'

SIXTEEN

Carys reached across the desk for the china mug emblazoned with the logo of an animated film franchise, then wrinkled her nose in disgust after taking a sip.

The tea was stone cold.

Turning the page of the witness statement she'd printed out along with four others, she ran her finger over the text and blinked through bleary eyelids.

Beside her, PC Laura Hanway's fingers pecked at a computer keyboard while she worked her way through another collection of CCTV footage received from the digital forensics unit at Headquarters, her mouth set in a fine line.

Three o'clock in the morning – over forty-eight hours since Alice had gone missing – and still no answers.

Carys raised her arms above her head and stretched, then glared at her watch.

'God, I need a break,' said Laura. 'Do you want another cuppa, ma'am?'

'Please.' Carys handed her the half-empty mug. 'Cheers – and don't worry about the formalities in here. Carys will do.'

'No problem, thanks.'

'How come you got the late shift?'

'I, er, I volunteered.' Laura stood next to her chair, her eyes downcast for a moment. 'I wanted to help.'

'You've applied to become a detective, haven't you? Do you want to work in major crimes when you've completed your exams?'

'I'd love to.' Laura's voice faltered. 'But I know how hard I've got to work. And I'm not doing this just to make a good impression with the DI. I want to find Alice.'

Carys smiled, and pointed at the two china mugs. 'Grab the tea, then. We're going to need more caffeine.'

'Right.'

Exhaling, Carys turned back to the paperwork she'd spread out over her desk and resisted the urge to sigh. She'd undertaken to review the statements from the previous day's house-to-house enquiries along the towpath and other footpaths and byways that led from the river.

Uniformed officers had worked with Alistair Matthews to ensure every property had been accounted for, but it was now her responsibility to double-check each one and find out if there were any anomalies or clues that might lead to a breakthrough.

She twirled a blunt pencil between her fingers as she pored over the information, keeping notes about anything she wanted to cross-check as she worked her way through, and determined to find something to give Kay and Barnes when they walked in the door at seven o'clock.

She'd seen the strain her two colleagues had been under since attending the crime scene the previous day, despite their best efforts at keeping their emotions to themselves.

Both had experienced pain and trauma in their lives, and she knew that Barnes especially would be haunted by Alice's kidnapping and that of his own daughter only a few years ago.

'Here you go. Tea.'

Laura's voice jerked her from her thoughts.

'Thanks. How's it going with the CCTV images?'

The police constable sank into her chair. 'Slow, but I've managed to discount anything from the streets around Tovil and that side of the river. I've just got the remnants of footage from private residents and business owners to go through now. There's no sign of her, Carys. Nothing at all.'

Carys bit her lip, the other woman's despair cutting into her.

'Keep going. Even if we don't find anything on

camera, we have to discount it. It's still important work, all right?'

Laura nodded, and turned back to her computer screen with renewed determination in her eyes.

Sifting through the last of the witness statements, Carys shuffled them into a stack and then reached into her tray for the next batch. She noticed that these had been taken from the employees of the wine merchant business that Robert Victor worked for.

All had been shocked at the news that his daughter was missing, and it became evident as Carys read through the notes that Alice had been a regular visitor to the offices in Sevenoaks.

Most of the interviews had been conducted by phone call, with two requiring home visits by uniformed officers earlier that day when employees hadn't answered their phones. The final interview had been conducted at five o'clock on Saturday afternoon, only hours before Carys had started her current shift.

A fresh wave of exhaustion threatened, but she squared her shoulders and forced herself to concentrate.

She reached the third statement in the pile, noted the officer's name at the top of the bespoke questionnaire that had been created for the purposes of the investigation based on knowledge gleaned to date, and ran her eye down the now familiar pattern.

Frowning, she reread the response to the penultimate question, and then snatched up the second and fourth statements.

'That's weird.'

'Hmm?' Laura's chair squeaked as she shifted her weight.

Carys didn't answer, and instead rose from her desk and hurried across the incident room to Sharp's office.

She paused as she heard him speaking in a low voice, and knocked twice on the door that was ajar.

'Guv?'

Sharp looked up from his phone screen and beckoned her in. 'How are you doing, Carys? Holding up all right?'

'I've been better.' She hovered at the threshold. 'Have you got a minute?'

'Of course. Come on in. What have you got?'

In reply, Carys held up Melissa Lampton's witness statement. 'Robert Victor's personal assistant told uniform that he landed in Paris at Charles de Gaulle airport on Monday morning. She said she spoke to him on Thursday to confirm some last-minute details.'

Sharp frowned. 'And?'

'Annette Victor told Kay and Barnes that she hadn't heard from her husband since he left the country,' said Carys. 'What sort of man speaks to his PA, but not his wife? I mean, even if he was busy with meetings and things, wouldn't he still want to speak to his daughter? Barnes said there were photos of Alice all over the place in Robert's study at the house. He obviously dotes on her, so why hasn't he been in touch?'

Sharp tapped his ballpoint pen on the desk and

leaned back in his chair, the ancient springs protesting as he shifted his weight. Finally, he spoke.

'I agree, it does warrant further investigation,' he said. 'Do any of the other statements from employees give you cause for concern?'

'No, but I wouldn't mind speaking with Melissa Lampton,' said Carys. 'It may be nothing—'

'But it's worth making sure.' Sharp tossed the pen onto the desk and clasped his hands. 'I agree, it's worth following up.'

'I'll take Laura with me and head over there before clocking off this morning,' said Carys. 'Hopefully they'll be open early, and we'll get some information to pass on for the day shift to work through.'

'If anyone can find a lead it's you, Miles.' Sharp managed a smile. 'I can't think of a better mentor for our new recruit out there.'

Carys swallowed, a prickle of heat flushing her cheeks. 'Thanks, guv.'

SEVENTEEN

Kay shoved her car keys into the side pocket of her handbag, then swiped a pile of messages from her desk.

As her eyes skimmed the notes, she reordered them into what would take priority and what could wait.

She frowned as her gaze fell upon her colleague's thin coat hanging on the back of the chair opposite.

'Is Carys still here?' said Kay.

'She took Laura with her and headed over to Wilkinson's Wine Merchants just before you got here,' said Sharp, emerging from his office. 'She was reading through the employee statements last night and found out that Robert Victor's PA spoke with him on Thursday. Annette Victor told you she hadn't heard from her husband since he left for his trip, right?'

'Yes.' Kay frowned. 'That's odd, isn't it?'

'Carys thought so, too. She said she wanted to

follow it up first thing today before clocking off, so I cleared it.' He managed a rueful smile. 'You know what she's like once she gets an idea into her head. Better to let her get on with it than get in the way.'

'True. It'll be interesting to hear what she finds out.'

Sharp waited while Barnes hurried towards his desk and nodded at the two senior officers. 'Did either of you get the impression the marriage was in trouble when you were over there on Saturday?'

'I didn't pick up on anything,' said Barnes. 'I had a quick look around upstairs after I'd finished in the guest room, but everything seemed normal. They're sharing a bedroom, at least.'

'And there were family photographs everywhere,' said Kay. 'Annette's demeanour was certainly one of a worried wife and mother when we questioned her. I didn't get the impression that she got involved in the business side of things, though.'

'There were some flyers and brochures for the local gym and a ladies' badminton group on the kitchen table,' said Barnes. 'As well as a letter that had been opened from a local private school. I imagine Alice would have been starting there within a couple of weeks.'

The room fell silent at his words, and he lowered his eyes.

Sharp cleared his throat. 'As you say, Ian – it all points to a normal family life at the moment. We'll see what Carys comes back with later this morning and if that has any bearing on the situation, then let me know.'

'Will do, guv,' said Kay. She took the sheaf of papers he held out to her and ran her eyes down the lines of text.

The evening shift had progressed without incident or breakthrough in the case, and she clenched her jaw at the thought of Alice spending a third night without her mother.

'I'm going to head off, but phone me if you need me,' said Sharp. He patted her arm. 'Someone out there knows where she is. Don't give up hope.'

He raised his hand in farewell to Gavin, who held a phone to his ear, engrossed in conversation.

Kay watched the detective chief inspector leave, and then turned her focus to her team.

'All right,' she said, as Gavin ended his call and wandered over, 'with Carys and Laura following up their enquiry with Melissa Lampton, we'll keep our focus on the river. Barnes – could you give the local stations at Gillingham and Sheerness a call to find out if there have been any sightings of Alice near the estuary? The all ports alert has been live since Saturday morning, but those things are never easy to police with this much coastline to monitor.'

'Will do.'

'Gavin – what's the latest from your side?'

The detective constable checked his watch. 'The

boat yard at Allington reopens at eight-thirty so I'll give them a call. They should've been back from their weekend jaunt last night, but I didn't hear from them.'

'Keep me posted on that,' said Kay. 'I can only presume that they don't take work mobile phones with them when they go away.'

Gavin cocked an eyebrow. 'That would explain why their business looks like it's on its last legs.'

Kay ran through the rest of the tasks she needed to delegate, then dismissed the team and turned to switch on her computer.

As Sharp's deputy SIO, she balanced a precarious amount of management tasks on top of leading the investigation with him. She contemplated the list of emails that had multiplied since leaving the incident room the previous night, and tried to focus on what she needed to do from a political as well as investigative angle.

It would do her no good if she accidentally caused friction amongst other senior detectives by seeking additional resources from an already stretched department or team.

A phone rang in the background, and her subconscious recognised Gavin's voice talking in low tones as he answered it. All around her, the sound of fingers on keyboards, urgent conversations and calls being answered filled the air with a constant hum of activity.

'Guv!'

She turned as the detective constable shoved his way between two abandoned chairs and hurried towards her.

'What's up?'

'That was the boatyard at Allington – they haven't got any record of a boat being hired in the name of Greg Victor—'

'Damn it—'

'But they did have one rented in the name of *Robert* Victor.'

'What?'

'He made the booking a week ago, but didn't show up to collect it on Friday night.'

Kay frowned, and ran her hand through her hair. 'Why on earth would Greg Victor hire one boat in his name, and another in his brother's name?'

'The lock at Allington has to be operated by a lock-keeper,' said Gavin. 'If Greg didn't know what time he'd be arriving there on Saturday, he might not have been able to phone ahead to have the lock opened. Robert might have hired the second boat, given that he was meant to be back on Saturday. Perhaps he was going to surprise his daughter. We can ask him when we speak to him.'

'Did the boat hire company at Allington confirm the phone number that was used to place the booking, or the bank card details?' said Barnes, scratching the fine stubble on his jaw.

'Yes. Exactly the same as the ones used to hire the first boat. In both instances, it was Greg's.'

'If he was using his own phone number and card details then, why on earth book it in his brother's name?'

Kay ran a hand through her hair. 'We're going around in bloody circles.'

EIGHTEEN

Carys squinted up at the Georgian façade of the stone-clad merchant's house, and slammed shut the car door.

A blue plaque on the wall stated that the building had once housed a semi-famous writer for all of seven days, and she automatically checked over her shoulder. There were no tourists – yet – and she relaxed a little in the knowledge that their visit to Robert Victor's place of work would go unnoticed.

Laura twisted her hair into a low ponytail. Out of uniform, the police constable wore a smart black trouser suit similar to that Carys was wearing, and exuded a new level of confidence beside the detective constable.

'What do you need me to do?' she said.

'We'll head in and introduce ourselves,' said Carys, and checked her watch. 'It's gone nine o'clock, so everybody should be in by now. I want to concentrate on Melissa Lampton this morning, though – none of the other statements raised a flag. If you take the notes, I'll lead the questions, but if we get to the end of the interview and you think I've left out something, then jump in. I'm not the sort of person who worries about her ego, and we still need to find a five-year-old missing girl. Ready?'

Laura nodded, and locked the car.

Carys hurried up a flight of three stone steps, and pushed against one of two brightly painted wooden double doors. She stepped into a wide reception area, the floor covered with a burgundy coloured carpet that soaked up the sound of her footsteps.

Off to her left, an elongated reception desk curved beneath an oak bannister. Large photographs hung on the walls, each depicting a scenic view across a vineyard at dusk or first thing in the morning, with mist clinging to ghostly wooden and wire framework.

'Can I help you?'

Carys crossed the carpet to the receptionist, who had risen from her chair and was poised with a pen in her hand, her brow creased.

'You're the police, yes?'

'That's right.' She held out her warrant card and introduced Laura. 'Sorry, you are?'

'Sharon Eastman.'

Carys recalled the name from the statements taken over the course of the weekend. 'We'd like to speak with Melissa Lampton, please.'

'Do you have an appointment?'

'No, but given the nature of the situation, I'm sure that won't be necessary.'

'Of course.' Sharon lowered her gaze and picked up a phone. 'Take a seat, I'm sure she won't be a minute.'

Laura crossed to a pair of sofas on the other side of the reception area that had been placed either side of an ornate fireplace.

A vase containing dried flowers had been arranged in the hearth, and Carys wondered what the building would have looked like when it was once a family home.

She reached out for one of the trade magazines that had been left on a table next to one of the sofas and flicked through it, trying to temper her impatience.

Fifteen minutes later, she was pacing the carpet while Laura stared through the window to the street beyond, nibbling at a fingernail as she watched the passing traffic.

'I'm so sorry to have kept you.'

Carys turned at the voice to see a woman in a blue blouse and navy skirt hurrying down the staircase towards them, her brown hair cut into a severe bob that brushed against her cheeks.

The woman held out her hand as she approached.

'Melissa Lampton.'

Older than she had expected, Melissa carried an air of efficiency that soon saw both police officers whisked up the staircase and shown into a meeting room at the back of the building.

Any noise from the street was blocked out as Robert Victor's personal assistant closed the door and gestured to the oval table in the middle of the room.

'Take a seat. Would you like tea, coffee – water, perhaps?'

'No, thanks.'

'Right.' Melissa twisted the ring on her right hand. 'What did you want to see me about?'

'Please, take a seat.'

Carys waited until the woman had perched on a chair to her left, and made sure Laura was ready to take notes.

'Have you heard from Robert Victor again since you spoke to him on Thursday?'

Melissa shook her head. 'Not a word. Mind you, the reception isn't great in that region.' She smiled. 'They might make fabulous wine, but their mobile signal leaves a lot to be desired.'

'I believe we're waiting for a copy of his itinerary.'

The PA raised her hands. 'I know, and I'm so sorry – when we got in this morning, it turned out our intranet was down. We can't access any of our work at the moment. The phones only got reconnected half an hour ago.'

'Do you have a printed copy available?'

'No, I'm sorry – we have a policy here that nothing gets printed out unless it's absolutely essential.' Melissa's mouth twisted. 'I know they tell us it's all about the planet, but I can't help feeling sometimes it's just a cost-saving exercise.'

'All right, can you recall what the hire car arrangements were for his trip?'

'Um… I know he wanted something special so he could travel in comfort. He was driving himself this time. Occasionally, we'll book a driver for him as well – especially if he's planning to see several vineyards across a wide area and do tastings. This time he was on his own, though.'

'Where did he fly to?'

'Paris. He would have collected the car from there, too.'

'Do you have the name of the hire company, and perhaps some phone details?'

'I've got one of their business cards stuck to my computer screen. Hang on – I'll get it for you.'

Carys exhaled as the door closed behind Melissa, and rolled her eyes. 'Good grief. This is hard work.'

Laura was biting her lip, her eyes amused. 'Some people have no sense of urgency, do they, ma'am?'

'It makes you wonder.'

The door opened, and Melissa hurried into the room. She held out a dog-eared business card to Carys.

'That's them. We've used them for the past two years.'

'Any problems?'

'No. They're one of the better ones.'

Carys passed the card to Laura and turned her

attention back to Melissa. 'What time did you speak to Robert on Thursday?'

The woman frowned. 'About half past four, I seem to recall.'

'What did you talk about?'

'He wanted some specialised information emailed across so that he could share it with a potential client that afternoon.' Melissa shrugged. 'We have our standard sales brochures and Robert always takes those with him while travelling, but if he hears about an opportunity not covered by those, we can send the information over. Most of our people who travel carry tablet computers with them so they can show the clients what we're capable of without having to cart around lots of documentation.'

'More cost savings?' said Carys.

Red splotches appeared on Melissa's cheeks. 'I suppose so, yes.'

'Have you spoken to him since Thursday?'

Melissa shook her head. 'No – there was no need. He was meant to be back here this morning. We've got a meeting with a supplier at two o'clock.'

'What do you mean? Haven't you seen him?'

'No. No-one has. We've been trying to phone him since the lines were reconnected,' she said, confusion sweeping across her features. 'There's no answer on his mobile number – it keeps going to voicemail.'

NINETEEN

Kay checked her notes, and then scrawled an update on the whiteboard in large block capitals that could be read at a distance, and underlined words for emphasis where required.

She re-capped the pen and took a step back, taking in the bullet points and angles of enquiry that were beginning to resemble a spider's web of information.

In the centre of the board, a photograph of Alice served as a reminder to everyone present about what was at stake.

And everyone wanted to be on shift when the little girl was found safe and well.

Kay swallowed. She wouldn't contemplate the alternative – not until she knew for sure.

She paused as the clatter of a helicopter overhead shook the windows, a reminder that her airborne colleagues were doing all they could to locate Alice.

She sifted through the paperwork in her hand, reading through the latest reports from dog search teams, from Harry Davis in his role as LPSM, and from other uniformed police officers who were coordinating wider search areas and liaising with eager members of the public requiring careful supervision.

She bit her lip. If she became overwhelmed, she wouldn't be able to lead her team.

Her shoulders sagged at the sight of the two women who walked towards her.

A fourteen-hour shift and the stress of Alice's disappearance had taken their toll on Carys and Laura, who both looked exhausted.

Carys rubbed at tired eyes as she approached, but managed a small smile. 'Morning, guv.'

'Morning. How did you get on?'

'Melissa Lampton confirmed she hasn't spoken to Robert Victor since Thursday afternoon, same as her original statement. But we did get this.' She held up the business card for the car hire company. 'I'll give them a call this morning – Melissa said Robert hired a luxury model, so it must've had a GPS tracker fitted to it for security purposes. Hopefully we'll be able to locate him and get in touch.'

'Tell you what,' said Kay. 'Give that to me and I'll have one of the others make the phone call. You two look shattered, and you need to rest.'

'But, guv—' said Laura.

'That's my final word.' Kay smiled to soften the

order. 'You're no good to me if you're tired, and you need to get home safely yet. What's it been, sixteen hours since you last slept?'

Carys mumbled a reply, then shrugged.

'Did you get anything else from Robert's PA?' said Kay.

'Only that their internet and phone lines have been down all weekend by the sounds of it,' said the detective constable. 'Which explains why we haven't received a copy of his itinerary.'

'What are your thoughts? Do you think he's been delayed somewhere?'

'Maybe he's having an affair,' said Laura. She shrugged, then blushed under Kay's scrutiny. 'I mean, he wouldn't be keen to get in touch with us if it meant breaking up his marriage.'

'Good point,' said Carys. 'But surely he would've seen the news? Alice's photograph has been on the telly up and down the country since yesterday morning, and the radio stations have been broadcasting the story about her disappearance since Saturday night.'

Dread spiked Kay's heart rate as an idea began to form.

She wandered across to the whiteboard, cutting off her colleagues in mid-sentence with a slight shake of her head, and stood before the swirls of handwriting – hers, Sharp's, Barnes's – that had been added as their enquiries grew and splintered into different avenues.

A dead man.

A kidnapped five-year-old girl.

And, underpinning it all, was the thought that she had no suspect – and no motive.

'Guv!'

Barnes's voice cut across the white noise and hum of conversation all around her.

'Who is it?'

'Harriet. Fingerprint results are in.'

'Ask her to send them across and we'll get someone to run it through the system to corroborate it's Greg Victor.'

'It's not that, guv – they've already had someone do that.'

'What's the problem, then?'

'Our victim isn't Greg Victor,' said Barnes. 'It's his brother. It's Robert Victor.'

TWENTY

Kay snatched the phone from Barnes.

'Harriet? How sure are you?'

'We've spoken with Lucas, and I'm confident we're within ninety per cent accuracy,' said the CSI lead. 'We got a full print on the door frame leading down into the cabin of the boat, and a partial under the window next to the door. We just had someone put our results through the system and Robert's name came up as a match.'

'Thanks, Harriet.'

Kay handed the phone back to Barnes, who murmured a response to the CSI lead before hanging up.

'Why is Robert Victor in our database?'

'He had a previous conviction for drink driving ten years ago,' said Barnes, his eyes scanning the screen. 'He received a fine and was banned from driving for a while, but no custodial sentence.'

'Sharp's office. Now. Carys, grab Gavin and meet us in there. Laura – write up your report and notes from this morning's conversation with Melissa Lampton please, and ask Debbie to phone the car hire company. After that, head home and we'll see you back here at seven o'clock tonight.'

'Ma'am.'

Kay snatched her mobile phone off her desk as she passed, then held open the door to Sharp's office for Barnes.

'What are your initial thoughts, Ian?'

'Maybe the two brothers had a falling out,' he said, perching on the windowsill, his arms folded across his chest.

'Some falling out,' said Gavin as he joined them and sank into one of the visitors' chairs opposite Sharp's desk. He gestured to the less shabby of the two seats and waited until Carys had settled next to him. 'And it still doesn't explain why Robert came back to the UK without telling his work colleagues – or his wife.'

Kay paced the carpet, aware that the hubbub of noise from the incident room had quietened as the rest of the team absorbed Harriet's news.

'Have we located where Greg Victor used to work?' she said.

'Yes – Harris and Sons. It's an abattoir just outside Kegworth,' said Barnes. 'I spoke with the bloke who used to supervise him earlier this morning. He said there weren't any issues with Greg's work.'

'So, why did he leave?'

'His boss said Greg mentioned something about having some family problems to sort out, and that he had to move south for a bit.'

'Anything from our colleagues in Nottingham to the contrary?'

'Nothing at all. He's clean as a whistle.'

'Damn it.' Kay stopped pacing and stared at the threadbare carpet. She checked her watch. 'Okay, here's what we're going to do. Barnes – I want you to head over to Annette Victor's to break the news. See what you can glean about Greg from her. When we last spoke to her, she hinted that not all was well with Greg staying under her roof – something about only expecting his stay to last a couple of weeks. Find out from her who he might have met with these past few weeks, and whether anyone turned up at the house for him. If he was close to Alice, find out where else he might have taken her.'

She broke off as the helicopter passed over the town once more and raised her gaze to the ceiling. 'He's hiding somewhere with Alice, probably scared. It doesn't seem as if Robert's death was planned, so he must have gone on the run with no supplies or any way of camping out.'

'I'll ask Annette if she's noticed anything going missing from the house or any outbuildings, too,' said Barnes. 'He might have circled back to collect some things before heading off again.'

'Sounds good. Gavin – I need you to liaise with

Alistair and Harry and be ready to widen the search area based on what Barnes comes back with after he's spoken to Annette.'

'Guv.'

'I'll phone Sharp and let him know we need to convene an urgent press conference to update the media about the latest developments,' said Kay. 'With any luck we'll get it broadcast ready for the radio news to broadcast for the commute home, and then the six o'clock television news.'

She turned to Carys, who blinked and sat upright under Kay's scrutiny.

'Miles?'

'Guv?'

'Time for you to head home.'

'But—'

'No arguments. You've done some great work this morning, but I need you rested and ready to go again this evening.'

'Okay.' Carys yawned, and rose from her seat.

Kay rested her hands on her hips as she surveyed her colleagues. 'Shit. This changes everything, doesn't it?'

Gavin frowned. 'What do you mean, guv?'

'What she means,' said Barnes, 'is that right now, Greg Victor is our number one suspect in the murder of his brother, Robert – and the kidnapping of his niece. And whatever happens, the press are going to have a field day with Annette Victor.'

Carys snorted as she turned to Kay. 'Blimey. Rather you than me fronting that press conference, guv.'

Kay rolled her eyes. 'Thanks a lot.'

TWENTY-ONE

'This is outrageous.'

Annette Victor stood in the hallway of her home, her chin jutting out as a uniformed police constable hurried past with a laptop computer under his arm and a thick leather desk diary.

'You can't do this.'

Barnes rested his hand on her arm and gestured to the living room. 'Mrs Victor, shall we sit down? I'm sorry – I realise this is a terrible shock for you, but we do need to search for anything that might have a bearing on your husband's death, and where we might find his brother.'

The woman dabbed at her nose with a scrunched up paper tissue, her shoulders slumping. 'Oh, this is terrible. I don't know what to do. Robert was always the one who was good at organising things. He was the one who—'

She broke off as fresh tears spilled over her cheeks, and allowed Barnes to lead her through the door and to an armchair away from the window.

Already, a dozen reporters were hovering at the low brick wall that separated the house from the avenue beyond, camera flashes reflecting off the walls of the room as the men and women jostled for space to get the perfect photograph of the grieving wife and mother.

'Bastards,' Barnes muttered under his breath, and drew the curtains across the front window. 'Hazel, can you have a word with one of our people and get those journalists moved away? Set up a cordon or something.'

'Guv.' The FLO rushed out to the hallway, closing the door behind her.

Dappled light shone through French doors at the far end of the living room, lifting the gloom created by the closed curtains at the front, and for a moment Barnes let his gaze drift over the patio and garden beyond.

A child's swing set had been placed in the centre of an immaculate lawn bordered by manicured flowerbeds, a leafy acer providing shade towards the rear of the property.

'She loves playing out there.' Annette's voice wobbled. 'She used to beg Greg to push her on the swings when he came back in the afternoons.'

Barnes took a seat at the end of the leather sofa nearest to her. 'Back from where?'

'Pardon?'

'You said "when Greg came back in the afternoons".'

'Oh.' She waved her hand in front of her face. 'Just a figure of speech.'

'Did your brother-in-law go out much?'

Annette wrinkled her nose. 'No, not really. I mean, he'd pop out during the day from time to time – job interviews, I suppose. But even those dried up in recent weeks.'

'Had he registered as being out of work?'

'I don't think so. He had some savings – the work might have been atrocious, but the abattoir paid well. I think he hoped to find something without having to ask for help.' A tight smile passed her lips. 'Robert was the same. He always wanted to do things his own way. Once Alice came along though, he decided he'd take whatever work offers came along.'

'What about you, Mrs Victor? Do you work?'

'Not at the moment – I was working as an admin assistant before Alice was born, but we decided that I'd wait until she settled into school full-time before I go back. It saves on childcare.'

'The owner of the wine merchants' business – Kenneth Archerton. How did your husband get on with him?'

Annette shrugged. 'All right, I suppose. I think they had disagreements from time to time, but everyone does, right? Robert was well looked after there, detective. All the staff are.'

Barnes looked down at his hands. 'I'm sorry, Mrs Victor, but I have to ask this next question. How have things been here at home in recent weeks?'

She sank into the armchair, twisting the paper tissue between her fingers. 'Like I said to you on Saturday, it's been strained with Greg being here. I really did think he'd only be around for a couple of weeks. Robert and I—' She sniffed. 'Well, we had been arguing lately, I suppose.'

'About what?'

'Stupid stuff. Money. His work. He'd been offered a promotion – they don't come up often. After the summer party in June, Robert was asked to take on a new role. It would've meant more money coming in, for a start.' She wiped at fresh tears. 'We – I wanted to start saving for Alice's future. Private school fees around here are going through the roof, and then of course there's university to think about later on.'

'Didn't your husband take the promotion?'

'No – and he refused to change his mind. Wouldn't hear of it.'

'Was he worried about the effect the longer hours might have on Alice?' said Barnes.

'I don't know.' Annette pushed herself out of the chair and wandered across to the window, peering through a crack in the curtains. 'God, look at them. You hear about this sort of thing on the news, don't you? You just don't expect to be the one who's *in* the news.'

'Have you heard anything from Greg since Friday?'

Annette let the curtain fall back into place. 'Nothing.'

'Any idea where he might be?' said Barnes. 'Do you know if he had somewhere he might go if he wanted some peace and quiet?'

'From all the arguing, you mean?' Annette's lips twisted. 'No. He loved the river. Liked fishing. I think he might have been a bit of a birdwatcher in his younger years. I saw some books upstairs – guides, that sort of thing.'

On cue, the sound of footsteps on the stairs reached Barnes.

'Are they taking everything?' said Annette.

'Only if it pertains to our investigation,' he said. He checked his notes, and then stood. 'Mrs Victor, my colleague DI Hunter and our DCI are organising another media conference for this afternoon to provide updates in relation to Alice's disappearance. I have to warn you, they will break the news that your husband has been murdered, and that your brother-in-law is now being sought in connection with his death and your daughter's kidnapping.'

'Oh, God.'

'Is there anything you can think of that could help us find them? Were there favourite places Greg used to take Alice when he was babysitting her for you?'

'I've already given Hazel all that information,' said Annette. 'I can't think of anywhere else.'

'Did Greg receive any phone calls or did anyone

turn up looking for him while he was staying with you? Anyone that gave you cause for concern?'

'No – not that I know of, anyway. He certainly didn't have anyone turn up here, and if he did make a call it was on his mobile. He'd either go upstairs to his room or outside.' She turned to the French doors. 'I used to see him pacing back and forth with the phone to his ear during the day sometimes. When Robert got home and I told him, he said not to worry about it. Said it was probably just frustration from the lack of work, things like that.'

Barnes leaned forward. 'Mrs Victor, one last question. All the time Greg was here, did you have any sense that he might do something like this? Was there any indication that he held a grudge against you or your husband?'

'No. Not at all. That's what makes it so hard. I didn't pick up on anything like that,' said Annette, her slight frame shaking. 'We were helping him to get back on his feet, and this is what he does to repay us. I should never have trusted him. I should never have let him into my home.'

TWENTY-TWO

Kay held a hand in front of her eyes as a camera flash went off too close to her face, and grimaced as four reporters shoved smartphones under her nose.

'Detective Hunter – why haven't you found Alice yet?'

'Is the brother-in-law known to police?'

'What is Mrs Victor feeling right now?'

She glared at the woman who asked the last question, then shoved past her and stalked up the steps to where Sharp stood in front of a wooden lectern.

A cloth with the Kent Police insignia emblazoned across it had been draped across the lectern, and the detective chief inspector adjusted the microphone as she approached.

Rather than set the media conference within the same room as they'd used on Saturday, Sharp had taken their communications adviser's guidance and elected to speak to the press outside the police station.

'It'll give the impression you're too busy trying to find Alice to talk to them, but that you need their help,' said Joanne Fletcher as she'd run through the notes she'd prepared for them.

We are, and we do, thought Kay.

Sharp wore a charcoal-grey suit cut perfectly to his frame, and his stern gaze was clear as he surveyed the throng at the foot of the steps.

They turned to the crowd of journalists as a forest of cameras, microphones on booms and outstretched hands holding phones were thrust upwards in anticipation.

'Thanks for coming at short notice,' began Sharp. 'We'd like to take this opportunity to bring you up to date with a series of developments in the hunt for Alice Victor.'

A silence fell upon the throng on the pavement, and Kay listened as he set out the actions that had been taken to date in an effort to find the missing child. She forced herself not to clench her fists, burying the fear and frustration that threatened, and instead kept a watchful eye on the reporters as Sharp led up to the most recent breakthrough in the investigation.

'We can confirm that the body of Alice's father, Robert Victor, was found near the scene of her abduction,' said Sharp, 'and we are actively seeking his brother, Greg Victor, in connection with his death and Alice's kidnapping.'

A cacophony of noise hit Kay's senses.

As one, the crowd surged forward, a barrage of shouted questions making it hard to work out who was talking.

Sharp held up a hand, refusing to speak until the noise had subsided.

'As I was saying—' he glared at a reporter who opened his mouth to speak and then lowered his head, chastened '—we have photographs available of both men, and we ask that you share the image of Greg Victor as a matter of urgency. Given the nature of Robert's death, we are warning the general public not to approach him, but to phone our dedicated enquiry line, or Crimestoppers if you wish to remain anonymous. Right – questions?'

'Why weren't we told about the murder on Saturday?'

Kay stepped forward. 'Due to the nature of the injuries the victim sustained, it's taken until now to obtain a definitive identification. As you can imagine, until we had all the information available to us, we weren't in a position to make that public.'

'Do you think the two brothers argued before Greg was killed?'

'We're not going to speculate on the circumstances during an ongoing investigation,' said Kay. 'Next.'

'How did Robert Victor die?'

'That information is not being made public until our enquiries are concluded,' said Sharp.

'Does Greg Victor have a previous record of violence?'

'Not to our knowledge,' said Kay. 'Again, our investigation is ongoing in that respect.'

As the questions peppered the air and Kay fielded each answer alongside Sharp, she began to notice a diminishing number of raised hands appearing.

Sharp raised his voice. 'That's all we have for you at this time. I'll reiterate that Greg Victor is not to be approached by members of the public and that, if you do see him, you should phone our dedicated enquiry line or Crimestoppers. We're working on the basis that Alice is with him, and may be in grave danger. We're doing everything in our power to bring that little girl back to her mother. When we have another update for you, we'll let you know. Thank you.'

He turned his back and led the way through the doors to the police station, setting a quick pace past the reception desk.

Swiping his security card across the keypad, he held open the inner door for Kay and then paused at the bottom of the staircase.

'What do you think?'

Kay folded her arms and leaned against the wall. 'I think now that Greg Victor's face is out there, we'll hear something soon. He's only been in the area for four months – he's been out of work in that time, and has no close friends that Annette is aware of. That means he can't reasonably harbour a missing child, not now. Even if he's managed to hole up somewhere with Alice, he's exposed now.'

'Have you heard anything from Hazel? Has Annette made any comments about what could've motivated him to kill Robert?'

'Nothing at all. Barnes said she seemed stunned by the news when he went over there earlier today, and she certainly couldn't offer any answers as to why it's happened.'

Sharp began to climb the stairs. 'We need a breakthrough, Kay. And soon.'

'Guv?' Kay pushed away from the wall as he paused.

'What?'

'What if Greg panics? What if he finds out we've put his photograph out there, that we know what he's done?'

'Then he'll make a mistake,' said Sharp. 'And if he does that, then he's going to break cover, and hopefully someone will spot him.'

'That's not what I meant,' said Kay. 'What if he decides that Alice is too much of a risk? What if he abandons her, or—'

'We'll find her, Kay.' Sharp began walking again, his shoulders rigid. 'We'll find her.'

TWENTY-THREE

Kay kicked off her shoes next to the bar stool at the kitchen worktop, then ran her gaze over the emails on her phone.

'Anything?' Adam wandered in from the garden, a pair of scissors in his hand that he washed under the tap and placed back in a drawer. He wiped his hands on the back of his jeans and moved until he was standing behind her, and massaged her shoulders. 'You're going to need your back seeing to after all this. Your muscles are too tight.'

'I know.' Kay closed her eyes and tried to relax under his touch. 'And no, no updates.'

She had stayed at the police station to watch the six o'clock news with the rest of the team, and then had agreed with Sharp to go home for a few hours' rest. He'd taken his own advice, instructing Barnes to maintain a watching brief over the team for an additional four hours so he could get some sleep before returning to manage the night shift with Carys.

Adam's thumbs moved to the base of her spine, and she groaned.

'Told you,' he said. 'Physio for you as soon as you can.'

He patted her arms, then kissed her hair before moving to the back door.

'How are the chickens settling in?' she said, turning in her seat.

'Happier.' He smiled. 'Hopefully within a week or so they'll perk up a bit more. They need to start growing some more feathers before the cooler weather comes.'

Picking up the sack of corn he'd opened, he disappeared from sight. Moments later, Kay could hear him talking to the chickens as he tossed a couple of handfuls of the food into the caged pen and then locked them away for the evening, safe from harm.

She grinned as he returned. 'Have you given them names?'

'I might have done,' he said, a sheepish expression crossing his face before he too broke into a grin. 'Yes, all right – I did. I kind of felt sorry for them not having names. It makes it feel like they're pets from now on.'

'You won't be giving them up for adoption at this rate.'

Adam winked, and ran water into a glass jug before heading back outside.

Kay picked up her phone, made sure there were no new messages, and then pushed it aside and rose from her seat. She busied herself sorting through the post that had been delivered that morning, threw all the advertising circulars into the recycling box under the sink, and then slid a notebook towards her and jotted down a reminder for supplies from the supermarket later that week.

By the time Adam had finished outside, she felt she'd at least organised one aspect of her life – even if her workplace was like a disaster zone.

Adam locked the back door, then turned to her with a frown on his face. 'I forgot to tell you – sorry – your parents phoned.'

'Everything all right?' Kay heard the fear in her voice, and bit her lip.

'Nothing to worry about. They were just calling to let me know what time they were planning to get here tomorrow afternoon.'

'Shit, I'd forgotten about that.'

Kay returned to her bar stool and twirled her wine glass in a pool of condensation. Months before, her father had been rushed into hospital, subsequently having a pacemaker fitted.

He'd undergone a series of appointments with specialists over the course of spring and early summer before receiving his consultant's blessing not to return for more check-ups for another six months. He'd been ecstatic, promptly booking a two-week holiday in

France – even if he'd had to agree to Kay's mother taking some of the driving responsibilities.

Kay had been terrified when his condition had first been diagnosed, but his steady recovery had made her realise that he was going to enjoy the new lease of life he'd been given.

His condition had also served to bring Kay and her mother closer together.

Her mother had never been happy with her choice of career, and after finding out that a wrongful Professional Standards investigation had led to Kay having a miscarriage that meant she could no longer have children, she'd been inconsolable. They'd been estranged for almost two years before Kay's father had nearly died.

'Kay? You okay?'

She shook her head to clear her thoughts. 'Sorry. Yes. Just thinking.'

Adam smiled, then turned his attention to the open refrigerator door. 'Do you think you could manage something a bit more substantial tonight? I've got some tuna steaks in here that need eating up. I could do them with a salad and some new potatoes.'

'Sounds perfect, thanks.' She stifled a yawn.

'Heard that.'

'You think I'm bad – you should've heard Gavin this afternoon. I think Barnes has banned him from drinking coffee. It's not working well.'

'I can't imagine what it must be like in that incident

room at the moment,' said Adam, seasoning the steaks and warming olive oil in a pan.

'You're right – it's not good. Especially with the realisation that it was Alice's father who was the victim.' Kay shivered. 'What sort of person kills their brother?'

'Do you think he did it?'

'I don't know. He's certainly our main suspect until we can start piecing together all the information we've got about the pair of them.'

'Are you in early tomorrow?'

'Yes. I thought I might set the alarm and go in an hour before I'm due, just so I can have a read through some of the new reports before we have the morning briefing and get a handover from Sharp.'

'Don't forget we were going to take your mum and dad to Elizabeth's grave tomorrow afternoon. They wanted to leave some flowers.'

She folded her arms on the worktop and frowned. 'I should phone Mum. Cancel. They'll be home quicker anyway if they don't divert here first, and it'll save them the expense of staying at the motel. The spare room's a tip at the moment – I've been sorting through all those boxes of books and stuff I was going to donate.'

'You'll only make her worry. She wants to spend the time with you. She'll be even more determined to come here if you try to put her off.'

Kay exhaled. 'I hate it when you're right.'

TWENTY-FOUR

Carys groaned as a red warning light flashed on the printer and the machine ground to a halt.

She slapped the documents she'd been clutching into the output tray, and then walked across to Debbie's desk and located the keys for the stationery cupboard. Out in the corridor, she grabbed two reams of paper before returning the keys and scribbling a note to the police constable to let her know what had been taken.

Debbie West had a reputation for guarding the stationery supplies better than the Federal Reserve at Fort Knox, and Carys didn't want to fall into her bad books.

She stuffed some of the paper into the printer tray, and then stood back as the machine whirred to life and went back to reading the report as the remaining pages emerged.

Before leaving for the night, Kay had requested that

Carys take a closer look at Robert Victor's employers. Unimpressed at the company's laid-back attitude with regard to providing information, the DI had decided that an audit of the company's public financial records and day-to-day activities be added to the lines of enquiry that the team were pursuing.

Grateful that she had some experience working with a forensic investigator in a previous case, Carys found she was actually enjoying reading through the information.

Wandering back to her desk, her eyes glued to the page, she pulled out her chair and sank into it while she finished the report.

The company had celebrated its first decade of trading the previous year, and Carys found a series of press releases on its website extolling its successes.

Originally set up in the kitchen of its owner's home, the wine merchant had won favourable contracts with some of the finest boutique vineyards on the Continent in a short space of time.

A photograph of the owner showed Kenneth Archerton as a sixty-something man with tanned features, the skin at his eyes crinkling as he posed for the camera with a glass of red wine in his hand.

Dressed in a chambray shirt open at the collar and dark-blue jeans, he leaned nonchalantly against an upright oak barrel beside lush green vines.

A light breeze had caught his hair when the

photograph had been taken against the setting sun, the effect giving him a rakish look.

'Is that the owner?' said Laura as she walked behind Carys's chair.

'Yes. Kenneth Archerton.'

'He looks pleased with himself.'

'Probably making a small fortune.'

'Nice to see someone doing well. It's not easy running a business these days, is it?'

'True.'

Carys lowered her gaze to her work once more. Typing the company name into the Companies House website, she located the recent balance sheet submitted for the business and made a note of the current assets and liabilities.

Laura's passing comment wasn't far from the truth – Kenneth Archerton was doing extremely well.

She moved through the available reports on the website, and made a note of the progress of the business. Archerton had had a rough start, setting up the wine merchants a few months after the financial crisis that had struck businesses at a worldwide level. He had been frugal, though, always making sure his liabilities were managed. Then, five years ago, his business had surged forward.

Carys closed the Companies House details and went back to the wine merchant's webpage.

She continued scrolling through the brief history of the company set out beside Kenneth's photograph, noting that he had turned his love for wine into a business after being made redundant from his role within a financial insurance brokerage firm.

"'It was my wife's idea," he said. "She told me if I wanted to continue drinking the vintages I enjoyed, then I'd better find a new job".'

Carys smiled at the clever branding. Bringing his wife and a little humour into the official biography lent a softer approach to an otherwise dry business proposition for suppliers and clients alike.

None of his staff members were mentioned on the website – a simple contact page provided a form that could be completed in lieu of an email address, as well as a main telephone number. The physical office address had been replaced with a post office box number, and Carys assumed that it wasn't the sort of business that encouraged its customers to call in.

Kenneth Archerton intrigued her though, and after pushing the reports to one side, she typed his name into a search engine.

A list of results was displayed within seconds, and she scrolled down until she found articles from local newspaper sites.

The first two links she clicked were stories based on press releases about new deals Archerton had secured for the business. The language used was dry, full of corporate speak, and accompanied by the same confidently posed photograph used on his website.

Carys close the tabs and scrolled further through the search results.

She ignored the listings relating to the company's social media pages, but stopped when she spotted an article posted by the *Kentish Times* the previous Christmas.

Wine merchants celebrate another successful year in style.

Carys skimmed the report, a puff piece about Kenneth's ongoing success, support for local charities, and a burgeoning list of clients and lucrative deals.

She yawned, moved the mouse to close the page, and then stopped as her eyes fell upon the photograph of Archerton with some of his staff, all raising their glasses to the camera. Each of their names had been printed below the image.

A familiar face stared at her from the screen.

'What the hell?'

Laura looked up from her work. 'What's up?'

Carys jabbed her finger at her computer screen, her heart racing. 'Robert Victor's boss – Kenneth Archerton – is his father-in-law. Why didn't Annette tell us?'

TWENTY-FIVE

Carys rapped her knuckles against the door, and then pressed the doorbell for good measure.

Footsteps echoed on the other side before Hazel wrenched it open, her face concerned.

'Everything all right?'

'Where's Annette?' said Carys, and stomped over the threshold. 'I need to speak to her.'

'Hang on.' Hazel closed the door. 'You can't speak to her given the mood you're in. What's up?'

Carys took a deep breath, exhaling slowly. Rummaging in her bag, she drew out a copy of the newspaper article and handed it to the FLO.

'This.'

'Bloody hell.' Hazel's eyes widened.

'That's what I said. Has she said anything to you about her father?'

'Nothing, no. She spoke with him earlier today after DI Hunter left, but she didn't mention anything about Robert being employed by him.'

'Any idea why?'

'No, not at all. Maybe she assumed we knew?'

Carys wrinkled her nose. 'Bit of a long shot.'

'What about her mother – has she mentioned her?'

'Died a few years ago, she said. 'Are you all right now? Calmed down a bit?'

'Yes. Sorry.'

Hazel smiled. 'I'd have been pissed off too, don't worry. She's out in the garden, on the patio. I just made myself a cup of tea. Do you want one?'

'I'm good, thanks.' Carys wandered through to the kitchen and then opened the back door.

She found herself on a wide-tiled patio that wrapped around the back of the house, screened on all sides by shrubs that provided privacy from the neighbouring properties.

A purple-blue twilight hugged the evening sky, the sun shredding clouds to pink and yellow tones on the horizon, and Carys lifted her chin to watch a lone passenger jet carve a vapour trail over the house. In another garden beyond the Victors' house, a family were being called in by their father, the desperation in his voice palpable.

She wondered how many other parents were keeping a close eye on their children tonight, perhaps double-checking the locks on the doors before heading to bed themselves.

Alice's disappearance had torn a gaping hole through the community, and she wondered if they would recover – or remain paranoid forever.

Annette sat with her back to her, and Carys detected a whiff of nicotine before noticing the tell-tale wisp of smoke above the woman's head.

'Excuse me, Mrs Victor?'

Annette spun around in her seat, her mouth open. 'Christ – you made me jump.'

'I'm sorry.' Carys held out her warrant card and introduced herself. 'Could I join you? I have a few questions I'd like to ask as part of our ongoing investigation into Alice's disappearance.'

'Sit down.' Annette gestured to a matching wicker chair beside her before picking up a glass of red wine and taking a sip. She grimaced, then took another drag on the cigarette before coughing. 'I don't usually smoke. These are – were – Robert's. He thought I didn't know he smoked. I found these stuffed at the back of his desk drawer earlier. I thought it might calm my nerves. He always told me that he only smoked because it helped him relax.'

Carys placed her bag on the paving stones as she eased into her seat, taking a moment to observe her.

The woman seemed shrivelled within her clothing, a tiny frame swamped within the folds of a thin cashmere jumper and jeans. Chipped nail varnish stained toes that poked out from tan leather sandals, and she'd tied her hair back into a loose ponytail that cast stray strands around her face and ears.

Annette turned to her with red-rimmed eyes that were slightly unfocused. 'What did you want to ask me?'

'I'd like to know more about Robert's work. How long had he been at the wine merchants?'

'Six years.'

Carys frowned, but before she could do the maths in her head, Annette spoke again.

'I met him there. Bumped into him – literally.'

'Oh?'

Annette shuffled in her seat, put the cigarette to her lips and inhaled. 'I was helping out for a few weeks there, admin stuff and the like while one of the personal assistants was away on holiday. Robert crashed into me while I was carrying a pile of new brochures that had just arrived. They went everywhere. He offered to buy me a drink after work to apologise.'

'You didn't take on a permanent job there?'

The woman choked out a bitter laugh, smoke spilling between her lips. 'God, no. Not my thing.' She contemplated her toenails, her mouth downturned. 'No, I wanted to do something different. And then I fell pregnant with Alice a few months later. Robert was his ever charming self about it and immediately asked me to marry him.'

Carys reached into her bag and pulled out the photocopied newspaper clipping. 'Why didn't you tell us your father was Robert's boss?'

Annette ran her eyes over the photograph, but she didn't reach out for it.

A single tear ran over her cheek as she dabbed the paper tissue to her nose. 'I'm sorry – I wasn't thinking. I was so upset about Alice, and then Robert, that it didn't occur to me.'

Carys bit back the reply that entered her head, and waited while the woman regained her composure before continuing her questioning.

'Did your father and Robert get along?'

'Yes, I think so. I never heard them arguing. Dad dotes on Alice.' She sat straighter. 'He says he wants her to take over the business one day – he's already putting aside money for her to go to university.'

Annette blinked, then turned her attention away from the photograph.

Carys folded it away.

'How much involvement does your father have in the business?' she said as she zipped up her handbag.

'Not so much these days. He probably goes in a couple of mornings a week. He tends to work from home.' She flicked ash from the end of the cigarette before taking another drag. 'He isn't very well.'

'I'm sorry to hear that.'

Annette shrugged, then stubbed out the cigarette on the sole of her shoe and placed the butt next to her wineglass. 'He went downhill earlier this year. Took weeks for a diagnosis because he refused to go and see a doctor. Typical man, right?'

Carys didn't answer.

'Anyway, he came back from an appointment with his doctor in late March, and told us he had MS – multiple sclerosis. He's seeing a specialist up in Manchester– some sort of new-fangled treatment offered by a clinic he found. I don't think he has a lot of faith in what the doctors down here are telling him. Some days are worse than others, so I think that's why he prefers to work from home.' She shook her head, sadness in her eyes. 'Dad sees it as a weakness. He thinks if his staff see him like that, they'll worry what will become of the business and leave. He doesn't want to lose them – he's got good people working for him.'

'Are any competitors making enquiries?'

'None that I know of. To be honest, I don't get involved in the business side of things much.' She tugged her cardigan sleeves over her wrists and shivered. 'I think that's why Dad is pinning his hopes on Alice. Better luck with the next generation perhaps.'

'Any idea why Kenneth didn't mention his relationship to Robert when he was interviewed at the weekend?'

'I don't know, sorry. I can only imagine that, like me, he's so wrapped up in Alice's kidnapping that it didn't occur to him to mention it. He's absolutely distraught.'

Annette's hand shook as she pulled another cigarette from the packet and lit it.

'All right,' said Carys, and rose to her feet. 'Thanks for your time, Mrs Victor. I'll see myself out.'

TWENTY-SIX

After another sleepless night, Gavin yawned before rubbing his hands together and casting his gaze over the array of items spread across the table in front of him.

It had fallen to him to sort through everything that had been collected and bagged up from Robert Victor's house, including personal items owned by his brother, Greg.

Gavin pushed aside Robert's laptop and turned to Andy Grey, the digital forensics expert.

'I'm not sure how much luck you're going to have with that,' he said. 'We're presuming he took his main work computer with him, and Harriet's lot didn't find it on the boat or in the river.'

'Don't worry,' said Grey. 'We might get lucky – he might've saved all his work to the cloud, or used this as a backup of some sort. I'll be in touch as soon as I know anything.'

He pointed to the mobile phone that had been placed in a plastic evidence bag. 'Is that the wife's?'

'Yes. We've already cloned it so we can work through the information,' said Gavin. 'I was going to drop it back to her this afternoon.'

'If you run out of time or can't get someone to go through the phone records for you, give me a call.'

'Thanks.'

As Grey left the room, Gavin turned his attention to the myriad of paperwork he had laid out to the right of the table.

Most of the documentation had been retrieved from Robert Victor's office and he had spent the morning organising it into different piles.

The shock of Carys's discovery that Robert Victor had been employed by Annette's father gave new impetus to the investigation, and Kay had ended the morning's briefing with clear instructions that she wanted more information about their business arrangements by the end of the day.

Bank statements and details of savings accounts had been split out from utility bills and other day-to-day household items, while a third stack of paperwork held membership cards from gym or social clubs the Victors belonged to. Letters and other correspondence, both personal and related to Robert's work, were in the final group.

Gavin scratched his earlobe, and wondered where to start.

'Bank statements,' said a voice behind him.

He glanced over his shoulder to see Debbie advancing towards the table.

She picked up the first pile and began sifting through its contents.

'What makes you say that?' said Gavin.

'Experience,' she said, and winked. 'Seriously, this part will take the most time, but at least we'll be able to see if there were any unusual transactions to or from their personal accounts.'

'Okay, well let's make a start, shall we?'

Gavin took half the statements from her, pulled out a seat at the end of the table and spun it around until he could put his feet up on the radiator under the window, then settled in to read.

Putting a line through items that were easy to identify – mortgage repayments, mobile phone charges, utility bills, regular supermarket visits – he gradually built up a picture of the normal day-to-day outgoings. On top of that, he added a note of the regular salary payments Robert received.

Eventually, he had put a line through most of the entries on the statements that depicted the household income and expenditure.

He checked his watch, and noticed with a shock that two hours had passed.

'How are you getting on?' he asked, pushing back his chair and stretching his arms above his head.

Debbie raised her head from her work, and gestured

to the documents before her. 'I've worked my way through all the store cards. I can't see any problems to flag – each one is paid off in full at the beginning of the month to avoid any interest charges. I think they've just got these to get the discounts and rewards. What about you?'

'I've just finished going through all the day-to-day stuff. There's not much left to do.'

'Shall we give it another hour, and then nip out to get a sandwich or something?' said Debbie. 'I could probably do with some fresh air by then – I'm getting cross-eyed looking at these.'

'Sounds good.'

Gavin pulled his chair over to the table, finding a space to lay out the remaining bank statements.

'Do we know when Alice's birthday is?' he said.

'Twenty-third of June,' said Debbie.

'Okay, thanks – at least that explains this cluster of payments going out.' He whistled under his breath. 'My parents sure as hell didn't spend this much on me when I was a kid.'

'I get the impression from Hazel that it was her father who tended to spoil her. I think Annette said in passing that she thought Alice had too many toys, but because Robert was always away for work I suppose he felt guilty – perhaps spoiling her was his way of making up for it.'

Gavin grunted under his breath, and turned his attention back to the documentation, determined to finish the task before taking a lunch break. He much preferred to be out and about speaking with people, or following up leads. Sitting in a meeting room going through someone else's financial background wasn't something that made him feel as if he was contributing to locating Alice, or her father's killer.

He picked up his pencil and began working through the remaining entries.

Turning the page, he ran his eyes over the scratched out lines and focused on finding the gaps in the information they had to hand.

He frowned as he noted a payment of four figures that had landed in the joint account earlier that year. The bank's reference details for the transaction were in a jumbled shorthand, which made no sense to him.

Gavin reached out for the preceding month's statement, but found no corresponding transaction. Frustrated, he tried the following month – and found an identical amount that had arrived midway through April.

Each month after that, a similar amount had been paid into the Victors' joint account.

'Debbie? What do you make of this?' Gavin held out three of the statements, and pointed to the transactions. 'Any idea what those reference numbers mean?'

The police constable's brow furrowed as she ran her gaze over the statements.

'I'm not sure. It's obviously an electronic payment made into the account, but each of the references are different. It could be a payment made from overseas perhaps?'

'What if—' Gavin broke off as his phone began to ring. 'Hello? DC Piper.'

'Detective, it's Alan Evershall.'

Gavin frowned as he tried to place the name, before the caller spoke again.

'We met on Sunday morning at Allington – I own the *Daisy Lee*.'

'Ah – Mr Evershall. Yes, I remember. What can I do for you?'

'Actually, I might have something for you.'

Gavin leaned forward and shoved the bank statements out of the way, pulling his notebook closer. 'Oh? What's happened?'

'I'm not sure if it's anything of importance, but I thought I should tell you.'

'Go on.'

'Well, I was cycling back along the towpath from Allington this morning – I tend to do my shopping at a little supermarket on the A20 and cut back home via the castle to vary the route. Keeps me healthy, see?'

'Yes.' Gavin bit back a sigh, and willed Evershall to continue rather than give him a blow-by-blow account of his shopping expedition. 'Did you see something?'

'I think so. I got back to the towpath just past the castle grounds – there aren't many boats moored there at the moment – I think there's a film crew there this week and the owners have to keep the private moorings clear.

I heard someone here at the yard mention it last week because all the boat owners have had to moor up this way for a bit. Wouldn't do to clutter up the scenery, would it?'

Gavin chuckled, and rolled his eyes at Debbie. 'Not at all, Mr Evershall.'

'Right, right. So about two hundred yards down the towpath, going towards the lock, there's an abandoned Canadian-style canoe.'

'A canoe?'

'Yes. You see a few of them around the place – they're really cheap to hire and a lot of the kids around here use them over the summer.'

'What made you think this one was suspicious?'

'It had been scuttled and pushed into the reeds. They get quite tall this time of year until the council comes along and tidies up the towpath. The thing is, there was a soft toy floating in the water inside it, stuck under the thwart – you know, the beam that goes across the middle of the canoe to strengthen the sides.' Evershall paused, as if collecting his thoughts. 'Of course, it might be nothing, but—'

Gavin began to pace the carpet. 'Where are you at the moment?'

'Back at the *Daisy Lee*.'

'And is the canoe still in the water near the castle?'

'Well, yes, I suppose so. I've only been back twenty minutes. I would've called you sooner, but I had to get the chicken livers in the refrigerator otherwise they'd go off in this heat. I—'

'Did you touch anything in the canoe, or did you remove the soft toy?'

'No, don't worry – I've seen enough of those crime shows on the television.'

'All right, brilliant. Mr Evershall, would you mind heading back to where you saw the canoe and make sure no-one else goes near it? We'll meet you there as soon as possible.'

'Of course, no problem at all.'

'Thank you.' He ended the call and turned to Debbie. 'Have you come across any foreign investments amongst this paperwork?'

'Not yet. I'll keep an eye out.'

'What about building societies? Did Robert have any other accounts – ones that aren't in joint names, I mean? Somewhere that money could've come from?'

'They didn't find any in his office, but you know as well as I do that doesn't mean he didn't have one somewhere.'

'That's what I'm thinking. Tell you what. Can you keep going with this, and I'll catch up with you later? I need to tell Kay and Barnes about this lead,' said Gavin, and hurried from the room.

TWENTY-SEVEN

Barnes squinted against the afternoon sun and glared at the row of catering company vehicles, large articulated trucks, and assorted cars that lined the narrow road that led past the castle.

He shook his head. 'No wonder they're always going on about how much films cost to make these days,' he said. 'Look at this lot.'

Gavin grinned. 'This is only for a TV commercial.'

'Is it? Bloody hell.'

The younger detective constable's mobile emitted a blast of music, and Barnes waited while he took the call.

To his right, a pair of actors posed beside a new sports car, its bodywork waxed and gleaming under the stage lights that surrounded it.

'Thanks, Hazel.' Gavin wandered over to where he stood, pocketing his phone. 'Harriet's team found a toy rabbit trapped in the hull of the canoe while we were on our way over here, and took a photograph. Annette Victor has confirmed it's similar to one Alice took with her the morning of the boat trip. Apparently, they'd spent the night at Kenneth's house for dinner and had breakfast there on Friday before Greg collected Alice to take her to Tonbridge. Annette said Alice fell in love with the rabbit as soon as she saw it that morning and insisted Greg pack it in her bag to take with them.'

'Shit.'

'Detectives?'

Barnes looked across a wide expanse of lush grass to where a uniformed constable beckoned to him from the taped-off towpath, and elbowed Gavin.

'Come on. Looks like Harriet's happy for us to take a look now. Where's this Evershall bloke who phoned you, anyway? I thought you told him to meet us down here?'

'Uniform cordoned off the path at the other end, past the canoe, so he's waiting for us there. I figured we could take a look at the canoe first and then speak to him once we've got our bearings.'

Barnes took the clipboard the PC held out to him, signed his name as a record of accessing the potential crime scene, and then ducked under the tape.

Despite several members of the public using the towpath over the weekend, it was imperative the team secured any evidence that might remain until it could be salvaged and recorded.

His shoes kicked up dust and loose stones as he and

Gavin hurried along the path towards a group of forensic specialists clad in white suits.

'When I called Harriet on our way here, she said they'd done an initial check on this stretch of the path, but didn't find anything else,' said Gavin.

Barnes swore under his breath as he almost rolled his ankle on the uneven ground. 'I don't remember any reports coming in about a stolen canoe, do you? I thought anything like that was supposed to be flagged to the task force.'

'No. Maybe the owner is away at the moment.'

'Make a note to have someone go through the statements uniform took from the property owners between East Farleigh and Tovil, just in case.'

'Will do.'

Barnes paused a few metres away from where Harriet and her team had congregated, then pivoted and looked back towards the castle, his thoughts tumbling over each other.

'What's up?' said Gavin.

'I was wondering – perhaps Greg didn't steal the canoe. Maybe it was his plan all along to use it.'

'That would make sense. After all, the second boat was hired in Robert's name.' Gavin began walking again. 'So, we'd have to find out where he'd hidden it, or who he arranged to borrow it from.'

'Ian, Gavin.'

Harriet Baker turned away from her colleague as they drew near, then beckoned them over. 'We've processed the riverbank here, so you can take a closer look.'

'Thanks,' said Barnes.

'I've left the canoe and everything in situ while we were waiting for you. I figured you'd want to see the scene as Mr Evershall found it.'

'Brilliant,' said Gavin. 'Have you met him?'

'Briefly – he's over there by the other cordon.'

'All right, we'll get our bearings here and then speak to him.'

Barnes followed Harriet to the water's edge where two CSIs were starting to pack away their cases of equipment.

Patrick, the photographer, stepped aside to let him pass.

'I'll upload some of these images as soon as I get back to the lab so you've got something to show the rest of your team,' he said. 'Probably easier than you trying to take photos and dropping your phone in the river.'

'Appreciated, thanks.' Barnes looked across to the opposite bank. Half a dozen uniformed officers milled about the towpath, keeping onlookers at bay. 'Have the media caught wind of this yet?'

'No – we've been lucky,' said Harriet. 'We plan to move the canoe once you've taken a look and we'll cover it with plastic sheeting before we carry it along to the trailer we've got on standby.'

'Let's have a look, then.'

Harriet gestured to the reeds at the water's edge.

'You'll need to be careful – the bank is quite slippery in places.'

Barnes heeded her warning. He didn't fancy returning to the incident room in a wet suit.

He'd never hear the end of it from Gavin, for a start.

He reached out and held back a clump of reeds, and spotted the sunken canoe close to where he stood.

The bright-red hull poked out of the shallow water by a few centimetres, and it seemed any attempts to scuttle it hadn't taken into the account the slope of the river bed.

He leaned out further as the water in the canoe eddied, and a light-blue toy rabbit spun in the gentle movement.

Barnes swallowed, stepped back and jerked his thumb over his shoulder.

'Do you want to take a look before they move it, Piper?'

'Sure.'

Barnes waited on the towpath and glared at the outline of the canoe.

At this angle, he could see how it had caught Evershall's attention.

'He did that in a hurry, didn't he?' said Gavin. 'You'd have thought he'd have pushed it out into deeper water.'

'Probably didn't think he had time,' said Barnes. 'Thanks, Harriet – we'll go and speak with Evershall and come back here when we're done, but I think you're okay to start moving this out of the water. Our luck with the media isn't going to last for much longer.'

He pointed at two cyclists standing on the opposite towpath a few metres away from the second cordon who both held mobile phones aloft.

'Dammit,' said Harriet.

Barnes gestured to Gavin to follow him as the CSI lead began to call out instructions to her team, and set off towards Alan Evershall.

'I'll let you lead this one,' he said as they drew closer, and pulled out his notebook.

'Mr Evershall, thanks for waiting,' said Gavin. 'Do you want to sign in so we can talk over here?'

He glared at a group of onlookers who hovered at the cordon, their eager expressions turning to disappointment as he and Barnes led Evershall away to a spot a few metres along the towpath.

'Was I right?' said Evershall. 'Is it to do with the missing girl?'

'We're still in the middle of preliminary enquiries, but you were right to call me. Can you take us through what happened this morning? You said you were out shopping?'

'Yes, that's right. I could've used the smaller supermarket over on the Chatham Road. It's closer, but I prefer the one in Allington. More choice, and it's a change of scenery on the bike.'

Gavin nodded, and said nothing. Evershall was staring at a point over his shoulder as he remembered the details of finding the canoe, and he didn't want to interrupt his train of thought. It was better to let the man recall what had happened in his own time rather than risk missing some vital information.

'Anyway,' he continued, 'I cycled back past the castle, thinking I'd have a look at what they were filming – I overheard someone in the shop talking about it. The towpath wasn't very busy – you don't see many people along here until lunchtime, when the pub opens down by the lock.' He frowned. 'I suppose I was daydreaming, just thinking about what I needed to do on the boat when I got back. I saw a flash of red between the reeds as I approached where you saw the canoe. It seemed so out of place that I stopped to take a closer look. I would've reported it to the lock-keeper anyway – can't have a boat hitting something like that, it'd cause all sorts of damage – but when I saw the toy rabbit, I thought I'd better call you.'

'Did you recognise the canoe as belonging to anyone along here?'

'No, never seen it before.'

'Have you heard of any thefts along this stretch in the past week?'

'No, and that sort of thing would have had us all on alert. News travels fast along here, especially after what's happened. Everyone who's a long-term resident on the river here is keeping an eye out for that little girl. It's all anyone's talking about.'

'All right – thanks, Mr Evershall,' said Gavin. 'You know where to find me if you see or hear anything else.'

'Okay, let's head back to the station.' Barnes closed his notebook as Evershall walked back towards the cordon. 'So much of this is going to come down to luck, isn't it, Piper?'

'I know. I hate it. If he hadn't been out shopping, if he hadn't taken that particular route home—'

Barnes slowed as they approached the CSI team, who were carefully lifting the canoe from the river, each step of the process being photographed by Patrick as they worked.

Water poured from a large hole in the hull, and Barnes watched as the last remnants of evidence were collected and bagged.

'Harriet, as soon as you've finished processing the toy, can you arrange to have it sent over to me?'

'No problem.'

'Thanks.'

'Why d'you want the rabbit, Ian?' said Gavin as they made their way back to the car.

'If Alice lost it when Greg Victor was moving her from here to wherever he's taken her, she's probably missing it,' he said. 'I want to make sure she gets it back when we find her.'

TWENTY-EIGHT

Kay leaned forward over the steering wheel as she slowed the car, and squinted at the brass numbers fixed to a brick gatepost on the right-hand side of the road.

Satisfied she had the right address, she turned onto the gravel driveway, lowered the car window and reached out to press the call button on the intercom under the numbers. While she waited for an answer, she took in the wrought-iron gates and the Tudor-style detached house beyond.

Dark wooden beams criss-crossed over the front of the building, stark against white render on the top level and red brick on the lower that matched the gateposts beside her. Two chimneys rose into the sky above a tiled roof, and she could see fir trees along the sides of the building that provided privacy from the driveway and any prying eyes from the road.

'Hello?'

A woman's voice carried through the intercom, and Kay turned so she could be heard clearly.

'Detective Inspector Kay Hunter. I'd like a word with Mr Archerton, please.'

'Do you have an appointment?'

'It's about his missing granddaughter. I was hoping I wouldn't need one under the circumstances.'

A rustling reached her ears, and she gazed back towards the house. She had no doubt she was being observed, and as if to confirm her suspicions, a curtain in one of the front windows fell back into place.

'Drive through,' said the woman eventually. 'Park over to the left. There's a door on that side of the house you can use.'

The line went dead before Kay could acknowledge the instructions, and then the gates swung inwards.

She accelerated forward as soon as there was enough of a gap to pass through, parked where she'd been told and crossed the gravel to the house.

Pausing for a moment to get her bearings, she estimated the property had at least five bedrooms and two reception rooms. The front garden had been landscaped to within an inch of its life and she wondered how much the maintenance cost.

Kay turned at the sound of the door opening and saw a woman with greying shoulder-length hair beckoning to her.

'This way.'

Kay wiped her feet on the doormat, and then stepped inside. 'Thanks. Sorry, you are?'

'Patricia Wells. I'm Mr Archerton's carer and housekeeper.' The woman locked the door, and gestured to Kay to follow her through an archway of dark beams that were similar to those on the exterior of the house. 'Mind your head. Mr Archerton is in his study this morning.'

Kay followed her into a wide hallway and across a thick carpet to a panelled door that remained resolutely closed. She looked to her right to see the front door bolted shut and a piece of material pinned to the slit window to the left of it.

'Reporters,' said Patricia, her lip curling. 'It's why I asked you to use the side door.'

'Have they been causing problems?'

'Not yet. I heard what happened at Annette's house, though.' She raised her hand to the door, then turned to Kay and lowered her voice. 'Mr Archerton has good days and bad. Today's a good day, but I would ask that you don't tire him out. He's under enough stress at the moment, and it won't take much to trigger a setback.'

'I'll bear that in mind.'

Patricia knocked, and a baritone voice answered.

'Come in.'

Kay's first impression of the room was that if she had the money, she'd have a study at home just like it.

Floor-to-ceiling bookcases lined the wall to her right while in front of her a pair of French windows opened out onto a wide lawn, the curtains billowing in a gentle breeze. To her left, a large oak desk had been placed in front of a fireplace, the empty grate stacked with pine cones.

'Mr Archerton, this is Detective Inspector Kay Hunter,' said Patricia.

Kay crossed to the desk as Kenneth Archerton hauled himself from a burgundy-coloured leather chair with the aid of walking sticks and appraised her with piercing blue eyes.

Apart from his obvious difficulty with walking, his chin jutted out defiantly as he gathered the sticks in one hand and leaned against the desk, his greying thin hair combed away from a high forehead.

'Have you found my granddaughter?'

'We're pursuing a number of enquiries, Mr Archerton. Can I ask why you didn't tell my colleagues at the weekend that you were Robert Victor's father-in-law?'

The man's brow furrowed for a moment, then his shoulders sagged. 'Did I not? I obviously wasn't thinking clearly. I answered their questions as quickly as I could so they could get on with finding Alice.'

He gestured to a seat opposite his desk, and waited until Kay sat down before he turned his attention to the carer. 'Patricia – would you mind fetching some coffee for us?'

'Of course.'

Soft footsteps preceded the door being closed behind

the woman, and Archerton eased himself back into his chair. 'Patricia is a godsend. She works part-time as my housekeeper but is a registered carer as well. I take it my daughter told you I have early onset multiple sclerosis?'

'She mentioned it to one of my colleagues, yes. I understand you work from home most days?'

'I go in one day a week for the staff meetings and to sign any new contracts. I was full-time until six months ago when my health took a turn for the worse,' said Archerton. He smiled. 'I wouldn't want my staff to think I'm shirking my duties.'

Kay reached into her bag for her notebook and pen. 'When did you last see Alice?'

Archerton leaned back in his seat as if he'd been struck, his smile fading.

'Thursday night. Greg picked her up from here the next day to take her on the boat. He turned up early, and I wasn't up so I missed saying goodbye to her.'

'Does she often stay here?'

He gestured to the open patio doors. 'She loves running around on the lawn. It's safe here. She likes the butterflies – my wife planted all sorts of shrubs and flowers for them when she was alive, and I've tried to keep that tradition. Of course, I have someone come in once a week and look after it all now.'

'When did you speak to Robert the last time?'

'Monday morning, before he caught his flight. I

wanted to provide him with some guidance regarding a potential new client.'

'Did he seem worried about anything?'

'Not at all. Business as usual.' Archerton tapped his fingers on the arm of his chair. 'We were planning to have a barbecue at the weekend. Sunday, in fact. I wanted to have my family around me.' He broke off. 'I'm sorry. It's just—'

'I understand, Mr Archerton,' said Kay, 'and I'm sorry if my questions seem intrusive. I'm simply trying to understand why this has happened.'

Nodding, he gestured her to go on.

She waited as the door opened, and Patricia appeared carrying a tray.

The housekeeper set out a coffee pot, cups, milk and sugar before retreating once more, and Kay poured out coffee for them both.

'Thank you, detective,' said Archerton as she passed him the milk. 'Now, what else did you want to ask me?'

'What's your relationship with Greg Victor like?'

His mouth twisted. 'We don't have a relationship,' he said. 'Obviously he drops by here from time to time if he's with the others, but I don't socialise with him. Not my sort of person really.'

'Did he ever approach you for work?'

'No. And Robert never mentioned he was after a job.'

'Annette said that he'd been living with them for

four months now, and that she only expected him to stay for a couple of weeks.'

'Yes, and she was none too pleased about it, either. Annette likes her privacy, same as me. I can imagine things were a little strained.'

'Did Robert seem worried about anything before he went away?'

Archerton sipped his coffee, then shook his head. 'I don't think so. If he was, he didn't say anything to me. Do you think he and Greg had a falling out or something?'

'It's not for me to say, Mr Archerton. Have you received any ransom demands?'

He blinked. 'No. No, I haven't.'

'And do you have any idea why Greg might have taken Alice?'

'No.' Archerton placed his cup into the saucer with a clatter. 'But if I find out he's harmed Alice in any way, Detective Hunter, I will make him pay.'

TWENTY-NINE

'How the hell did no-one see him?'

Barnes glared at his computer screen. In his left hand, he held a printout containing a list of mooring points along the River Medway that he waved in the air.

Kay lifted her chin so she could see across the top of her screen to where he sat. 'I take it you've had no luck?'

'Nothing. Zip. Nada.' He threw the paperwork to one side, his lip curling in disgust. 'There's no way Greg would've been able to paddle that canoe all the way through Maidstone without being seen. Friday night? You know what it's like down by the river this time of year.'

'Crowded,' said Parker as he doled out copies of the latest briefing agenda. 'I know – I was on patrol.'

'Down by the river?'

'Yes. Didn't see a man and a kid go by in a canoe, though. There were the usual cruisers and narrowboats jostling for space before the sun went down, but I don't recall seeing anyone that could have been Greg Victor and Alice.'

'What about closer to midnight? He might have been able to paddle past without being noticed.'

Parker shook his head. 'It was still busy along there with pedestrian traffic. We extended our patrol along past the Archbishop's Palace and then over the bridge to the leisure centre a few times due to some rowdy groups larking about. I'm pretty certain a canoe going past would've stayed in people's minds, simply because it would've been dangerous at that time of night. It's why they insist on boats being moored by sundown, isn't it?'

Kay pulled her keyboard closer, and typed into a search engine. 'Were there any special events on?'

'No,' said Parker. 'It was just the usual weekend crowds. People making the most of the last of the long evenings, I guess. We had a bit of trouble at one of the pubs near Fairmeadow, but that was about it. All things considered, it was a quiet shift.'

'So much for that idea, then,' said Kay, and shoved her keyboard away again as Sharp appeared at the door. 'Get yourselves over to the end of the room and we'll kick off the briefing. I want updates from all of you, so make sure you're prepared.'

She collated her notes and walked across to the whiteboard.

Sharp joined her as she was reviewing the major tasks that had been listed, and loosened his tie. 'We're not getting much ticked off that list, are we? How's morale?'

'Everyone's getting frustrated,' she said, and turned to face the room as the team began to congregate around them. 'They're still one hundred per cent focused though – and completely committed to finding Alice.'

'I knew they would be. All right, I'll take a seat and let you run with this. Drop by my office before you head home – I'll let you have an update about staffing levels for the next week.'

'Thanks.'

Kay waited a moment while the last of the group settled into seats or leaned against a wall close by, made sure that the night shift team had all arrived and were given a copy of the agenda, and then began. After running through the conversation with Barnes and Parker, she jabbed her finger at the map of the river, indicating the town centre.

'Before we move on to other business, does anyone have any thoughts about this?'

Gavin raised his hand. 'Guv, since we got back I've been going through the statements we got from residents along the river between East Farleigh and Tovil, as well as reviewing the call logs from Friday night. We've had no reports of a canoe being stolen amongst those people. I was thinking, though – given how busy we know that part of the towpath to be on a Friday night, Greg could have carried Alice along there, and no-one would've batted an eyelid. It's not like he was a complete stranger who kidnapped her – she knew him.'

'Nothing turned up on CCTV,' said Debbie, 'so perhaps he left the towpath before getting to the Archbishop's Palace and cut around the back roads until he could reach the river again.'

'Exactly,' said Gavin. 'And then he could've seen the canoe moored up somewhere and stolen it. By then, both he and Alice would've been tiring. If she'd had a tantrum or something due to being exhausted, it would've caught people's attention.'

Kay nodded when Gavin finished speaking. 'I think you're onto something there. I want you to coordinate with uniform to extend their enquiries to properties between Maidstone and Allington, and if they find out someone's on holiday, do all they can to trace them and ask if they have a Canadian canoe like the one found.'

'Will do, guv.'

'In the meantime,' said Kay, 'where the bloody hell is that itinerary of Robert's we're waiting for? I thought Melissa Lampton was supposed to be emailing that over last night?'

'I left a message for her before I left this morning and asked that she call the incident room when she got in,' said Carys. 'Hasn't she sent it yet?'

'We haven't heard back from her,' said Debbie, looking up from her computer. 'No-one's recorded a conversation with her in HOLMES2 today.'

'Bollocks,' said Barnes. He crossed the room to his desk and snatched up his mobile phone and car keys. 'I'll go over there and get it myself.'

THIRTY

Kay smoothed down her hair as she hurried past the hatchback parked haphazardly on her driveway.

Despite her father's insistence that his doctor had told him he was fine to drive, Kay's mother had taken it upon herself to chauffeur him from place to place.

A smile feathered across Kay's lips as she imagined the conversations between them as her father was ferried around.

Adam's four-by-four was parked in front of the garage, and the familiar taint of barbecue smoke wafted from the back garden as she turned the key in the lock.

'I'm home!'

'We're through here.' Her mother's voice floated from the kitchen.

'All right – let me get changed first.'

She took the stairs two at a time, tossed her work clothes into the washing basket and pulled on a favourite pair of jeans and a thin long-sleeved black T-shirt before tying her hair back in a ponytail.

Walking into the small en suite, she checked her appearance in the mirror.

Thankfully, she didn't look too tired.

She and her mother had tentatively started to mend their bridges earlier in the year, with her mother realising that no amount of snide remarks or derisory comments were going to make Kay quit her role with Kent Police, and admitting her anger had been a way to deal with a fear that she might lose Kay forever.

Kay still wasn't sure her mother had forgiven her for keeping her miscarriage a secret for so long, but they were making slow progress, and today was the third time they'd all congregated for a family meal over the course of the summer.

Abby, Kay's younger sister, was still bemused by the turn of events, but vocal in her relief that the rift between her mother and Kay was healing. They had shared many phone calls over the course of the summer to chart progress.

Kay dabbed a little concealer under her eyes to ward off the dark shadows that had formed since she'd left the house that morning, and then headed downstairs.

She put her mobile phone on the worktop and then hugged her mother. 'When did you get here?'

'A couple of hours ago. Adam had only just got in from work, so we nipped up to the supermarket to get the bits and pieces he wanted for the barbecue.' She held

Kay at arm's length, her eyes sweeping over her. 'How are you holding up? We heard the news while we were away.'

Kay bit her lip. 'I'm all right. I just want to find her.'

Her mother nodded, but said nothing. At that moment, her father stepped through the doorway linking the kitchen to the garage, his face beaming as he strode towards her.

'There's my girl,' he said.

Kay felt the air get knocked from her lungs as he enveloped her in a bear hug. 'Steady, Dad.'

He grinned, and loosened his grip.

'You're looking great,' said Kay. 'Good holiday?'

'Perfect,' he said. 'Just what we needed after the year we've had.'

They turned at a loud cluck from the back door, to see a sandy-coloured chicken peering around the frame.

'What do you want, Mabel?' said Kay's father.

'Mabel?' Kay looked from him to her mother. 'I told Adam he'd regret giving them names, otherwise they'll never get rehomed – you know what he's like. We'll end up with them.'

Her mother shrugged. 'Your father decided she looked like a Mabel – Adam had already named the other two. The brown one out there is Gretchen, and the white one – well, she'll be white when she's grown some more feathers – is Snowball.'

'I need a drink.'

Laughing, her mother picked up a bowl of salad and headed out to the garden.

Kay turned as her mobile phone vibrated on the worktop, and snatched it up as she saw the name displayed.

'Ian?'

'Sorry to disturb you, guv. I've got a copy of Robert Victor's itinerary at last.'

'Good work. Where are you at the moment?'

'Just driving back from his offices.'

'Anything on the itinerary that might help us?'

She glanced up as her mother returned and went across to the refrigerator before pulling out a bottle of Sauvignon Blanc and raising an eyebrow.

Kay stuck up her thumb.

'It's going to take some work,' said Barnes, his voice carrying over the noise of his car engine. 'The beginning of the week should be easy, as there are hotels and potential clients listed. It looks like he was driving in the mornings and then meeting with different vineyards or individuals over the course of the afternoons. There's less information about the latter half of the week, and no hotels listed. It only notes two locations – Le Mans and Laval. I took a look at a map of the area on my phone before I left their offices.'

'Can you do me a favour before you go home? Leave a message for Carys to phone any vineyards between Le Mans and Laval to find out if Robert had made appointments to visit them and if so, arrange interviews as soon as possible either by phone or video conference call.'

'Will do, guv.'

'All right, Ian – thanks. Get yourself home once you've dropped off the itinerary and I'll see you in the morning.'

She ended the call, and slid the phone back into her bag. When she turned around, her mother was standing in the doorway with a glass of wine in each hand and a quizzical expression on her face.

'Sorry, Mum. I had to take that.'

'Was it about the missing girl?'

'Yes. Thanks.' She took the glass her mother held out to her.

'Do you think she's been taken to France, then?'

'What? Oh – no. Barnes got a hold of the victim's itinerary. He was travelling for work last week. We're trying to find out his movements.'

'He was a wine merchant, wasn't he?' Her mother blushed. 'I heard it on the news.'

Kay smiled, acknowledging her mother's tentative interest in her work. 'That's right, yes.'

'It's ready!' Adam's voice drifted from the garden.

'Come on. Let's go and eat.'

Her mother headed back out to the garden, stepping to one side as a chicken ambled across the doorstep, clucking under its breath before shoving its beak into a pot of oregano next to a drainpipe.

'Well, these look like they're settling in, don't they?'

Kay grinned. 'Making themselves at home, as you can see. It's just as well he keeps them locked in the pen at night, otherwise I think they'd be taking over the house.'

'I can just imagine them sitting on the sofa watching a film with him.'

Her father handed a laden plate of sausages and steak to Kay as she sat in a chair next to him, then turned back to the barbecue and helped Adam dish out the rest.

Kay added a portion of the salad and a dollop of sauce on the side of her plate, then closed her eyes as the first mouthful hit her taste buds.

'Oh my God, that's good.' She opened her eyes to find her family smiling at her, their own plates piled high. 'What? I'm starving, all right?'

Adam laughed. 'It's a good job I cooked extra.'

She ate as the conversation turned to her parents' holiday, with Adam adding a note to his phone about a bed and breakfast property that Kay's father recommended for future reference.

'Kay?'

'Yes?' She turned to her mother.

'I couldn't help overhearing your conversation. On the phone.'

Kay swallowed the last of her food and set down her knife and fork before leaning back in her chair with a sigh. 'Barnes was looking into our victim's last movements, that's all.'

Her mother's lips pursed. 'Look, I don't mean to pry
– and it's none of my business, I know – but I heard you
mention a wine merchant, and a place called Laval.'

'Our victim was there sourcing new clients who
want to export their wine over here.'

'That's the thing, though.'

'What is?'

'That area you mentioned. There aren't any
vineyards there.'

'Where's that?' Kay's father broke off his
conversation with Adam.

'Laval,' said Kay's mother. 'I was telling Kay –
there are no commercial vineyards, are there?'

'No. None that I recall, anyway. We didn't get over
that way this time but we were there two years ago.
Drove straight past Le Mans and then out to Rennes. I
don't remember seeing any signposts for vineyards.' He
winked. 'Your mother would've insisted on stopping
otherwise.'

Adam and her parents laughed as Kay's mother
playfully slapped her husband's arm, but Kay frowned.

*Why would Robert Victor visit an area with no
vineyards?*

Kay pushed back her chair. 'Sorry – I've got to
make a phone call.'

THIRTY-ONE

Carys brushed her fringe from her eyes, blew a loose strand out of the way and tried to concentrate on the itinerary Barnes had obtained from Melissa Lampton.

It seemed to her that Victor's colleagues were disorganised at best, and she could only imagine what Barnes had said when finding out the information had been available twenty-four hours beforehand.

It jarred with the professional image that was conveyed on the website she'd been looking at the night before, and she wondered if standards had slipped since Kenneth Archerton had become ill.

On the screen in front of her was a map she'd found of the area where Robert Victor had been travelling while in France. After receiving a call from Kay who had told her that there were no vineyards in the area Robert visited at the end of the week, she printed out a copy and used a highlighter pen to mark off the major towns along the route. She began to piece together information about each of those, following the DI's request to investigate what extracurricular activities Robert might have been pursuing, especially given Laura's suggestion he might have been having an affair.

She moved her mouse across the screen and selected the option to view the map as a satellite image, and zoomed in closer.

Most of the buildings that abutted the main road on the route appeared to be industrial in nature rather than residential. From time to time, roadside cafés jostled for space beside tumbledown garages and car spares suppliers.

She wrinkled her nose.

Definitely no vineyards, either.

So why go there?

She glanced over her shoulder at the sound of footsteps to see Sharp approaching. 'I've got no idea what he was up to, guv. But Kay is right – there are no vineyards around here.'

The detective chief inspector leaned on the desk and gestured towards her screen. 'Did he visit any vineyards at all?'

'At the beginning of his trip, yes.' Carys picked up the itinerary and turned the page back. 'There's one here at Orléans, which he visited on Monday after picking up the car. He stayed at a motel nearby, and then drove to a different one on Tuesday morning. It's after that when things seem a bit strange.'

'In what way?'

'Well, at the beginning of this trip he's setting quite a fast pace. Laura managed to get hold of the GPS information from the hire company and reckons the only way he managed to do the distance is if he was speeding. It is almost as if he was trying to get his work commitments out of the way before this extracurricular stuff.'

'Can you work out any addresses from the GPS data?'

'Only the streets, not the actual building he might've visited. There was nothing programmed into the satnav, either. Wherever he was going, whoever he was meeting with, he knew how to get there. We've only got this much because the hire company fits a GPS tracker to all their high-end cars in case they get stolen.'

'What does Robert's itinerary say for the remainder of the week?'

Carys flipped the page. 'Not much. It looks like Melissa booked accommodation for the first two nights but, apart from that, I've got nothing.'

'Okay, well, I suggest tomorrow you get someone from uniform to head over to the office and take a formal statement from Melissa Lampton.'

Carys turned her chair to face Sharp. 'Do you think I was right, then? Do you think someone else might have been involved with Robert's death?'

'Maybe. Whatever the case, we need to find out if there is any correlation between what you're holding in your hand and where Robert actually went while he was in France. If necessary, get on to our colleagues over in Coquelles and see what they can tell you about these areas.'

'Okay.' Carys bit back her disappointment. The only problem with working on a night shift was missing out on the inroads the rest of the team were making during the day.

She knew what she was doing was contributing to the investigation, but envied Gavin for his position within the day shift – and the progress he had been making the past two days in her absence.

Her eyes moved to the window as one of the plainclothes police constables opened the blinds, and saw with a shock that the sun was already up. She checked her watch.

'The time goes quicker than you think,' said Sharp. 'That's the problem, isn't it?'

He straightened, and then gestured to the computer screen as her desk phone began to ring. 'This is good work you're doing, Carys. Keep it up.'

'Thanks, guv.'

Her phone began to ring as he walked away, and she picked it up, unable to keep the weariness from her voice.

'DC Miles.'

'Ma'am, it's Sergeant Tasker over at Snodland – we've got a report of a possible sighting of Alice Victor.'

THIRTY-TWO

Kay reached out blindly for her mobile phone as the opening bars of an Aerosmith song blasted her awake.

Next to her, Adam groaned and rolled over before pushing back the sheets and staggering sleepily towards the en suite.

'Carys. Have you found her?'

'Morning, guv. Not sure – we've just received a call about a possible sighting near Wouldham Common. Thought you might want to join us.'

'I'll be ready in ten minutes.'

'Okay, I'll have someone pick you up on the way.'

'Thanks.'

She ended the call as Adam flushed the toilet and wandered back into the bedroom.

'Good news?'

'There's been a possible sighting of Alice,' she said, pulling clean underwear from a drawer and throwing it onto the bed. She pulled her vest top over her head, tossed it into the wash basket and hurried into the bathroom. 'Carys is going to get someone to pick me up in ten minutes.'

'I'll make you coffee to take with you. Are you hungry?'

'No, don't worry – I'll grab something later. Thanks.'

She stepped under the hot jets of water, quickly showered and then dressed.

Eight minutes later, she was standing in the lane outside the house, takeout coffee cup in hand when a red four-door vehicle hared around the corner towards her and slid to a stop.

'Morning, guv,' said Laura.

'Morning. Who phoned it in?' Kay stuffed her handbag into the footwell and fastened her seatbelt as the police constable turned left at the roundabout and powered the car through the housing estate towards the main road.

'A man by the name of David Sykes. He's a keen birdwatcher, apparently. Went up onto the Common in the hope of spotting something or other at first light, and reckons he saw a man with a young girl. 'Course, from up there he's got a view of the whole of the village and across the marshes down to the River Medway. You can see for miles.'

'Are you familiar with the place?'

'I had family in Meopham, guv. Used to spend my school holidays kicking around there.'

'Good. Stick with me this morning – I know you've just done a full shift but I could do with someone who knows the local area well on this one.'

'Thanks, guv.'

Kay noticed Laura sit up straighter in the driver's seat as she shifted down a gear and steered the car past the golf course to their left, and recalled Sharp's comments about bringing on board the police constable as part of the investigation team.

'How long until you hear about your application to become a detective?'

'Six weeks, guv.'

'Thought about any specialisation you want to do when you've passed your exams?'

Laura shot her a smile. 'This, guv. Major crimes.'

Kay sipped her coffee and watched the landscape flash past the window.

Laura slowed the car as they approached the turn-off for the Rochester Road and then steered it expertly along a winding lane through Burham village. She took a right-hand turn a few miles later, and the car began to climb.

'There's a team already setting up along here,' she explained. 'Sykes – the bloke who called it in – says he saw them walking along the perimeter of a field down near the playing fields. DCI Sharp has two more teams in plainclothes down in the village.'

Kay frowned. 'I wonder if Greg has run out of food or water? He's taking a risk getting that close to the village. Have there been any phone calls to Annette Victor?'

'Hazel hasn't reported anything to her,' said Laura. 'Sharp told her not to say anything to Annette yet – not until we're sure, anyway.'

Kay dug her fingernails into her palms. A possible sighting involving both Greg Victor and Alice was good news, especially if the little girl looked well, but they couldn't afford to have the man panic when approached. Despite all the work the team had undertaken since Robert's body was discovered, they still hadn't fathomed a motive for his brother's actions – or ascertained if his brother was responsible for the shooting.

She hoped she would soon have the answers she sought, and she would insist on being present when Greg Victor was interviewed.

She exhaled, and forced her attention to the task in hand.

They had to find him first.

Laura swung the car in next to an ambulance parked beside a picnic bench, and Kay climbed out.

Spotting Carys talking to a group of uniformed officers, she wandered over to join her and gestured for her to continue her briefing.

The detective constable held out a map to the group,

fighting against a breeze to keep it flat while she pointed out the search area.

'David Sykes says he spotted a man and a girl fitting Greg and Alice's description here,' she said, pointing to a copse of trees at the edge of the marshes. 'It's a fair way from the river, but it avoids the new river-walk and the most built-up fringes of the village. Sykes says there are a few houses along here, and it might be that Greg has run out of food or water. He could be trying to find somewhere to break into and steal a few supplies.'

'If he's down there, guv, why are we up here?' said a junior constable.

'We've got two teams down in the village, but Greg will be alert to anyone trying to approach him,' said Carys. 'If he makes a run for it, our position here gives us two advantages. One, we can observe where he runs off to, and second, if he heads this way, we can apprehend him.'

'One thing everyone needs to bear in mind is that Alice is going to be a very tired and scared little girl,' said Kay, 'so corralling Greg into a space where he feels threatened is something we need to avoid. If he runs, let him – he'll be exhausted from being in hiding for the past five days and won't last long out here. We can track him once he's out in the open.' She turned as a van pulled up alongside, a loud barking emanating from the inside. 'And I don't want the dogs used until it's absolutely necessary. I don't want that poor kid terrified, understood?'

'Guv.'

The chorus of voices died down, and Kay beckoned to Carys.

'Are you okay to continue? Not too tired?'

The detective constable shook her head. 'I wouldn't want to be anywhere else right now, guv.'

THIRTY-THREE

Gavin glared at his mobile phone screen and swore under his breath.

'Any news?' said Barnes.

'Nothing.'

'Come on then. The sooner we do this, the sooner you can go back to checking your phone.'

Upon reaching the incident room that morning, Sharp had provided both men with an update regarding the possible sighting of Greg Victor and Alice.

Eager to join the search, Gavin had been disappointed when the DCI had tasked them with speaking to the business owners who Greg had been having job interviews with since arriving in Kent four months ago.

'We need to know what their impressions of him were,' said Sharp. 'The statements taken by uniform only provide confirmation that he had meetings with them. I want to know what he told them. The more information we've got before we interview him, the better.'

Gavin couldn't argue with the DCI's logic, and bit down his frustration that, despite working four night shifts in a row, Carys was now leading the search for Alice.

He got on well with his colleague, but there had always been an underlying competitive edge to their working relationship. A year ago, he'd been convinced she was going to apply for the role of detective sergeant that had been advertised within the team at Maidstone, and was surprised at her admission that she didn't feel ready for such a task.

'Oi, Piper.'

Barnes's voice dragged him from his thoughts. The detective sergeant was holding open the door into the carpet retail shop, his eyebrow raised. 'Are you coming, or what?'

'Sorry.'

Gavin hurried after him, and blinked as his eyes adjusted to the artificial lighting inside the shop.

An overwhelming smell of chemical compounds assaulted his senses, the air thick with the stench of new carpet and rugs. To his left, rolls of carpet samples had been stacked along the wall, the varying vibrant, mock antique, and muted tones providing a plethora of choices for the shop's customers. Piles of rugs in different shapes and sizes had been stacked along the shop floor to his right.

At the far end of the shop, two men in short sleeves and wearing ties broke off from their conversation and watched as he and Barnes approached.

Barnes held up his warrant card. 'Who's the manager here?'

The shorter of the two, a man in his mid-forties with a receding hairline and wireframe glasses, almost raised his hand before changing his mind at the last minute and pointing at his chest.

'Me. What's this about?'

'Sorry – your name is?' said Barnes.

'Clive Morton.'

'Is there somewhere we can talk in private?'

Morton turned to his colleague. 'Charlie, can you give me a shout if it gets busy?'

The other man gave a curt nod, his mouth downturned. 'Sure.'

Morton beckoned to Gavin and Barnes, and then walked past a wraparound desk laden with catalogues and an ancient computer, before swiping a security card over a panel next to a door at the back of the shop and holding it open for them.

'There's a kitchenette down by the fire exit on the left-hand side,' he said. 'We can talk in there.'

Gavin entered the cramped space, wrinkled his nose at the dirty cups piled on the draining board and the stain-covered microwave door, then turned to face Morton and pulled out his notebook.

'What's this all about?' said Morton. He folded his arms over his chest and leaned against the door frame, his eyes moving from one detective to the other.

'Greg Victor,' said Barnes. 'We understand you interviewed him for a job here. Can you confirm when that was?'

Martin scratched his chin. 'I thought the name sounded familiar. He's the bloke who's gone and done a runner with that little girl, isn't he? I thought there was something about him.'

'When did you interview him?'

'Must have been about eight or nine weeks ago. Charlie out there was the successful applicant, and started about a month ago, so yeah – eight or nine weeks.'

'What were your impressions of him?'

Morton frowned. 'I can't really remember.'

'You just said you "thought there was something about him",' said Gavin.

The man's face flushed. 'It was only a figure of speech. I do recall he was early for the meeting. I was running late, coming back from our head office at Ashford, and he was wandering around the shop when I got here. Megan, who was working here that afternoon, said he didn't talk much once he had introduced himself.'

'What did he tell you about his previous employment?' said Barnes.

'Nothing much, other than what was already on his CV. I mean, come on, he killed animals for a living, right? He didn't seem enthused about it, that's for sure.' He shuddered. 'If I was him, I'd have been looking for a new job, too.'

'Do you still have a copy of his CV on file?' Gavin looked around the cramped kitchenette, but couldn't see a filing cabinet.

'Probably not,' said Morton. 'Head office deal with all that. The only CVs I keep on file are for those people I end up employing.'

'We'll need a name and number for someone we can speak to there,' said Barnes. 'Why didn't you give him the job?'

'Because I had two other applicants who were better qualified,' said Morton. 'I was spoilt for choice.'

After concluding the interview, Barnes led the way back to the car and paused next to the driver's door, tossing the keys from one hand to the other.

'Well, despite Kay's assertion that these interviews are going to help to build up a picture about Greg, I can't help feeling that he's a bit of a grey man. He's not exactly mister personality by the sound of it, is he?'

'It was only a job interview,' said Gavin. 'How many people have you interviewed over the years that you can recall, despite our training?'

Barnes grimaced. 'Who's next on the list?'

Gavin checked his notes. 'There's a builders' merchants about half a mile away from here in the Tonbridge direction. According to the paperwork we found in his room at Robert and Annette's house, Greg had an interview there at the beginning of August.'

'That was only a few weeks ago.' Barnes wrenched open the car door. 'Let's hope they remember more about him.'

Gavin said nothing, put his notebook away and then pulled his mobile phone from his pocket. There were no new messages, no missed calls.

The passenger window went down.

'Trust me,' said Barnes, 'if they find Alice, Carys will let you know. Come on.'

Gavin scowled, and got in the car.

THIRTY-FOUR

Barnes wrapped his fingers around the steering wheel, gritted his teeth and willed the traffic lights to turn green.

Beside him, Piper flipped through the apps on his phone screen muttering under his breath. The young detective constable turned his attention to the road as Barnes accelerated once more.

'What road is this builders' merchants on?'

'Just off the London Road,' said Barnes, and lapsed into silence once more.

It was all he could do not to pull over and check his own phone.

The thought of Alice Victor being taken across the marshes by her uncle brought back painful memories of his own daughter's kidnapping and near drowning.

It had only been the quick thinking of a police constable and a sergeant that had saved Emma's life.

Barnes didn't know what he would have done if he'd lost her – or what he would have done to the man who had taken her.

He tried to fight down the sickness in the pit of his stomach and vowed he would call his daughter that evening when he finished his shift. Now that she was at university, their conversations had become all too brief for his liking. He suspected she thought of him as being overbearing sometimes, but had the kindness to understand what drove his fears.

'What?' His colleague's voice jerked him from his thoughts. 'Sorry – didn't catch that. What did you say?'

Piper pointed out the windscreen. 'It's this turning off to the left up here.'

'Okay.'

The builders' merchants took up a large lot on the corner of the junction, the entrance on one road and the exit on the other. Sandy-coloured dust covered the concrete apron, and Barnes suppressed a groan as he saw a man wielding an angle grinder cutting concrete paving slabs on one side of the yard near the car park.

'This car is going to look like it's crossed the bloody Sahara by the time we leave here,' he said.

Piper snorted. 'Well, you're the driver, so it's your turn to clean it.'

Barnes rolled his eyes, switched off the engine and climbed out. He blinked as the breeze wafted a fresh cloud of dust towards them, sneezed, then locked the car and hurried towards the warehouse-sized building.

He dusted a fine powder from his shoulders as Piper followed him between a pair of unmanned service counters, and ignored the cheerful pop music that blared from speakers in the far reaches of steel rafters that soared above his head.

Eight rows of tall shelving units ran from one side of the store to the other, and signs hung from girders proclaiming where to find plumbing supplies, bathroom fixtures and fittings, or kitchen appliances.

'Nightmare,' said Piper, as a family of four led by a harassed-looking father brushed past him, their bickering voices disappearing around a corner and into a row labelled "lighting".

'Another few years, and that'll be you,' said Barnes. 'Couple of ankle-biters at your feet, nagging wife, the lot.'

He grinned as his colleague shuddered, then spotted a man in a bright-yellow polo shirt pushing a handcart laden with rolls of wallpaper.

'Excuse me?'

The man slowed to a halt and looked Barnes up and down, then Gavin. 'You the police?'

'We were wondering if we could have a word with the manager?'

'Stephen? He's out the back. Go along here, then turn left. You'll see an office – he's in there.'

'Thanks.'

The man grunted an acknowledgement, then wheeled the trolley away, the squeak of a wheel an indication of his slow progress as Barnes turned and walked in the opposite direction.

He spotted a double set of windows at the back of the warehouse-like building where the staff member had directed them, and rapped his knuckles on the open door.

A waif-like twenty-something spun around from a laptop he'd been peering at, and jumped to his feet. 'Who are you?'

Barnes made the introductions. 'We're looking for the manager.'

'That's me. Stephen Francis.'

'Really?' Barnes cleared his throat to hide the surprise in his voice, and wondered when everyone had started to look so young. 'How old are you?'

'Twenty-nine. Why?'

'We wanted to speak to you about Greg Victor. I understand you interviewed him for a job here about three or four weeks ago.'

'Oh. Him.' Francis flopped back into his seat, and ran a hand through his collar-length hair. 'Yeah, I'm kind of glad I didn't employ him now. What a nightmare that would've been.'

'What can you tell us about him?'

'Nothing much.' Francis's top lip curled. 'I don't think he fancied reporting to someone younger than him. As soon as he clapped eyes on me, he sort of clammed up. He could've done the work – I mean, stacking shelves and operating a cash register isn't difficult – but I could see that he was going to be trouble. I gave the job to someone else.'

'Do you still have a copy of his CV?'

'I think so. Hang on.'

Barnes moved out of the way as Francis pushed his chair back and crossed the tiny office to a four-drawer filing cabinet in the corner of the room.

The store manager stooped as he opened the bottom drawer and rummaged through the contents before pulling out a two-page document and thrusting it at him.

'Here you go.'

'Can you give us a copy?'

'You can keep that one. It's not like I'm going to employ him now, is it?'

Barnes didn't respond, and instead ran his gaze over the contents of the CV. It matched exactly with the one that had been found at Annette and Robert Victor's house, and provided no new information about Greg's background.

He resisted the urge to sigh. 'Okay, thanks for your time. We'll call you if we have any further questions.'

'You're right,' said Gavin as they left the builders' merchants and crossed the dusty car park. He finished flicking through the CV and then folded it. 'Nothing out of the ordinary. Makes you wonder why he's gone off the rails like this.'

'Doesn't it? I mean, kidnapping his niece is bloody extreme.'

Barnes stopped walking as his phone began to buzz

in his pocket. He fished it out and swallowed to counteract the lump in his throat as he read the message.

Gavin's phone vibrated a second later.

'They've found her,' said Barnes, his voice croaking. 'They've bloody found her.'

THIRTY-FIVE

'Give me those binoculars.'

Kay snatched them from the outstretched hand of the police officer beside her, and then trained them on the flat marshy land below the Common.

'Where?' she said.

'Find the goal posts on the playing field,' said Laura, shielding her eyes from the sunlight. 'Then come forward until you see the outer reaches of the marsh. There are some scrubby trees in the middle. I saw a flash of blue amongst them, and then a man and a little girl.'

Kay held her breath as she followed her directions, and then let out a gasp.

'Bloody hell, Hanway – good spotting.' Kay passed back the binoculars and took the radio Carys held out to her. 'I need two teams heading back towards the recreation field now. We have a likely sighting on the marshes, but I don't want to make him run. We need to think of Alice's safety.'

She turned to PC Morrison. 'Dave – where's the water patrol? I need a boat down by the river walk, just in case.'

'I'll get on to them, guv.'

Handing back the radio, she caught Carys's gaze as the detective constable lowered her mobile phone. 'Did you tell Barnes and Piper?'

'Yes.'

'Okay. Have them go back to the incident room and start phoning around to get the nearest available ABE in for a briefing as soon as Alice has been recovered. Make sure they check the cells, too – I don't want Greg Victor trying to self-harm while he's in custody. Twenty-four-hour watch, got that?'

'Guv.'

Carys moved away and held her mobile to her ear, her instructions to her colleagues carrying on the slight breeze that rustled the tree branches above Kay's head.

The Achieving Best Evidence officer would be the only person allowed to interview Alice about what had happened on the boat and her subsequent kidnapping. Even Alice's mother wouldn't be allowed to be present, but a specialist intermediary could be appointed if Annette wished.

Kay knew how vital Alice's evidence would be, and how critical her management of the little girl's rescue and return to her mother would be analysed by her superiors, the Crown Prosecution Service, and Greg Victor's defence solicitor.

'Who's leading the two nearest search teams?' she said to a nearby police sergeant.

'Hughes is down there, nearest the recreation field, guv,' said the woman, 'and Tasker is moving towards the marshes from the lower end of the Common.'

Kay raised her hand to her brow and shielded her eyes against the glare off the river from the rising sun. It beat against the back of her neck, a reminder that summer wasn't yet over and that a little girl was out in the open, exposed to the elements.

She watched the ambulance crew that hovered at the perimeter of the gathered officers, and swallowed as she watched them check their equipment and supplies. They would have all that they needed to treat Alice should it be required, but she knew from her own experience that keeping busy was also a way to counteract the nerves, and the fear that something could go wrong.

'Guv, look.'

Her attention snapped back to the marshland below at the sergeant's voice, in time to see a man leading a child away from a copse of trees.

His shoulders slumped with exhaustion – yet, when the child stumbled on the uneven ground, he didn't hesitate and swept her up into his arms. He dragged his feet towards the houses that backed onto the recreation field, his whole body language depicting a man defeated.

'He's giving up,' said Kay. 'Get that team down there to fan out – don't crowd him. Let him have some space in case he changes his mind. We've got no idea what his motive is, and I don't want anyone spooking him.'

'Got that, guv,' said the sergeant, and raised her radio to her lips.

'What's going on, guv?' Carys appeared at her shoulder, her mobile phone still clutched in her hand. 'Is he moving?'

'He's broken cover,' said Kay, pointing to the figure that was nearing a hedgerow behind one of the goalposts. 'Have you got a map?'

'Here.' Carys held up her phone, then zoomed in on an image. 'There's a footpath in the corner of the field that leads to the road.'

'Did you get that?' Kay turned to the sergeant beside her.

The woman nodded and relayed the information, and Kay watched as a third group of officers poured onto the road from a deep thicket, cutting off any hope of escape.

'Carys, have you got your car keys?'

'Yes.'

'All right – get me down there. Laura – come with us.'

Carys hurried towards a blue four-door hatchback parked haphazardly behind two patrol cars, and threw it into gear as soon as Kay closed the door and Laura tumbled onto the back seat.

The detective constable passed her mobile phone across, and accelerated past a cyclist.

Kay gripped the hand rest. 'Laura, can you maintain radio contact with Hughes for me? Let him know I'm on my way.'

'Ma'am.'

The countryside sped past the window in a blur as Carys steered the car around a sharp bend that curved downwards towards the marshes.

Barked commands amongst the uniformed teams between bursts of static over the radio added to the surge of adrenalin that coursed through Kay.

What if Greg Victor panicked?

What if Alice was sick? Was that why he was giving up?

A flash of blue caught her attention in the door mirror and she angled her head until she could see the patrol car in their wake.

'Laura? Get them to switch those bloody lights off. There's no need to announce our arrival.'

The police constable's voice carried from the backseat as she relayed Kay's instructions, and then leaned forward.

'Done. And Hughes says they've got a visual. They're about four hundred metres from them.'

'Okay.'

Kay hung on tight as Carys took the last bend and

slid the car to a halt behind two Kent Police vehicles in a lay-by.

'The recreation field is just up there to our left, guv,' she said, and ripped the keys from the ignition.

'Let's go.'

Kay kept to the verge on the left of the road as it rose up towards the village, and resisted the urge to run.

She had three teams now encircling Greg Victor, and she had no wish to frighten the man. The hedgerow beside her was a tangle of blackberry bushes, hawthorn and hazel, and, as she hurried towards the footpath boundary that Carys had identified on the map, she tried to peer through the greenery.

It was no use – she couldn't see a thing.

'Laura, make sure your radio volume is down, won't you?' she said over her shoulder.

'Yes, ma'am. Hughes says Victor is now two hundred metres away from the road. He's entered the footpath and he's moving this way.'

Kay's stomach twisted. 'Is Alice still with him?'

'Yes, he's carrying her.'

Her attention snapped towards the brow of the hill at a commotion.

A man emerged beside a sign pointing towards the recreation field at the same time as eight uniformed police officers burst from a gate next to a property bordering the road.

Kay could hear Hughes's voice carrying towards her as he gestured to Alice.

Greg's shoulders sagged as he lowered the little girl to the ground, and raised his hands.

Alice hugged herself to his side, cowering behind his right leg as he spoke with the police sergeant and the rest of the officers encircled him, cutting off any means of escape.

'She's terrified,' said Kay, and jogged towards them.

As she drew closer, Greg's gaze moved away from Hughes and he stared at her, his eyes pleading.

'Don't scare her,' he said. 'Please. She doesn't understand.'

Kay ran her eyes over the five-year-old, noting the grass stains on her jeans, mud around the hems, and torn threads on the green jumper she wore.

Bright-blue eyes shone out from under a blonde fringe, and Kay forced a smile.

She crouched in front of the little girl. 'Hello, Alice. I'm Kay.'

'Where's my mummy?'

THIRTY-SIX

Ignoring Greg Victor's shouts, Kay swept up Alice into her arms and raced towards Carys's car.

The detective constable had already started the engine and turned the vehicle around, and as Kay secured Alice into the back seat and stuffed her jacket alongside her to fill out the seatbelt, Carys called over her shoulder.

'I've spoken to Barnes – he's heading over to Kenneth Archerton's house. Gavin has been in touch with Annette, but her place is still besieged by reporters. She doesn't want to have the reunion there – she wants to keep Alice away from the cameras.'

Kay moved around to the passenger door and climbed in. 'Okay, go. I don't blame her – they're going to be like vultures now.'

Carys's eyes moved to the rear-view mirror, and she smiled. 'Are you warm enough, Alice?'

Turning to face the little girl, Kay saw that she was staring out of the window, her thumb in her mouth.

Her eyes were wide as she watched the landscape flash by, and then she turned her gaze to the front seats.

'Where's my mummy?'

'She's waiting for you, Alice. We're taking you to her now. Are you cold?'

'No.'

'Okay.'

Carys's mobile phone began to vibrate in the cradle on the dashboard, and Kay picked it up.

'Gavin?'

'Guv – we've got the ambulance following you to Kenneth Archerton's house so they can give Alice a check over. We've also got a specialist on her way. I've asked Annette to bring a change of clothes for Alice as well.'

'Thanks, Gav. We're probably twenty minutes away now.'

'We'll be there.'

Carys's car slowed behind a stream of traffic heading into Maidstone, and Kay battened down the temptation to keep turning around to check on Alice. She didn't want to give the child cause for concern, and add to what must have been an already confusing time for her.

Despite the little girl's dirty clothing, she hadn't noticed any bruises or scratches on her face or hands, but it would be up to the female ambulance officer travelling in their wake to conduct a thorough examination while she was reunited with her mother.

Kay gritted her teeth, unsure what she would do if it transpired that Greg Victor had harmed his niece in any way.

Moments later, Carys slowed the car as the gates to Kenneth Archerton's house came into view, and Kay breathed a sigh of relief.

There were no reporters hanging around outside, and a patrol car was parked on the verge next to the driveway. The driver raised his hand to Kay and Carys before they passed through the gates.

The front door opened as their vehicle crunched over the gravel towards the house, and Barnes appeared. The older detective turned and beckoned to someone in the house as the gates closed behind the car.

Annette Victor appeared on the doorstep beside him, her hand over her mouth.

'Mummy!'

Carys braked to a standstill at Alice's cry, and Kay leapt from the passenger seat. She wrenched open the back door before Annette stumbled down the front steps towards them as the ambulance turned into the driveway. Releasing Alice's seatbelt, Kay lifted the girl to the ground.

'She's here, Alice. Your mum is here.'

She took a step back as a sob escaped Annette's lips and the woman crouched on the driveway, her arms outstretched.

The little girl tumbled into her mother's embrace, and Kay blinked away a tear as Annette rose on shaky feet and clutched her daughter to her chest.

She smoothed down Alice's hair, ran her fingers over her face, and then turned to Kay.

'Thank you – thank you.'

Her voice broke as tears streamed down her face.

Kay nodded, and took a deep breath. 'Shall we go inside? The ambulance crew will want to give her a check over to make sure she's all right.'

Annette turned as the female paramedic crossed the driveway towards them, a canvas bag in her hand.

The petite blonde stopped a few paces away and waited for Kay's signal.

Alice wriggled in her mother's arms, kicking out her feet, and Annette lowered her to the ground, keeping a firm grip on her hand.

'Of course,' she said. 'Everyone else is in the kitchen – your detectives, I mean. And a woman who says she's a specialist in this sort of thing.'

'It's to make sure we do everything in Alice's best interests,' said Kay. 'Is your father here?'

'He had to go into the office – something urgent came up. He's on his way back. I phoned him as soon as I heard the news.'

'Okay, well before Kenneth gets here we're going to need you to change Alice out of these clothes, so that we can take them into evidence,' said Kay as she followed Annette through to the kitchen. 'After that, we'll need to arrange for Alice to be interviewed tomorrow morning, while her recollection is still fresh.'

'But – but she can't. She needs to stay here with me. She needs to recover.'

'I understand your concern, Annette, but her evidence is vital in our investigation as to why Greg kidnapped her, and what happened while they were on the run.' Kay caught the ABE officer's eye. 'Bethany here is going to conduct the interview with Alice. She's very experienced in doing this, and your daughter will be in safe hands.'

Alice slipped from her mother's grip and edged towards the back door, her hands against the panes of glass as she stared at the vast garden beyond.

'But I'll be with her too, won't I?' Annette looked from the brunette police officer to Kay, then back.

Bethany moved away from the kitchen counter she'd been leaning against, her face passive. 'We'll have a specialised suite set up for interviewing Alice, and she'll be made as comfortable as possible. It's essential that we speak with her alone because—'

'But I want to be with her—'

'Mrs Victor—'

'Annette.'

'Annette, I know it's difficult for you, but there's a risk that Alice may not tell us everything if you're in the room with her,' said Bethany. Her eyes softened. 'She may feel embarrassed, or want to protect you from hearing something that she'd otherwise tell me without your being present in the room.'

'It's very important that we do this the right way,' said Kay. 'As Bethany said, you can't be in the room with her. We're only allowed to do this once, so we have to make sure we do it right and listen to every aspect of Alice's story.'

Annette paled. 'Do you think he harmed her?'

'If you could let the paramedic here examine her while you're getting her out of these clothes, I'd be grateful. Bethany will come with you, too, in case she needs to note anything.' Kay gestured to the ambulance officer who hovered on the threshold, her eyes full of concern for the five-year-old who had turned away from the back door and now gazed up at her mother, silent.

'Oh.' Annette blinked, then gave a slight shake of her head. 'Okay. Shall we go upstairs, Alice? Get you out of those dirty clothes?'

Alice gave a small smile, then slipped her hand into her mother's and followed her meekly from the kitchen.

'Gavin, can you go with Lucy and Bethany and wait outside the room to bag up those clothes?' said Kay.

'Guv.'

Kay took a deep breath as the voices receded down the hallway and up the stairs. 'Carys, head back to the station and start making some headway on the formal interview plan, please. Ask Fiona Wilkes to assist – we could use her input on the psychological aspects of this one. I'll get a lift back with Barnes and Piper.'

'Will do, guv.'

'Get yourself home after that – I want you in at seven o'clock tomorrow morning.'

The detective constable nodded, then shot from the room, the front door slamming shut in her wake before Kay turned to Barnes and exhaled.

'Are you all right?' he said.

'Yes, I think so. You?'

The skin at the corners of his eyes crinkled. 'I am now. That was a good result, Kay. Where's Greg?'

'In custody at the station by now. Sharp is still there – in fact, I don't think anyone went home this morning. Once we've got Alice's clothes into evidence, we'll head back. I'll interview Greg with Piper, but I'd like you to observe with Carys.'

'Reckon he'll talk?'

'You didn't see him at the marshes, Ian. He gave up. Five days on the run, and then – nothing.'

'Maybe he's feeling a bit of remorse?'

'I don't know. It's why I want Fiona's input. She'll think of an angle we might miss.'

The interview specialist had been working with Kent Police for a number of years providing analysis and input into some of the more difficult interviews that had been conducted, and Kay respected the woman's work ethic. Requesting her help wasn't an indication of defeat – it was another aspect of ensuring she had the most carefully phrased questions when she began talking to Greg Victor.

She glanced up at soft footsteps padding towards the kitchen to see Alice dressed in fresh jeans and a white sweatshirt, her wet hair curling around her cheeks.

A fresh scent of strawberries and hibiscus filled the air as the little girl meandered across to the kitchen table and climbed onto one of the pine seats beside it, her eyes hopeful.

'Someone's hungry,' said Annette as she entered the room, a relieved smile crossing her lips.

'That's great,' said Kay. 'Before we go, I think Ian has something for you, Alice.'

Barnes pulled the blue rabbit from behind his back and mimed it bouncing across the table to Alice.

The little girl's face brightened, a wide toothy smile creasing her features as she reached out for it.

'Thomas!'

Barnes smiled. 'Is that his name?'

'Yes.' Alice clutched the rabbit to her chest. 'He escaped.'

'But now he's back with you, isn't he?'

Her face fell, and she nodded. Her bottom lip wobbled, and Annette put her arm around her, pulling her close.

'It's alright, my darling. It's all over.'

Alice wiggled away from her mother's embrace, and held out the rabbit to Barnes.

'My daddy said I had to keep Thomas safe, but I didn't.'

'That's okay. You got him back, right?' said Barnes, his voice thick with emotion.

'You found him.' The little girl pushed the toy rabbit towards him. 'I want you to have him.'

THIRTY-SEVEN

DCI Devon Sharp paused in the corridor outside the interview suites and gestured to Kay to wait.

'I've been here since six o'clock last night, so I'm about to head off and get a few hours' rest. Before I go, I want you to know how proud of you I am. You've only been in this role eighteen months, and yet you've proven to me and others that you were the right one for the job. Larch should never have held you back.'

Kay took a step back. 'Thanks, guv. I appreciate that.'

'Credit where credit's due, Kay. You've got a great team upstairs, but that's down to the way you manage them. I know the Chief Super's impressed, too.' He broke off as Gavin appeared. 'All right – see you tomorrow morning.'

The detective constable nodded to the DCI as he left, and then handed one of two manila folders to Kay.

'Fiona Wilkes had some thoughts about a couple of the questions,' he said. 'There's a summary on the top for you.'

Kay flipped open the folder and ran her eyes over the interview specialist's suggestions. 'This is good. Did everyone go home who was working here last night?'

'Yes,' he said. 'Even Carys.'

'Thank goodness – she looked dead on her feet at Archerton's house.'

Gavin pointed towards the interview room. 'Ready, guv?'

'You bet I am. Lead the way.'

Gavin pushed open the door to interview room three, and stood aside to let her pass. He waved a uniformed constable from the space, and Kay took in the dejected figure slumped in one of the plastic chairs surrounding a metal table.

Greg Victor had been reduced to a pathetic creature. Since arriving at the police station, his clothes had been taken for forensic analysis and he'd been subjected to a thorough strip search before DNA swabs were taken.

Now, he sat in a crumpled paper suit and bootees, his wet hair sticking up on end and dark circles under his eyes.

He lowered his gaze to his folded hands when Kay pulled out a chair opposite him, and she noticed his fingernails had been bitten to the quick.

As Gavin pressed the "record" button on the

machine next to him and recited the formal caution, Greg winced and shifted in his seat.

Beside him, his solicitor loosened his tie, evidently resigned that he was going to be in for a long day.

'State your full name and address for the record, please,' said Gavin.

Greg Victor stuttered his response, then wiped the back of his hand across his mouth.

'How long have you lived at that address?'

'Since the end of May.'

'And where were you prior to that?'

Greg took a shuddering breath and confirmed his ex-wife's Nottingham address. 'We split up. I caught her having an affair. My daughter, Sadie, lives with her.'

'Let's talk about what happened last Friday,' said Kay. 'What time did you leave Kenneth Archerton's house with your niece, Alice?'

'About eight o'clock.' Greg cleared his throat and lowered his gaze to his hands. 'Yeah, eight o'clock. I had the boat hired from ten, and I knew traffic would be slow getting through town that time of the morning.'

'Why was Alice at Kenneth's house?'

'She and her mum had stayed over the night before.'

'Why did you take Alice with you?'

'I promised her I'd take her out on the river before she started school. She overheard me talking about it at a barbecue a few weeks ago and kept on about it.' He raised his head. 'Annette and Robert were fine about it.

I'd been babysitting for them on and off since I came down here. She had a life jacket.'

'Where did you hire the boat from?'

'Toppings. I saw their advert on social media. They're based in Tonbridge.'

'What time did you leave Toppings?'

'It was after ten o'clock by the time I'd gone through the handover process with them and made sure Alice understood the dangers. We stopped for lunch at Yalding.' He rubbed a knuckle at his eye, then lowered his hand to the table, his fist clenched. 'Is she okay? I tried to make sure she kept warm, and we only ran out of food this morning. She lost her rabbit. It's a blue one – have you found it?'

'Did you touch her in any way?' said Gavin.

'What?' Greg's eyes opened wide, and then he grasped the edge of the table and sneered at the detective constable. 'No, I bloody didn't. She's my *niece.* What sort of monster do you take me for?'

'The sort of monster who kidnaps a little girl and disappears for five days, leaving her mother traumatised.'

'I didn't touch her. I didn't harm her. I was just trying to keep her safe.'

'If you were trying to keep her safe, why didn't you go to the police? Why run?'

'Look, I know it was stupid. I should've come to you, but when I heard that gunshot, I knew I had to get Alice away from there as fast as possible. It wasn't until yesterday that I realised I'd probably made things worse.'

'Did you shoot your brother?'

'No!'

'Who were you trying to keep Alice safe from?' said Kay.

'I don't know,' he said. 'Robert turned up that night and said there was a problem. He told me to get her away from the boat.'

'Hang on,' said Kay, and frowned. 'Back up. You said you stopped for lunch at Yalding. What happened after that?'

A sad smile crossed Greg's features. 'It was a perfect afternoon. Only a few boats on the river between there and Teston. Alice saw the swings next to the picnic area before the bridge and wanted to go and play so I moored up there for an hour or so. She got bored eventually, so we set off again. I made her stay inside when we went through the lock because I couldn't keep an eye on her and get the gates opened and closed, but apart from that she was happy to stand on the deck with me. She likes spotting the water voles.'

'When did Robert get in touch with you?'

Greg's face clouded. 'He phoned me just before we got to Barming. I was surprised – he'd been in France all week, and wasn't due back until the Saturday. He said he'd got the ferry back to Dover that morning and needed to see Alice. I told him I'd be back the next morning, but he said it was an emergency.' He sighed.

'He sounded angry – and scared. By then, Alice was giving me a funny look because she could hear his voice, so I told him to meet us at East Farleigh lock. I knew I'd need to moor up just past there for the night, and Alice was starting to get hungry so I thought Robert might as well join us for dinner.'

'What time did you reach East Farleigh?'

'By the time we got through the lock it was going on half past six. Most of the commuter traffic had passed over the bridge and things were starting to quieten down. There were a couple of dog walkers that went past while I was checking the mooring lines, but that was about it.'

'What time did Robert turn up?'

'Seven, give or take.'

'Take me through what happened when he arrived.'

'Alice was pleased to see him. We had dinner, and then let Alice sit up for a while to play.' He frowned. 'We went up on the deck – Robert said he needed to talk. He had a cigarette – Annette didn't let him smoke in front of Alice. We could see her through the window, though.' Greg exhaled. 'I was asking him about his trip to France and why he needed to speak to me in such a hurry, because he hadn't said anything since turning up. I suppose he didn't want to scare Alice. Anyway, I don't know – he spotted something, or someone, back towards the East Farleigh direction. He told me to shut up when I was mid-sentence, and sort of craned his neck, and then told me to go and get Alice.'

'Who was it?'

He shook his head. 'I don't know. I couldn't see anyone, but the light was fading by then. He swore blind there was someone under the bridge looking at us.'

'What did you do?'

'Nothing, at first. I thought he was having me on. Then he started getting scared, pleading with me, and told me Alice was in danger and that I had to get her away from there.'

'Is that when you shot Robert?' said Gavin.

'No, I told you – I didn't shoot him. Someone else did.'

'Who?'

'I don't know. Robert told me to take Alice and make a run for it. I didn't know what he was going on about. I told him if he wanted to get away, we should take the boat if he was scared, but he said it wouldn't work. He tossed his cigarette into the water, and then headed into the cabin and made Alice put on a sweatshirt. She was crying, because he was shouting at her to hurry up.' He shook his head. 'He put some cans of food and a couple of water bottles in a backpack and threw it at me. I tried to calm down Alice, and I shouted at Robert, told him he was making her scared, and that's when he shut up. He – he was terrified, I realise now. Alice was standing in the middle of the cabin, bawling her eyes out, and then he saw the toy rabbit she'd got from Kenneth. Robert shoved it at her, I suppose to try to calm her down because I told him she hadn't let it out of her sight since that morning. And then he pushed both of us up to the deck, and told me to piss off. He said whatever happened, I wasn't to return to the boat, and that I should use the one he'd hired at Allington instead.'

'You knew about the second boat?'

'That was the first time I'd heard about it.'

'Why steal the canoe, then?'

Greg ran his hand over his close-cropped hair. 'Alice was too tired to walk by the time we reached Maidstone, and I knew I had to do something. We managed to avoid the crowds, and then I saw the canoe hauled into some undergrowth by the rowing club. I didn't think – I dragged it into the water and set off. I didn't realise there was a bloody hole in the side of it until we were nearly at Allington.'

'Where were you planning to go?'

'At first, I thought I'd take the boat that Robert had hired, but then I realised I didn't have the bloody keys. In his haste to kick me off the boat, he'd forgotten to give them to me. I was scared by then. I thought maybe I'd been followed, that they might have found the keys on him. I mean, if they knew he'd travelled to East Farleigh, they might have known to look out for me at Allington, right? I carried Alice along the towpath as far as I could before daylight, and then we slept rough under the bridge that goes under the M20. I didn't have a plan after that. I just wanted to keep her safe – you have to understand that.'

In the silence that followed, Kay could hear the clock ticking on the wall behind her and the faint sound of voices along the corridor towards the door through to the front desk.

The solicitor turned the page of his notebook, the crackle and crunch deafening to her ears as she narrowed her eyes at Greg Victor.

'How far along the towpath did you take Alice before you went back and shot your brother?' she said.

'I never shot Robert,' he said, his voice low.

'Then who did?'

'Look, I did what he asked. I left the boat and headed off in the direction of Maidstone. I got about half a mile along when I—' He took a shuddering breath and ran a hand over his eyes. 'I heard a *bang*, from behind us. I've never heard a gun before, not in real life. But I knew that's what it was. I knew he'd been killed. And I knew I couldn't go back there. I picked up Alice and started to run.'

'Have you any idea who would want to kill your brother?' said Kay.

'No, but he was scared. I should've asked him why, but there wasn't time. When we were talking after dinner, he said he was going to speak to Annette about moving out of the area. Said he'd had enough.'

'Had he ever said anything about moving away before?'

'Not to me.'

'Five days on the run, Greg. What happened today? You expected to get caught, didn't you?'

The man in front of her visibly crumpled, his eyes reddening. 'Because I thought you'd be better at keeping her safe than me. I'm a father, detective, and Alice's uncle. I'm not a fugitive. I'm not some evil bastard who goes around kidnapping little girls. I was trying to save her, like her dad – my brother – told me to.'

Kay checked her watch, and signalled to Gavin to end the interview. She slapped shut the manila folder and stood, her mind reeling from Greg's statement and the revelations she'd heard.

As she opened the door, she heard the sound of a chair scraping across the tiled floor and turned, ready to defend herself.

Instead, Greg Victor stood beside the table, his hands by his side and his face distraught.

'Please, look after Alice – I think she's still in danger. I didn't kill my brother – someone else did. You have to believe me.'

THIRTY-EIGHT

Kay led the way into the incident room, dropped the folder she'd been carrying onto her desk as she passed, and called the investigation team to attention.

'Everyone – briefing, now. We've got a lot to get through, and not much time.'

She strode over to the kitchenette at the end of the room and heaped instant coffee into a chipped mug, adding two sugars. She turned as Fiona Wilkes, the interview specialist, joined her.

'What do you think?' said Fiona, a frown creasing her features.

'We've got a long way to go with this one,' said Kay. 'I've spoken to Sharp and he's sanctioned another twelve hours to interview Greg in order to give him enough breaks, but I've also put in a request with a magistrate to hold him for longer if we need to, based on the severity of the kidnapping charges.'

'That's probably for the best. I'll review the recording and let you know if I can offer any suggestions for the next interview.'

'Thanks, Fiona.'

As soon as the last team member took their seat, Kay moved to the front of the room. 'Greg Victor is, as we suspected he would, denying he had anything to do with his brother's murder and has stated that there was a third party involved in the shooting of Robert Victor.'

A ripple of conversation swept through the gathered officers, then died away as their attention returned to Kay.

She checked the list of items on the whiteboard. 'What happened with regards to our enquiries about the canoe? Did we find out where that came from?'

'Yes, guv.' PC Phillip Parker raised his hand. 'Eve Henderson from Penenden Heath. She came forward when we were chatting to regulars at the rowing club earlier today. She got back from holiday yesterday and found out the canoe was missing when she turned up there. She was about to report it when we arrived. She was surprised it was taken – she said it was hit by a narrowboat back in July and wasn't safe to use.'

'Thanks. It seems Greg stole it to put some distance between himself and the town centre and didn't realise it was damaged – he confirmed in his interview that it leaked, which was why he abandoned it,' said Kay.

'What if he's telling the truth, and he didn't shoot

his brother?' said Gavin. 'What about his comment to you that Alice isn't safe?'

'If he's telling the truth about Robert's killer, then perhaps he's worried that person will turn up at the house,' said Barnes. 'I'll organise a surveillance team after this briefing, but Annette and Alice are staying at Kenneth's house at the moment.'

'So they should be safe there,' said Kay. 'And there's a twenty-four-hour watch on the gates – get in touch with uniform and alert them to what Greg's told us. I won't have them put in danger if he's telling the truth, so tell them to stay alert.'

'Guv.'

She paused as Debbie's phone began to ring, and waited while she briefly spoke to the caller and then ended the call.

'We've been granted a further extension in addition to Sharp's to interview Greg Victor,' she said. 'In light of the seriousness of what he's done, and given Alice won't be interviewed until tomorrow morning, the magistrate signed off the paperwork a moment ago.'

'That's good news. Thanks, Debbie,' said Kay. 'All right, some of you have been here since the early hours of this morning so I'm calling an early finish. We've had a fantastic result today, and I'm very grateful to you all for your tenacity and dedication to getting Alice Victor home safe. Debbie – can you pass around the roster for this evening and the remainder of the week? That way we can get you all back to your own families as soon as possible. Okay, everyone – you're dismissed.'

She moved back to her desk and picked up her mobile phone, then smiled at the text message displayed on the lock screen.

Well done. Love you – Adam.

A thought occurred to her, a warmth growing in her chest as she typed a response.

'Are you heading off?' said Barnes as he swept up his car keys from his side of the desk.

'Yes,' she said, and smiled. 'It's a couple of hours until my parents head back home, and I've got something I need to do.'

THIRTY-NINE

Kay pulled into the car park beside Adam's four-by-four, pushed the door open and brushed her hair from her eyes as a light breeze carried across the rolling landscape.

Grey clouds tumbled on the horizon, while a late summer storm that had been forecast for the evening rumbled a few miles away.

Her heels sank into the light layer of gravel as she crossed towards the green expanse of the cemetery, and she buttoned her jacket with one hand while clutching a flower bouquet in the other.

A group of three people stood together at the brow of the hill, and she could make out Adam's tall figure as he stood waiting for her with his hands in the pockets of the light coat he wore.

Her mother and father hovered beside him, her

mother's eyes full of concern as Kay drew nearer. Her father held another bouquet of flowers in his hands.

Adam smiled and pulled her into a hug when she reached him, then kissed her.

'This was a good idea,' he said.

She smiled, then turned to her parents. 'Thanks for waiting. I wasn't sure if I was going to get out in time to see you before you went.'

'Don't be silly,' said her mother. 'We could have always stayed an extra night or two if we needed to. Your father doesn't have to be at the hospital for his next check-up until early next week.'

'Have you been here long?'

'We got here about twenty minutes ago,' said Adam. 'Your mum and dad wanted to stretch their legs before the drive back, so we've had a walk around the boundary while we were waiting for you.'

Kay exhaled, letting out some of the stress from the past five days.

She turned until she could see down the hill towards the open fields behind the police headquarters beyond the cemetery grounds. It never ceased to amaze her that within minutes of leaving work, she could be out in the open countryside. It was why she and Adam had chosen to set up home in the town, and why she could never see herself leaving.

No matter what her job threw at her, she knew now that she could cope.

'It's a pretty spot,' said her mother.

'You're right, it is.'

She threaded her fingers through Adam's, and squeezed his hand. 'Shall we?'

They walked down the incline until they reached a row of simple graves, the stone ornaments newer and less worn than the others. Flowers and soft toys had been left beside more than one, but Kay kept her eyes averted from those and concentrated instead on the one she sought in the middle of the row.

There was too much pain here, too much sadness, and she couldn't bear to absorb others' grief while she was still coping with her own.

It came to her in waves, crashing down on her at the most unexpected moments, jolting her awake or delivering a punch to her sternum while she daydreamed in the middle of management meetings.

Finally, they were there, the precision of the bronze lettering across the mottled granite stone catching the afternoon sunlight.

Elizabeth Hunter-Turner. Beloved daughter, taken too soon.

Adam pulled her into his chest and kissed her. 'Love you.'

'Love you too.' She pushed the bouquet into his hand and turned to her mother and father, who had stopped a few paces away to give them some time alone. 'If you wait here, I'll go and get some fresh water for the vase.'

She didn't wait for an answer, and turned away before they could see her tears.

Clearing her throat, she walked along the row to a standpipe that had been installed under a yew tree, rinsed out the metal vase and leaned on the tap as she refilled it.

Alice's kidnapping and rescue had unearthed emotions that she had desperately tried to bury, and as she wiped her eyes with the back of her hand and sniffed, she wondered how she would have coped if she were in Annette Victor's place.

It was why she had been prepared to do anything to find the five-year-old. It was why she had driven her team to work so hard.

She twisted the faucet and turned back to the graves.

Adam crouched at the base of Elizabeth's grave, talking to her parents as he pulled out tufts of long grass that threatened to obliterate the dates inscribed below their daughter's epitaph. He smiled as she reached him, and took the vase from her.

'Come here,' said her mother. She stepped closer and put an arm around Kay's waist, resting her head against her shoulder.

They stood in silence as Adam and her father arranged the flowers, and she realised how thankful she was that she and her mother had been reconciled. She had been afraid of what her mother's reaction would be to her miscarriage, afraid of rejection, and instead had kept the truth from her for a long time. Her mother had been inconsolable when she had found out, isolating herself from Kay.

Time, and Kay's father's illness, had helped to heal her resentment.

'I wish I'd known her. I wish we'd had the chance.' Exhaling, she pulled away from her mother and smiled at her father. 'Thanks for coming here with us.'

He nodded, unable to speak.

Adam tapped him on the arm. 'Tell you what, Phil – let's wander back to the car and let these two have a moment, shall we?'

Kay watched as the two men wandered back to the main path, their voices a low murmur.

'Will she be all right? The little girl you found?'

She turned to her mother. 'I hope so. The specialist is interviewing her tomorrow, and we've given her mother the note of a psychologist who can help if needs be.'

'Did he hurt her?'

'We don't know for sure. Not yet. I hope not.'

They began to stroll towards the car park, the breeze wafting across Kay's shoulders and rustling the leaves in the maple and silver birch trees. The colours were beginning to change, with a subtle tone of yellow and orange in the boughs that bordered the cemetery, and a scattering of early fallen leaves covered the grass.

Her mother stopped walking, and reached out for her arm. 'Wait.'

'What's wrong?'

'Nothing.' Her mother took a deep breath. 'I just wanted to tell you. Now I understand why you do this, Kay. I'm so proud of you.'

Kay blinked back tears, and put her arm around her mother's shoulders.

'Thank you.'

FORTY

The following morning, Kay drained the dregs of her third coffee and shoved the mug across the desk.

The team had spent the time since the morning briefing helping Bethany to set up interview room two in such a way that it wouldn't intimidate Alice.

Barnes and Piper had wrestled a small coffee table and two comfortable armchairs that had been rented for the day across the car park and into the building, and these had been set out next to a colourful rug and a box of toys. The older detective had disappeared at nine o'clock, much to Kay's consternation, until he reappeared half an hour later with a small collection of toy cars.

'Annette told you that Alice wanted to be a racing driver, remember?' he said. 'I thought these might help.'

Kay had smiled, knowing that Alice's abduction had brought back painful memories for her colleague, and was touched that he had put so much thought into Alice's wellbeing for the forthcoming interview.

She pulled her chair closer to her desk as her phone rang, the station's reception number showing on the caller ID.

'Hunter.'

'It's Hughes on the front desk, guv. Mrs Victor is here with Alice.'

'Thanks, I'll be right there. Can you show them through to the room that we've set up so that she can get Alice settled in?'

She replaced the receiver in the cradle, and signalled to her two detective constables.

'Carys, Piper – get yourselves over to Ken Archerton's offices and speak with Melissa Lampton. See if she can shed any light on Greg Victor's statement that Robert was in danger. Ask her if he received any threats while he was at work. After you've done that, head over to Ken's house and find out whether he's had any threats against the business or his employees. Hopefully with Annette out of the way, he'll feel more inclined to talk.'

'Will do, guv,' said Gavin. 'Good luck with Alice.'

'Thanks,' said Kay. 'This isn't going to be easy for any of us. Barnes – are you ready?'

'Yes, guv.'

Kay gathered up her notebook, mobile phone and a couple of pens and began to walk towards the door behind him, when Gavin called out.

'Hey, Ian.'

Barnes stopped and looked over his shoulder. 'What?'

Carys held up the toy that now took pride of place on his desk.

'Don't forget to take your rabbit,' she said.

'Very funny.'

Barnes rolled his eyes as the incident room filled with laughter, and Kay grinned.

'You knew you were asking for it, leaving it on your desk,' she said, giving him a gentle shove towards the door. 'Why didn't you take it home?'

'Because I've got nowhere to put it there – anyway what would Pia say?' He reached the top of the stairs and paused. 'To be honest, I like it there on my desk. It reminds me why I do this.'

Kay smiled, and then followed him down the stairs towards the interview suites.

The door to interview room two was open, and as she walked in Bethany and Annette fell silent and turned to her.

Alice stood next to her mother, her face downturned.

Kay took one look at the child's red-rimmed eyes and turned to Annette. 'I realise this is going to be upsetting for both of you, but it's an essential part of our ongoing investigation as to why all this happened. We'll try our best to make it as easy as possible for Alice, and she'll be made comfortable here.'

Annette dabbed a crumpled tissue to her eyes, then

sniffed and forced a smile as she looked at her daughter. 'Are you going to help Detective Hunter and her team this morning?'

The five-year-old lowered her gaze to her feet, bounced the toe of her shoe on the tiled floor, and shrugged.

'Yes,' she said.

'I brought you some new cars,' said Barnes. 'Do you want to see what they are?'

Alice's face brightened as she took the toys from him and wandered across to the coffee table.

Kay turned back to Annette. 'Before we start Alice's interview, I wanted to ask you about some entries on Robert's bank statements. One of my colleagues noticed there have been some large deposits of money made each month since April.'

'Oh, he told me they were some sort of performance bonuses he'd received, that's all,' said Annette. 'He made a couple of good deals for the business earlier in the year.'

As the sound of Alice's attempts at engine noises and sudden braking filled the room, Kay gestured to Bethany. 'We should let them talk, Annette. Do you want to come with me? I'll find someone to get you a cup of tea or something, and you can wait in our canteen area.'

The girl's mother took a deep breath, and then nodded. 'All right. I suppose the sooner you start, the sooner it's over and done with, isn't it? I'll be back in a bit, Alice.'

'Okay, Mummy.'

Bethany adjusted the ear piece she wore. 'Guv, give me a couple of seconds to make sure I can hear you properly when you get in the observation suite, please.'

'Will do.'

Kay sent Annette off to the canteen with a police constable and then settled in one of the chairs opposite the monitors in the observation suite next door.

Bethany had been playing with Alice and now each of them sat in an armchair, the toy cars zooming back and forth across the table between them.

Kay spoke into the microphone next to the monitor, and Bethany took a moment to ensure Alice was preoccupied before glancing up at one of the cameras and nodding.

She sat back in her seat and forced herself to relax. The communications link was the only way she and Barnes would be able to interact with Alice now, and she bit her lip as she listened to the ABE officer guide Alice through the carefully prepared script.

Each question had been formed in such a way as to coax information out of the little girl without causing her undue distress.

'Here we go,' Barnes muttered under his breath. 'Come on, Alice. You can do this.'

FORTY-ONE

Gavin fell into step beside Carys, shielding his eyes from the sun as he crossed the busy road beside her.

He emitted a low whistle as he gazed up at the stonework of the wine merchants' office building, and then chuckled at the blue plaque on the wall above one of the front windows.

'Some office.'

'I know – wait until you see the inside. Bloody luxury compared to ours.' Carys grinned, and pushed open the front door.

As he took in his surroundings, Gavin let his colleague take the lead and watched as she approached the woman sitting behind the reception desk.

The two women spoke in low voices, but after seeing confusion sweep across Carys's features he wandered over.

'Is something the matter?'

'This is Sharon Eastman,' said Carys. 'Ms Eastman was just telling me that Melissa Lampton no longer works here.'

'What?' Gavin frowned. 'Why not?'

The receptionist's lips narrowed. 'I'm sorry, I'm not allowed to talk about personnel matters.'

'When did she leave?' he said.

'Yesterday morning.'

'Were you here at the time?'

She sat down and ran her gaze over her computer screen and keyboard, her face miserable. 'Yes.'

'What happened, Sharon?' said Carys, her voice softening.

Gavin raised his gaze to the staircase off to his left and the landing above the reception area, but the space was quiet. Beyond a closed door, he could hear a woman's laughter, and then voices. His gaze fell back to the receptionist.

'You can tell us, Sharon. It might help.'

The woman pulled a crumpled paper tissue from the sleeve of her blouse, and blew her nose. She blinked.

'I can only tell you what I heard. I didn't see anything.'

'All right, go on,' said Carys.

'It happened just after I got here, so about twenty past eight. I like to get here ten to fifteen minutes before I'm supposed to start at half eight – it gives me time to sort myself out and get a coffee before I take the phones off the night-time answering service.'

Gavin remained silent, his jaw clenched.

'I'd just sat down here and was about to put my headset on when I heard someone shouting upstairs. At first, I thought someone was larking around, but then he sounded angry.'

'Who sounded angry?' said Carys.

'John Lavender – he's in a similar role to what Robert was doing.'

'How long has he worked here?'

'Six months. Ken brought him on when his health took a turn for the worse after the winter, so he could take on some of his workload.'

'Go on.'

'I heard a woman speaking then, as if she was trying to calm him down, and recognised Melissa's voice.'

'Could you hear what was being said?'

Sharon shook her head.

'What happened next?' said Gavin.

'I heard a door opening.' The receptionist lowered her voice and leaned closer. 'John's office is the one at the far end of the corridor – left at the top of the stairs. I heard it slam, and then footsteps across the landing above my desk here. It must've been Melissa, because I heard her speaking to one of the girls in the admin office, and then she came down here. She handed me her key card to the front door, and the mobile phone she uses for work.'

'Did she say anything to you?' said Carys.

'Yes. She said that John had asked her to leave. She

said he'd told her that with Robert dead, they couldn't afford to keep her on because there was no need for a spare personal assistant. She was shaking by the time she walked out the front door.'

Gavin exhaled, and raised an eyebrow at his colleague before turning back to Sharon. 'I don't suppose you have an address for her, do you?'

Sharon bit her lip. 'I can't – I'll get into so much trouble. You'll have to ask Mr Archerton or John when he comes back into the office later.'

'He's out at the moment?'

'Yes, he had a ten o'clock meeting in Hythe.'

'All right,' said Carys. She pulled a business card from her bag and handed it over. 'Thanks for your time. Can you give that to Mr Lavender when he comes back and ask him to call us?'

The phone beside Sharon began to ring as she turned the card between her fingers, and she nodded. 'I will.'

Gavin walked across the plush carpet to the front door and held it open for Carys. He paused on the pavement and stared up at the building.

'That was a bit sudden.'

'Wasn't it just?'

'I wouldn't mind hearing Melissa's side of the story.'

'Me too. Come on – I'll drive while you see if you can trace an address for her.'

Moments later, Carys was steering through traffic as Gavin held his phone to his ear.

'Who's this John Lavender bloke she was talking about?' she said. 'I'm trying to remember him from the statements.'

'He's a sales rep like Robert was,' he said. 'A couple of years younger, though. I think he's from Staplehurst way.'

'We ought to speak to him this afternoon if he doesn't phone us back.'

'Hang on,' said Gavin. He pressed the speakerphone option as his call was answered. 'Debbie? Can you find out an address for Melissa Lampton for us? She's not at work – apparently she left yesterday and won't be back.'

'No problem.'

He heard the shuffle of paperwork, and then the deft strike of keys as Debbie ran an online search.

'Here you go – she must be one of the last people around here with a landline phone number that isn't ex-directory. It's an address in Borough Green. I'll text it through.'

'Thanks, Debs.'

'Are you going to call her first?' said Carys.

'No.' The phone emitted a *ping*, and he read out the address. 'I don't want to give her an excuse to go anywhere before we get there.'

He gave Carys the address and then settled back for the short ride. 'What do you think is going on?'

She shrugged. 'I don't know. Maybe Robert was working behind Ken's back to try to do a deal with another supplier or something. I mean, at the moment, we don't even know if Greg's telling the truth about what happened. It could have been him. He could've shot his brother and he's lying through his teeth. I guess we won't know unless Alice can shed some light.'

'She comes across as a good kid, doesn't she? Bright, I mean.'

'Let's hope so,' said Carys. 'Because we're clutching at straws at the moment, aren't we?'

He could hear the frustration in his colleague's voice, but there were no platitudes he could offer.

FORTY-TWO

Melissa Lampton lived in a semi-detached property in a cul-de-sac off the main road through Borough Green.

Carys pushed through a wooden gate into a neat garden with concrete pavers that led to a brightly painted front door, and noted that the 1930s-built house had been undergoing a revamp. Pots of varying sizes had been placed on the doorstep, the steady hum of bees accompanying a waft of fragrances from strongly scented lavender and abelias.

After pressing the doorbell, she gave the letterbox a rap for good measure, and then stifled a yawn.

Making the switch from night shifts to day always left her wretched and discombobulated for at least forty-eight hours, and she didn't miss her time as a police constable. She always struggled to sleep, and had no idea how people managed eight hours or more – or why that was considered normal.

'Do you want to get a coffee after this?' said Gavin, his eyes concerned.

She managed a smile. 'Good idea. Your round, isn't it?'

'Very funny.'

They turned back to the door as it opened and Melissa Lampton appeared, her grey eyes wide as her gaze moved from them to the street beyond and then back.

'What are you doing here?'

'We wondered if we could have a quick word, Ms Lampton. Can we come in?'

'I suppose so.'

Carys stepped into a hallway that was in the process of being decorated. A stepladder had been folded up and leaned against the wall behind the front door, while a bundle of dust sheets covered the carpet beside the staircase. Various tins of paint were lined up alongside the ladder, with two brushes balanced across the lids.

'I can't decide which colour to go for,' said Melissa. She crossed her arms over her chest. 'What do you want, anyway? I've already given my statement and spoke to you on Monday.'

'We understand that you no longer work for Wilkinson's Wine Merchants,' said Carys. 'Could you tell us why?'

'You'll have to ask John Lavender. Or Ken.' The woman spat the words out, her distaste clear.

'Ms Lampton, could we perhaps sit down

somewhere?' said Gavin. 'We'd like to hear your side of things.'

'Oh, all right. Come through to the kitchen. The living room's a mess – I was going to get someone in to sand the floorboards at the weekend but I don't know if I should now. I don't know if I can afford it.'

As she followed the woman into a kitchen at the back of the house, Carys ventured a further question. 'Do you live here alone?'

The woman's mouth twisted. 'Yes, thank goodness. Got divorced five years ago. Won't be making that mistake again.'

'Right.' Carys nodded, and guessed that a cup of tea wasn't going to be offered.

'Before you ask, yes, I was made redundant yesterday. By John Lavender, of all people. You know he's only been with Ken for six months? Bloody cheek. Sharon probably told you – I knew she was eavesdropping the moment I saw her face when I came down the stairs, but it wouldn't have been difficult. I think the whole office heard us.'

'I take it that his decision was a shock,' said Gavin.

'Came right of the blue.' Melissa took a shuddering breath, and blinked back tears. 'Five years I'd been there. Worked all sorts of hours after my divorce went through. I don't know what I'm going to do now.'

'You received no warning that they were going to let you go?'

'None at all. I mean, I know Ken is ill and

everything but you'd have thought after all this time he'd have had the decency to tell me himself.'

'Going back to your work with Robert Victor,' said Carys. 'Did he ever give you any indication that he thought his life was in danger? Or that he was being threatened in any way?'

'No. Otherwise I would've said something on Monday when we spoke. It was business as usual until—' Melissa broke off, wiping at her eyes. 'What a bloody mess. Thank God you found his daughter.'

'Did you ever meet her?'

'Alice? Once or twice. Annette came into the office with her if they were in town to meet Robert for lunch. Lovely kid. Will she be all right, do you think?'

Carys thought of the interview currently being conducted by the ABE officer at the station, and forced a smile. 'We hope so. Are you sure there isn't anything else you can think of? Something that might help us understand why Robert was killed?'

'I don't think so, no.'

'Okay, thanks for your time. We'll get out of your way.'

Disappointed, Carys inclined her head towards the door, her thoughts turning to the questions they would have to put to Kenneth Archerton, and followed Gavin back along the hallway.

'Detective?'

Carys turned on the step, her hand on the door frame. 'Yes?'

Melissa held on to the door as if she was steadying herself. 'There – there was something. I wondered yesterday whether I should've phoned you when I realised.'

'Realised what?'

Melissa bit her lip. 'I gave your colleague the wrong itinerary.'

'Pardon?'

'Robert's itinerary. For his trip to France. I was in a rush once our computer system was up and running properly on Monday when I printed out the itinerary. I didn't realise. I only read the front page, because that was the same, and didn't bother checking it. I was going to read the rest before I emailed it to you, but I got talking to Sharon and forgot about it. I left it at reception – there was a panic on regarding a delivery of Chablis that was running late and I was the only one around to sort it out. She must've put it in one of her trays to give back to me and it slipped her mind until your colleague turned up demanding a copy late Tuesday afternoon. She assumed that's what it was there for – to pass on to him.'

'I don't suppose you can remember what was different about the one you were meant to give us?'

'Originally, he was meant to be visiting a vineyard a few miles from Vallaire for the last two days. He phoned me to cancel that part of the trip the Sunday night before he flew out. I had to dash into the office early the next day to make his excuses to the owners and arrange for him to go back next month to meet with them.'

'Did he say what he was going to do those last two days he changed his plans?' said Gavin.

'Only that he had some personal things to sort out and that he'd catch the same flight back to Gatwick I'd booked for him.'

'Why didn't you mention this to us before?' said Carys.

'I'm sorry. I didn't think of it at the time.'

Carys bit back her frustration. 'Just one more question. Was the itinerary amended in any way after Robert's death?'

The woman frowned. 'No. Not that I know of, anyway. Why would it be?'

'No matter. Thanks for your time.'

'You can't tell anyone you've been here, all right? I don't want them to know you've spoken to me.' Her eyes widened. 'I need that redundancy pay – I don't know how long it's going to take me to find another job if they don't give me a reference.'

'We'll be as discreet as possible,' said Carys.

FORTY-THREE

'Wow – nice place,' said Gavin as Carys drove through the wrought-iron gates and up the driveway towards Kenneth Archerton's house.

'Every time I see a house this big, I wonder how much time it takes to keep it clean,' she said. 'What a nightmare.'

'If you can afford this, you can afford staff. He's got a carer, hasn't he? Wonder why he answered the intercom?'

'Probably just passing when I pressed the button. I mean, it's not like she's waiting on him hand and foot, is it?'

'Kay said to use the side door. Apparently the front one is locked again because of the reporters who were at Annette's place.'

'The road's silent now though, isn't it?' Carys checked her rear-view mirror. 'I didn't see anyone.'

'It's old news now that Alice has been found. I heard the Chief Super pulled the pin on the patrols here and at Annette Victor's house earlier today, too – not enough staff on roster to provide cover.'

'Jesus.'

Climbing out the car, she gazed up at the top floor windows, blue sky and white clouds reflected in the sparkling glass, and then blinked at movement at the far end of the house. A face appeared at one of the downstairs windows – eyes glaring at her from under bushy eyebrows that contrasted with his thinning hair.

She raised her warrant card, and the man nodded.

'He's not taking any chances,' said Gavin as he followed her along the path.

'I don't blame him. It's going to be as bad, if not worse, when this goes to trial.'

Carys didn't bother knocking when they reached the door – she could hear Kenneth Archerton unlocking the solid mortice lock, and stepped back as he opened it.

'Yes?'

'DC Carys Miles, Mr Archerton. This is my colleague, DC Gavin Piper. We wondered if we could come in, please? We have a few more questions we'd like to ask as part of our ongoing enquiries.'

'Of course. Has he said anything yet?'

Archerton moved to one side and beckoned them in.

'I'm afraid I can't comment on that.' She waited while he relocked the door.

'Come this way.'

He shuffled towards the kitchen, the soft *thud* from the base of his sticks echoing off the tiles as he crossed to the worktop.

'Patricia is out at the moment, but I can offer you coffee,' he said, gesturing to a state-of-the-art machine that gleamed under the bright lights.

'Thanks, but we're okay, Mr Archerton,' said Carys. 'Would you like to sit down?'

'I would, as much as I hate to admit it. Bloody disease.' He grimaced, then gestured to a long table that had been constructed from a single tree trunk, the whorls and eyes left in situ. Eight chairs were placed around it, and he gravitated to one at the head of the table before sinking into it with a groan then balancing his sticks against the chair beside him. 'I thought you were talking to Alice this morning?'

'She's being interviewed by a specialist at the station at the moment, Mr Archerton. I doubt they'll be much longer.' Carys ran her eyes over her notes. 'Did Greg Victor have anything to do with your business interests?'

Archerton frowned. 'No, nothing at all.'

'Had you met him?'

'A few times, like I told your colleague. Since he moved down here, I've probably seen him once or twice over at Annette and Robert's during the summer.'

'Has he ever been here?'

'Not as a guest, no. Perhaps a couple of times to collect Alice when he's been looking after her for

Annette. And, before you ask, it never occurred to me that I should invite him. We weren't what I would call "close".'

'What about Robert – how did you get on with him?' said Gavin.

Archerton ran his fingers over the whorls in the table. 'I liked him. I liked him a lot. He cared so much for Annette and Alice. He couldn't have been a better father.'

'Did you have any problems with him at work?'

'Not that I can recall. He was someone I found I could confide in – we'd work through negotiations together, issues that might crop up, that sort of thing. He's irreplaceable. I don't know what we're going to do without him.'

'Were there any issues between him and your clients that gave you cause for concern?' said Carys.

'No.' He rubbed a hand across his chin. 'Do you think Robert was killed because of something to do with my business?'

'That's what we're trying to ascertain,' said Carys. 'His movements in France seem to be erratic. He changed his itinerary to cancel meetings at short notice, and the two places the rental car show him visiting on the GPS are nowhere near known vineyards.'

Gavin passed him a photocopy of a map that had been marked up with the two streets in the towns identified by the GPS. 'Do you have any business interests in either of these two locations?'

Archerton took the map from him, pushed his glasses up his nose and squinted at the page. 'They're nowhere near any vineyards, as you say, so why would I?'

'What was your daughter's marriage like?' said Carys. 'Did you see or hear anything that worried you?'

'No. Robert was a good father to Alice, he was easy to get along with, and he was an asset to my business.' Archerton's face fell. 'I don't know what Annette is going to do without him. I've mentioned to her that perhaps she should sell the house and move in with me. The place is big enough, after all.'

'How was Alice last night?'

'Happy to be here. Confused by her father's absence, and why she can't see her uncle.' His top lip curled. 'Annette told her last night after dinner. That her father wasn't coming home. Poor mite.'

Archerton reached out for his sticks, slowly got up and shuffled across the tiles until he was looking out of the window to the landscaped garden beyond.

'Alice is so sad at the moment, I just want to see her smile again.' He sighed. 'Hopefully the specialist she has to see on Monday will agree, but I think she ought to start school as soon as possible. At least it'll give her some sort of routine in her life while we work through this mess.'

Carys turned the page of her notebook, letting a silence descend on the kitchen for a moment, and then leaned forward.

'Why did John Lavender make Melissa Lampton redundant yesterday?'

'Why? Has she made a complaint?'

'Not at all. We went over to the office to speak to her, and were surprised to find out that she no longer works for you.'

'It wasn't an easy decision,' he said. 'But John and I – he's my other business sales manager – went through the figures on Monday night, and what with Alice's kidnapping, and Robert's murder… well, let's just say some of the sales we'd built into our cash flow for the next six months probably won't eventuate. We're losing clients because of Greg Victor, detective. That means I'm losing money. With Robert gone, I can't afford to hang on to a personal assistant who is now an assistant to no-one. A couple of years ago, I would've been able to keep her out of a sense of duty, but these days my sense of duty is to my business. Otherwise, I'll have nothing to pass on to Annette and Alice when I'm gone. Of course, once the business stabilises again, I might be able to consider inviting Melissa to join us once more.'

'Are you saying your decision was purely a business one?' said Gavin.

'I am, yes. Look, I'm not proud of myself for it, and that's why her redundancy pay is several months more than I'm required to give by law. At least she'll be able to finish the renovations on her house while she's looking for work.'

Carys pushed back her chair. 'Thanks for your time, Mr Archerton. We'll let you get on.'

'Not a problem, detective.' His face contorted into a grimace as he shifted the sticks in his grip.

'We'll see ourselves out, Mr Archerton,' said Gavin.

FORTY-FOUR

Later that afternoon, Kay took one look at the exhausted faces of her investigation team and walked over to Debbie's desk.

'Can you order a dozen pizzas to be delivered?' she said, handing over her debit card. 'I have a feeling I'm not the only one who's going to need some carbohydrates to get through the briefing.'

The police constable grinned and picked up her phone. 'At least that way you'll get their attention.'

'That's what I'm planning on.'

Movement by the door caught her eye and she nodded to Carys and Gavin as they moved towards their desks. She'd let the team collect their thoughts and update their notes into the HOLMES2 database, and then start.

'How did Alice's interview go?' said Sharp, pausing by her desk with a cup of coffee in his hand.

'Bethany was brilliant,' she said. 'It's the first time I've worked with her, and I was really impressed. Alice was a little trooper, too.'

'Do we have enough to charge Greg Victor?'

'I'd say we do for the kidnapping after the conversation I've just had with Jude Martin from the CPS.' Her mouth twisted. 'Not sure about the murder.'

'Well, we've got him for a few more hours, thanks to the magistrate. Let's see what we can turn up in that time regarding the murder. Otherwise we'll charge him with offences relating to the kidnapping and keep working our way through what we've got,' said Sharp. 'Didn't Alice hear anything?'

'She said she heard a bang, but I think she's too young to put two and two together.'

'Damn. So, at the moment, we only have Greg's word that he had nothing to do with his brother's death?'

'Yes.' She jerked her chin to where Carys and Gavin sat at their desks, hunched over their computer keyboards. 'Unless those two can shed any light on someone else having a motive.'

'Well, we'll see what comes out of this briefing, and then I think you and I should interview Greg again. Can you get someone to call his solicitor and have him here by five o'clock?'

'Will do.'

'I'll join you for the briefing.' Sharp blew across the

top of his coffee. 'I'll just see what Debbie's managed to sneak into my in-tray first.'

He winked, and crossed the incident room to his office, pausing to stop and talk to different team members as he passed.

Kay spent the next ten minutes at her desk, scrolling through the list of emails that had appeared since that morning and delegating what she could, and then looked over the top of her computer screen as Sergeant Hughes appeared at the door with a stack of pizza boxes balanced in his arms.

'Bribing the troops again, guv?' said Barnes.

'It works, doesn't it? You're still here.'

He laughed, gathered up his notebook and phone, and began pushing his chair towards the front of the room. 'I'll see you over there.'

She locked her computer screen, wandered over to the whiteboard at the end of the room, and then cleared space on one of the tables beside it for the pizza boxes.

'All right, come and get it while it's still hot. Can someone grab some paper towels for napkins?'

Picking up a slice topped with ham and pineapple, she stepped to the side. As one, her team swarmed towards the food, their cheerful banter filling the air as they jostled for their favourite toppings.

The atmosphere had changed since Greg Victor's arrest and Alice's return, and although she sensed they were no less driven, she acknowledged that some of the fire had gone out from the investigation now that the urgency had subsided.

It would be up to her to maintain their focus in order to bring a compelling case to the Crown Prosecution Service, and she had no intention of abandoning Annette Victor and her daughter in their cause to find justice for what had happened to them.

Sharp towered over the last of the queue for the food, took his share and then leaned against the door frame to his office while he ate, his gaze wandering over the throng as they found seats or somewhere else to perch.

Kay finished eating, snatched up another slice before the whole lot disappeared, and set it aside on a paper towel on the table next to her before wiping her fingers.

'Let's get started, then.' She gestured to the whiteboard. 'Before I get to today's tasks, I'll give you a quick update about Alice's interview this morning. Bethany spent just over an hour with her, and myself and Barnes were observing via video link. After creating a rapport with Alice, Bethany asked her about her relationship with her uncle. It seems that since he moved in with Annette and Robert, he's spent a lot of time with Alice, collecting her from kindergarten from time to time and babysitting to give her parents some time off in the evenings. She says he talked a lot about his own daughter, Sadie, and that she was keen to see her cousin again.'

'Happy families, then,' said Gavin.

'Indeed. When she was asked about the boat trip, Alice became agitated – grumpy, rather than distressed though. She'd been looking forward to it, and said that Greg had promised to take her on a boat "all summer". She confirmed what Greg said about stopping for lunch at the pub in Yalding, and that she played on the swings at the park – that's the one near the Teston Bridge. Bethany asked her why she was cross, and Alice said that her dad spoiled it. When asked how he did so, Alice said that he turned up at the boat, and her uncle seemed annoyed to see him. She said they tried to be cheerful, but that she could see it was an effort for them.' Kay paused and checked her notes. 'When Greg was cooking dinner, he was "making a lot of noise, slamming cupboard doors and things". After dinner, she was told to play with her toys, and the pair of them went outside on to the deck.'

'Could she hear anything of their conversation, guv?' said Parker.

'No, not that Bethany could ascertain. After a while – Alice couldn't say how much time passed – Robert came back into the cabin and told her that she had to go. He started throwing some of her clothes into a bag. She said she was upset because he was "scrunching stuff up instead of folding it" and that her mum would've been cross if she'd seen that. He told her to pick a toy to take with her but she couldn't make her mind up fast enough for him, so he gave her the rabbit.'

Kay waited while her team caught up with their note-taking, and then continued. 'Bethany asked Alice if her dad said anything to her before she left the boat, and she said that he told her she was a good girl, and gave her a hug. She said she told him she wanted to stay on the boat with him, but he crouched down and said that there was a bad man after him, and that she had to go with her Uncle Greg because he would take her away and keep her safe.'

A silence descended as Kay finished speaking, and she tossed her notebook onto the table. 'She doesn't recall seeing anyone else near the boat as they left, but says she did hear a loud bang. She said Greg stopped walking for a moment and turned back to the boat, but then changed his mind. He picked her up, and started running in the opposite direction.'

'Bloody hell,' said Barnes.

'How was she by the time Bethany finished?' said Carys.

'Bored.' Kay managed a smile. 'And you'll be glad to know that Bethany managed to coax out of her that Greg didn't touch her inappropriately, which supports the examination by the paramedic yesterday, so that's something.'

A collective sigh of relief flitted through the room.

'She got a bit upset when Annette came to take her back to Ken's,' said Kay, 'Annette said that Alice has been demanding to go home, because she wants to be where her daddy was happy.'

'They've told her, then?' said Sharp.

'Yes, last night. Annette said she felt it was for the best.' Kay blinked, and exhaled. 'Right, let's hear from everyone else. Carys and Gavin – what have you got to report?'

Gavin gestured to his colleague to take the floor, and Carys moved to the front of the room so she could be heard.

'We went to the office first to speak with Melissa Lampton, except she got made redundant yesterday.'

The detective constable let the ripple of questions die down before speaking again. 'We went to speak to her at home, and although she was reluctant at first to talk to us, she did confirm what we'd been told at the office – that the remaining sales manager, John Lavender, had informed her when she arrived yesterday morning that, with Robert deceased, her role was no longer tenable. We thought that might be all we'd get from her, but as we were leaving, Melissa said that she made a mistake in handing over the wrong itinerary to us earlier this week.'

'What?' Kay spun around from the whiteboard where she'd been making notes.

'That's what she said, guv – she said the itinerary we got wasn't Robert's original one, and that she was going to send us the one that had his original route included – the one with the two vineyards he was meant to be visiting. We got the revised one, the one she had to change at the last minute because Robert phoned her Sunday night to cancel his plans for the last two days.'

'What did Ken Archerton say when you spoke with him?'

'He said Lavender spoke with Melissa the previous day on his behalf, and stated that Robert's murder has had an adverse effect on their cash flow forecast, but didn't elaborate further. We showed him a map showing the two locations Robert visited, and he confirmed he has no business interests there, and had no idea why he would visit those towns. He also says he's not aware of any issues between Robert and their clients.'

'Okay, thanks, you two.' Kay bit into the second slice of pizza, ran her eyes over the notes on the board while she chewed, and wondered if her team would get the breakthrough they so desperately needed.

FORTY-FIVE

Kay paused at the bottom of the stairs and checked her messages while she waited for Sharp to join her.

She'd been intrigued at Carys's report that they'd been given a different itinerary according to Melissa Lampton.

'Ready?' said Sharp as he descended the last few treads. 'You looked lost in thought.'

Kay lowered her phone. 'I was thinking about Melissa's statement. What if we weren't meant to know about the changes to his plans or the fact that he visited someone in those two towns?'

'We would've found out via his GPS anyway.'

'No, we wouldn't, because we only sought the GPS information from the hire company after getting the itinerary to try to work out where he'd been. That's how we found out he deviated from the wine regions.'

Sharp rubbed his chin. 'Good point.'

'Look, I'll get Carys and Gavin to look into it in the morning. There won't be anyone around at the car hire company's head office over there at the moment – they're an hour ahead of us. We only received the high-level GPS information anyway that told us the suburb where Robert went. They must have the exact coordinates. We can then get someone over there to take a look for us, can't we?'

'Even with local support, that could take a couple of days to get the paperwork signed off,' said Sharp. 'And there's no way the Chief Super is going to let us have additional funding to fly someone out there.'

'We can at least get it moving,' said Kay. 'It might be that we don't need the information if Greg starts talking, but I'd like to rule it out. If anything, it'll help to corroborate the data we've got.'

'Okay, then I'll sign the paperwork. Have Carys or Gavin get it to me by ten o'clock tomorrow though – I'm in meetings at Headquarters from half ten.'

'Thanks. Shall we go and see what Greg has to say for himself?'

When she opened the door into interview room two, the first thing she noticed was that all the soft furnishings and toys provided for Alice's interview were nowhere to be seen. Instead, the room was back to its sparse decor, with a table and four chairs the only furniture.

Greg Victor's solicitor nodded to them as they took their seats, and Kay reached out to start the recording before reading out the formal caution and noting that their conversation was a continuation of the previous interview.

'Have you spoken to Alice?' said Greg. 'Is she okay?'

'What can you tell us about John Lavender?' said Kay.

'I don't know him.'

'Are you sure? Because it seems he's very much involved in Ken's business. Holds a similar role to your brother's.'

'Robert might have mentioned him once or twice.'

'When?'

'Over the summer.'

'What did he say about him?'

Greg patted his hand on the table, and then stopped. 'He said he was new, that Ken brought him in a few months ago once his health started failing.'

'Was he upset that Lavender took a greater role in the business?'

'A bit. I think he thought that when it came to succession planning he'd be the obvious choice, but Ken seemed to be taking the business in a different direction.'

'In what way?'

'He didn't tell me. He clammed up then, because Annette came into the room.'

'Did Robert mention John Lavender while you were talking on the boat last Friday night?'

'No. He started to say something, but that's when he told me he'd seen someone back by the bridge. And then he told me to take Alice and get away from the boat.'

Sharp signalled to Kay to end the interview, and then moved into the corridor and closed the door.

'What do you think?'

'I think we're getting closer, guv. We're not there yet, but I think we need to speak to this John Lavender under caution before we go any further with Greg.'

'Didn't Carys and Piper ask Archerton about him?'

'They weren't aware of the context in relation to what we've learned from Greg since.'

'Head back there – find out how Archerton knows Lavender, how he recruited him and what his background is. We might as well know who we're dealing with so we can form a strategic approach to the interview.'

'Okay. I'll take Barnes over there first thing.'

FORTY-SIX

The next morning, Kay turned the page of an internal report as Barnes changed down a gear, slowing the car.

'Ay-up. Who's this?' he murmured.

She lifted her head and looked through the windscreen as a sleek black four-door car pulled out from Ken Archerton's driveway and accelerated away in the opposite direction.

'Did you get the licence plate?' she said, pen held ready.

Barnes recited it from memory, then braked and turned into Archerton's property. 'Did you recognise it?'

'No, not someone I've seen before. God, I hope it wasn't another reporter.'

She saw her colleague's jaw clench as he braked to a standstill in front of the house.

'At least he'll have them on camera if it was,' he

said, jerking his chin at the shining lens pointed at them from under the porch roof.

'All right, let's go and have a word with him.'

Before Kay could head off down the side of the house, the front door was wrenched open, and Patricia Wells stared out from behind it, her face pale as she clutched the oak surface.

'Has he gone?' Her voice shook, and she stepped backwards as Kay approached.

'Do you mean the owner of the vehicle we just saw leaving here?'

'Yes.'

'I believe so, Mrs Wells – we saw it heading off down the road towards Hurst Green. Who was it?'

'Hold on.' She disappeared behind the door for a moment, and Kay heard the mechanical whirr as the wrought-iron gates across the driveway began to move. Patricia smoothed down her shirt as she returned, and stood to one side to let them in. 'Sorry about this.'

'Who was it?' said Barnes. 'A reporter?'

'No – although I almost wish it was. He said he worked with Mr Archerton when he buzzed the security intercom, so I thought it would be okay.'

'What happened?' said Kay. 'Do you want to take us through to the kitchen so you can sit down?'

'I-I — Yes, that's probably a good idea. I'm sorry. I'm just a bit shaken up, that's all.'

Kay let the woman walk on ahead, and then raised an eyebrow at Barnes.

Her colleague shrugged.

'Come on.' Kay entered the kitchen to find Patricia pouring a glass of water from a filter jug.

'Do you want some?' she said.

'We're fine, thank you, Mrs Wells.'

'Please, call me Patricia. "Mrs Wells" makes me sound like my ex-mother-in-law.' She managed a small smile, then leaned against the worktop and drained half the glass. 'Oh, God. Look at me. What a state.'

'Take your time,' said Kay. 'Is Mr Archerton here?'

'No – he had a doctor's appointment in town, so he left half an hour ago. I couldn't take him because I have a lady I have to go and clean for at ten o'clock.'

Barnes gestured to the cluster of chairs around the table. 'Do you want to have a seat and tell us who that was?'

'Okay.' She sat, and took a sip of water. 'I feel so silly about it now. I was probably just overreacting.'

'You looked like you'd had a fright,' said Kay.

'He was so rude, that's all.'

'Who was he?'

'I don't know – I've never met him before. He said he works for Mr Archerton. That's obviously why he came here. He was looking for him. When I told him he was out at an appointment, he said I should tell him that he had to stop avoiding their phone calls and get in touch.'

Kay frowned. 'Any idea who he meant?'

'No – I haven't got a clue. I'm not aware of any

missed calls – Mr Archerton still has a landline here so that I can answer the phone in case he can't get to it.'

'I presume he has a mobile?'

'Yes, but he carries that on him all the time.'

'Could you describe the man who was here?'

Patricia rocked back in her seat, and turned her gaze to the window. 'Let's see. Mid-forties, perhaps – dark complexion, as if he has Italian or Spanish heritage. Taller than me – about your height, detective. Perhaps a bit more. He was wearing a grey suit and a blue shirt. Brown eyes.'

'Are the security cameras working, Patricia?' Barnes rested his hands on the back of one of the chairs and leaned forward. 'Perhaps we could take a look at the footage?'

To Kay's surprise, the woman smiled.

'Oh, I'm sorry,' she said. 'They're not real. Mrs Victor put those up as a way of warding off people. We've had some of the locals driving past here and slowing down to stare through the gates, so she thought she'd fit those above the doors in case they got any ideas about ringing the bell.'

Kay craned her neck until she could see back along the hallway. 'Where are Annette and Alice?'

'Annette drove her father to his appointment, and she took Alice along with them. She said she was going to pop into town while he was seeing his doctor so she could buy Alice some new shoes for school.' She rolled her eyes. 'That girl is growing so fast, she didn't want to risk getting them at the beginning of the summer, and I think she thought it might cheer her up – you know, a treat for being so good with the interview and everything.'

Kay pushed back her chair, and handed one of her business cards to Patricia. 'If you're going to be okay, we'll see ourselves out. Can you ask Mr Archerton to give us a call when he gets home? We have some details we need to clarify with him as part of our enquiries.'

'Of course,' said Patricia.

As Barnes drove the car out onto the road, Kay checked her notes and found the licence plate she'd written down.

'Are you thinking what I'm thinking, guv?' said Barnes.

Kay put her phone to her ear, and waited for Debbie to answer. 'If our hunch is right about that car, then we need to speak to John Lavender sooner rather than later.'

FORTY-SEVEN

Barnes slowed the vehicle as Kay's call was answered, and he shot her a smile as she put her phone on loudspeaker.

'Debs, can you run this plate through the system for me?' she said, and recited her notes. 'I'll hang on while you do that. Barnes is here with me.'

'Will do, guv.'

He could hear the tapping of fingers on a keyboard as the police constable searched. 'What do you think, guv? Five quid bet?'

'I don't fancy the odds,' she said. 'It's going to be him, isn't it? Has to be.'

She fell silent as Debbie's voice returned.

'I've got a vehicle registered to a John Michael Lavender of twenty-six Hazelhurst Close in Staplehurst,' she said.

'Bingo.' Barnes banged the steering wheel with the palm of his hand. 'Got him.'

'Thanks, Debs. We're heading over there now.'

'See you.'

Kay ended the call and shifted in her seat until she was facing Barnes. 'All right. What do you think is going on?'

'Patricia could have been overreacting,' he said. 'I mean, she'd never met Lavender before.'

'Maybe, but she seemed pretty shaken up, and after what Carys and Piper said about Lavender firing Melissa Lampton yesterday, he doesn't come across as a people person, does he?'

He wrinkled his nose. 'I don't know. Is Lavender trying to make a move on the business? Putting pressure on Ken to hand it over before his health deteriorates even more? Annette told you she wasn't interested in it, didn't she?'

'More or less.' Kay stared out the windscreen and bit her lip. 'Do you think Greg Victor is telling the truth, then? Do you think Lavender was the one who shot Robert?'

'Bit extreme, don't you think?' said Barnes. 'Murdering your colleague in order to position yourself as the next in line to the throne?'

'People have been doing it for centuries.'

'Ooh, listen to you, the history buff.'

She smiled. 'Saw something on telly about it the other night.'

'I knew it.'

She laughed as he indicated right and followed the winding road into Staplehurst, and cast her eyes to the fields that flashed by the window, ripe for harvesting.

Barnes slowed and indicated left before reaching the main road that cut through the centre of village, entering a maze of avenues and cul-de-sacs that clung to the fringes, caught between countryside and an increasing urban sprawl.

Hazlehurst Close was a dead-end street comprising twelve terraced houses that looked about thirty years old. Barnes spotted number twenty-six on the end of a row beside a shared driveway.

'I can't see his car, can you?' he said.

He slowed as Kay craned her neck to peer around a brick wall that had been erected in front of the houses.

'Turn around at the end, and we'll take another look,' she said.

He lowered his window as they passed a second time.

Only three cars were parked outside, and none of them matched the black four-door vehicle they had seen leaving Kenneth Archerton's house.

'Okay, park over here and I'll go and knock on the door,' said Kay.

Barnes pulled to the kerb and waited while she crossed the road to the three townhouses. She rang the doorbell for the end property, and then moved to the window and shielded her eyes against the reflection.

After a moment, she turned away and walked back to the car.

'Not there?' said Barnes. He wound up his window as Kay climbed in.

'Doesn't look like it.' She checked the time displayed on the dashboard. 'He must have gone straight to the office.'

'Onwards,' said Barnes, and pulled away.

It took him nearly an hour – a journey that involved a lot of cursing under his breath at the remaining tourists that still packed the Kentish roads – but when he pulled into the council-owned car park opposite Kenneth Archerton's offices, he sat upright and pointed towards a row of vehicles at the far end.

'He's here, look.'

'There's a space next to his car,' said Kay, and released her seat belt. 'I'll jump out and then you can block his driver's door, just in case.'

He grinned, and did as she suggested before they hurried across the street to the old merchant's house.

Following Kay through the front door, he hovered in the middle of the reception area while Kay spoke to Sharon Eastman, the woman's eyes opening wide at the sight of the police entering the building once more.

'Can I tell him what it's about?'

'Our ongoing enquiries in relation to the death of Robert Victor,' said Kay.

'I thought I heard voices.'

Barnes took a step back and raised his gaze to the

top of the stairs to see a man in his forties running his hand along the banister as he walked down.

He matched Patricia Wells's description perfectly, his brown eyes sweeping from Kay to Barnes and back. 'I'm presuming you're the police?'

'Detective Inspector Kay Hunter. My colleague, Detective Sergeant Ian Barnes,' said Kay. 'Can we have a word in private?'

'Of course. Come through here – there's a meeting room we can use. Do you want coffee or something?'

'We're fine, thanks,' said Barnes.

He hung back and watched Lavender as the man led them through a side door and into a room that must have once been a living room when the building had been a home.

A high ornate ceiling hung above plain-coloured walls that continued the company's branding theme with landscape photography depicting scenic views across vineyards around the world.

Lavender adjusted his cufflinks, then gestured to the oval table in the middle. 'Please, take a seat. I've already provided a statement to the uniformed officers who were here last week. Now, if there's anything further I can do to help, just—'

'Before you continue, Mr Lavender, I do have to tell you that this is going to be a formal interview so we'll run through the caution first,' said Kay. After she finished reciting the words, she paused. 'Do you have any problems with that? Would you like to have a solicitor present?'

Lavender smiled. 'No, that's fine. I have no problems speaking with you.'

'Good. Why did you go to Kenneth Archerton's house this morning?'

'What's that got to do with—?' He paused, then: 'Sorry. I suppose you have to ask about everything, don't you? I went over there to get him to sign off some urgent paperwork. You know he only comes into the office once a week? This couldn't wait until Tuesday.'

'Why not?'

'It was the payroll documentation for Melissa Lampton's redundancy payment. Ken's health might be failing, but his mind isn't. He's the only one who can sign off anything financial for the company.'

'When we spoke with Mrs Wells, she seemed quite shaken by your visit.'

Lavender reached up and loosened his tie. 'God, sorry. I didn't mean to frighten her. She can be infuriatingly protective of Ken. I was frustrated that I had to go there in the first place, to be honest. I've tried telling Ken that he needs to start letting me take on some of the monetary aspects of the day-to-day business activities if he can't do it. I mean, he could set a limit on the level of spending if he's worried I might make a financial decision he disagrees with, but it can't go on like this. That's why I had to drive over there this morning.' He leaned back in his seat. 'Look, I didn't deal with having to let Melissa go in the best way, and I feel bad about that, really I do. So, I figured if I could get her final salary organised as soon as possible, it'd go some way to apologise for that.'

'Whose decision was it to make her redundant?'

'Mine. Not an easy one, either. I know she'd worked closely with Ken and Robert these past few years and I'm the new guy, right? I can imagine how it felt, but it wasn't a decision taken lightly. I'd gone through all the financials with Ken when we found out about Robert – Ken's had a crisis management plan for the company ever since he was diagnosed with MS, just in case something happened to him and he took a turn for the worse, but he didn't factor in his key sales manager being murdered, or the subsequent media interest. It made some of our clients uncomfortable. So much so, that our ability to negotiate deals to import wine and then sell it here has diminished in the past few days. We had no choice but to make the decision not to recruit a replacement for Robert until such time as the business stabilises. And that's why I made Melissa redundant as well.'

'How closely did you work with Robert Victor?' said Barnes.

Lavender shrugged. 'Not that closely. We ran separate accounts. He had his clients, I had mine. Same with suppliers. It's the way Ken set up the business. He didn't want us to be in competition with each other, only other wine merchants.'

Barnes slid across a copy of the map Gavin had used to depict Robert's movements in the final days before his murder.

'What's here?' he said, tapping the page.

Reaching out for the map, Lavender spun it around. 'Looks like industrial units, or the sort of thing you see small businesses using. I've got no idea. Where is it?'

'North of Le Mans. It's where Robert went after cancelling his meetings for the Wednesday and Thursday of his trip.'

'That doesn't make sense,' said Lavender. He pushed the map back to Barnes. 'Why would he do that?'

'Where were you last Friday?' said Kay.

'Here. Working.'

'Until what time?'

'I left here about seven o'clock. I had a late telephone conference call with a vineyard in California – it's the only problem about being tasked with our American and southern hemisphere accounts,' he said. 'Late nights, or early mornings with the time differences.'

'Where did you go when you left here?' said Barnes.

'Home, and then I got changed and met some friends for a few drinks down the pub. We went for a curry at a new place that's just opened.' He frowned. 'I told the two policemen who took my statement all this. I left the restaurant at half ten and went home.'

'How much had you had to drink?'

'Too much to drive, detective, so if you're insinuating I had anything to do with Robert's death, you can think again.' Lavender's jaw clenched. 'I went home, watched television for an hour or so, and then went to bed. First thing I heard about Robert was when Ken phoned me on Sunday morning with the news.'

Kay turned to a clean page in her notebook and shoved it across the table to Lavender. 'We'll need names, addresses, and phone numbers for the friends you say you met with on Friday night.'

He pulled a pen from his shirt pocket. 'I thought you might.'

FORTY-EIGHT

Barnes eyed the contents of his desk with a sigh, then flipped his thumb through the paperwork Debbie had stacked in the top filing tray.

Deciding that none of it was urgent, he ran a hand over tired eyes.

Kay had left for Headquarters as soon as he'd parked behind the police station, summoned by the Chief Superintendent and accompanied by Sharp, who was tasked with providing an update regarding the murder enquiry.

Barnes wished he had more help to give her.

He gave himself a mental shake and swept remnants of his sandwich off his desk before logging in to his computer. He spent the next half an hour responding to various requests and clarifications in response to his enquiries, and was relieved to find out that the main suspect in a spate of burglaries across the north of the town had been sentenced that morning.

At least he was getting results somewhere.

His gaze moved from the computer screen as a man moved into his line of vision.

'What've you got for me, Parker?'

'Results from our calls to John Lavender's friends,' said the police constable. 'They all said the same thing – John was at the pub from seven forty-five, and then they went to the curry place. He was there all night with them, they left around ten-thirty, and he went straight home. One of them – Mark Price – lives four doors up from John and says he picked up a bottle of red John had promised him before he headed off to his place. He reckons he left there about eleven o'clock.'

'Which doesn't give Lavender enough time to drive over to East Farleigh and confront Robert,' said Barnes, and tossed his glasses onto his keyboard. 'Okay, thanks.'

'You all right, Ian?' Laura handed him a mug of tea, then flopped into a spare chair next to him. 'You don't look happy.'

'Thanks for the tea.' He took a slurp, and set it to one side. 'I'm frustrated, that's all. Same as we all are. I thought we had something earlier, but it turns out it's nothing.'

'What happened this morning?' said Carys as she joined them. She pulled out Kay's chair and sipped her tea.

He told them about the trip to Kenneth Archerton's, and the subsequent interview of John Lavender.

'The thing is,' he said, 'I sort of felt sorry for the bloke after we left. There he is, trying to keep Ken's business going for him, but Ken won't let him do it. You'd have thought with his health in decline he'd have handed over some of the financial responsibility.'

'Maybe he was thinking of doing that with Robert,' said Carys. 'You know – keep it in the family as it were.'

'Maybe not,' said Gavin. The younger detective constable leaned against Kay's desk. 'Sometimes that's the worst thing you can do with a business, isn't it? Think of the number of times you've heard about family feuds wrecking successful businesses over the years.'

'I'd imagine Ken's the sort of person who would set up something like that so it's legally bombproof,' said Carys. 'After all, he's made it quite clear in his statements that it's his intention to leave the business to Alice. Even Annette told me this – she admitted to me she's got no interest in it.'

Barnes exhaled. Reaching out for his mug of tea in the hope it had cooled enough to drink, amazed that Carys had almost finished hers, his eyes rested on the blue rabbit balanced on the top of his computer screen.

He plucked it down from its all-seeing position and turned it over in his hands, wondering why someone would kill a little girl's father.

'What if someone didn't want Alice to have the business?' he said.

Gavin wrinkled his nose. 'I don't see it. Robert wasn't a factor in Ken's plans for it, so killing him served no purpose at all in that respect. Alice would still inherit.'

Barnes grunted, running his hands absentmindedly over the plush material, the tips of his fingers tracing the seams. Piper was right – Robert had no claim to the wine merchants' business over his daughter.

He frowned as his thumb caught on a rough surface.

'Dammit,' he said, and pulled his reading glasses from his shirt pocket. 'Can't see a bloody thing without these.'

'Getting old, Ian?' Carys grinned.

He paused to stick up his fingers at her, smiled, and then stared at the back of the rabbit once more.

'You beauty,' he murmured.

'What's up?' said Laura.

He didn't answer, and instead moved around to where Carys sat. 'Out the way, Miles. I need to get into that drawer. I know Hunter's got a pair of scissors in there somewhere.'

Carys grinned and rolled her chair out of the way. 'I'll tell her.'

'It's an emergency.'

He bent down, reached into the drawer, and plucked out a pair of needlework scissors he'd seen Kay using the previous month. Returning to his desk, he sat and began to cut away at the rough seam on the toy rabbit.

'What are you doing?' said Laura, a hint of alarm in her voice.

'This has always been about Alice, hasn't it?' he said, pulling on a pair of protective gloves from a box between the desks. 'Greg says he tried to protect her, and Robert saw something in France that scared him and he came racing back to her, only to be killed. So, what's so special about her?'

His colleagues stared at him in silence while he continued to snip away at the stitches. He swore under his breath as the scissors caught on his thumb, and then continued. 'According to Annette, when Hazel showed her the photograph of the rabbit, Alice said her grandfather gave it to her. When I tried to give it back to her, she said that her dad told her to keep it safe before sending her away from the boat. So, why give it to me?'

Carys shrugged. 'Maybe she wanted you to have it because you rescued it out of the river after she dropped it. That's what she told you, wasn't it?'

'That's what I thought, but I was wrong.' He smiled as the seam tore, then held up the rabbit and cupped his hand underneath it. 'I think her dad knew about this.'

Laura's mouth fell open as a stream of pink tablets spilled from the soft toy and poured over Barnes's hand onto his desk.

'Bloody hell,' said Gavin.

FORTY-NINE

'What's going on? Barnes – are you nicking stuff out of my drawer again?'

Kay headed towards the group of detectives gathered around her and Barnes's desks, then stopped and frowned when her joke fell flat amongst the cacophony of voices.

'All right, what's all the excitement about?'

Carys turned to her, wearing a wide smile. 'Barnes has only gone and cracked it.'

Kay saw the obliterated toy rabbit lying on the detective sergeant's desk, and frowned. 'I don't think Alice meant you to turn that into roadkill, Ian.'

'Very funny,' he said.

Her gaze travelled over the pink pills that had spilled over the surface next to it.

Both Barnes and Piper were crouching on the floor, picking up stray pills that had tumbled onto the carpet, their movements meticulous as they made sure they accounted for each one.

'What's going on?'

'It was the rabbit,' said Barnes. 'It's why Alice wanted me to have it. Harriet's team wouldn't have known to look for this – there was no trace of any of this when this was found in the canoe.' He rose to his feet and picked up the toy, holding it out to her. 'Look, the inside has a waterproof lining. We might be able to get some prints off it. I only found it because the seam had been re-stitched and had a rough edge. It got me thinking, that's all.'

Kay pulled on a pair of gloves, and then turned over the rabbit between her hands. 'Well, well, well – did you notice the label on its bum? *"Fabriqué en France".*'

Barnes nodded. 'That's what got me wondering.'

'Bet that was made north of Le Mans, then,' said Gavin. 'It must have something to do with where Robert Victor went.'

Kay handed back the rabbit and picked up her phone. 'Have a look to see if there are any toy manufacturers in either of the two locations we know Robert stopped at. I'll give Sharp a call to bring him up to date about all this. We're going to need help from our colleagues over there now.'

'Guv.'

Gavin shot back to his desk and began to work, and she turned to Barnes.

'Nice work, Ian.'

'We might never have known,' he said. 'It was luck. I just couldn't fathom why Alice would give a complete stranger her toy.'

'Maybe she knew what was in it,' said Carys. 'Or, at least, that there was something wrong with it. And knowing you're a policeman means that – given her age – she trusts you.'

Barnes shrugged, a slight blush rising to his cheeks. He took off his glasses and polished them against his shirt before dropping them into his pocket.

Kay walked a few steps away as her call was answered. 'Guv, it's Hunter. We've had a breakthrough on the Victor case, and I think you'll want to see this. Okay, see you in fifteen.'

She replaced the phone and, raising her voice, addressed the rest of the team in the room. 'Briefing – now.'

'What do you want me to do with all of these?' said Barnes, gesturing to the pills. 'Shall I bag it all up and send it off for analysis?'

'Please,' said Kay. 'And tell them it's urgent. I know they'll say it always is, but tell them we believe it's a strong contender for the motivation of Robert Victor's killer.'

She squeezed past two police constables and made her way to the front of the room, the team falling silent as she joined them.

'Okay, so Kenneth Archerton gives his granddaughter the toy rabbit that's been manufactured in

France – are we assuming that the drugs were inserted prior to it leaving the country, or once it arrived here?'

'Before it got here,' said Carys, tapping her pen against her chin as she stared at the whiteboard. 'So either he went over there on the pretence of a business trip – hardly likely, given his health – or, someone brought it back with them.'

'Robert, or John Lavender?' said Kay.

'John's new to the company, and his background checks out,' said Laura. 'What if a third party – perhaps someone from the factory in France – brought it over, Ken gave it to Alice, and Robert found out? He'd be livid, but he'd want to see the set-up for himself before confronting Ken.'

'Which is why he deviated from his planned itinerary.' Kay nodded. 'Good. Okay – so what's going on? Why give the rabbit to Alice of all people?'

'Maybe this is a test,' said Gavin, taking a seat next to Barnes. 'Perhaps they wanted to see if they could get that rabbit through customs without getting caught before sending over a bigger shipment? And then to avoid any suspicion, Ken could've given it to Alice for safekeeping. Only he would know what was inside it.'

Glaring at the photograph of Kenneth Archerton that had been pinned alongside those of the rest of his family, Kay shook her head, then turned to face them.

'He's had us fooled, hasn't he? We've only got his word that he's ill.'

'Guv?' said Laura.

'What evidence do we have to suggest he has multiple sclerosis? One, he told us. Two, we know he has a carer, Patricia Wells. Three, he uses sticks to get about. That's it.'

Barnes whistled under his breath. 'And because he's Alice's grandfather, we've put him above suspicion. Christ, what a fu—'

'I want Patricia Wells brought in now for questioning. Let's see what she has to say about her employer's health. Carys, Gavin – that one's yours.' She ran a hand through her hair. 'Guess we'd better have another word with Greg Victor as well.'

'He's been moved to the remand wing at the prison until he appears in court next week. I'll have to phone them to get an appointment,' said Carys. 'What about Ken Archerton?'

'Hold fire,' said Kay. 'Let's find out if Greg can tell us anything first. Ken probably knows Barnes has the rabbit, but he might not realise we know its significance yet. Not given the way our last two conversations have gone with him, anyway.'

'Do you think it's him?' said Gavin.

'Slow down,' said Kay. 'One step at a time. Let's get these other witness statements together first. Given what that family's gone through in the past two weeks, we can't afford to make a mistake. We need to be sure we're right about this. Speaking of which – Debbie, can you phone Andy Grey and ask him to get his team to work through the CCTV images from last Friday night again in the vicinity of East Farleigh. What sort of car does Patricia Wells drive – anyone?'

'A black four-door hatchback, guv,' said Laura.

'Right – that's what they're looking for, Debs.'

'Guv.'

Kay raised an eyebrow. 'Well, don't just sit there, you lot.'

The team scrambled out of their chairs, and within seconds the incident room was a cacophony of noise. She signalled to Barnes as Sharp walked in, and brought the DCI up to date.

'Where are you off to now?' he said.

'The prison, to interview Greg Victor. We'll come back here afterwards to debrief with Carys and Gavin to find out if there's anything that ties in his statement with that of Patricia Wells.'

'Good,' he said. 'Once we have those, we'll make a decision about Ken Archerton. And, Barnes – good work.'

FIFTY

Gavin adjusted his tie, attempted to flatten down his hair, then gave up and slammed shut the locker door.

Wrenching open the door into the main corridor, he sidestepped a female police constable concentrating on the radio clipped to the front of her vest, and hurried to join his colleague.

Carys swept the case files into her arms and pushed back her chair as he strode towards her.

'Ready?'

'Yeah. Has she calmed down?'

'Quiet as anything once she was shown into a cell.' The detective constable grinned. 'It was only a glass of water. Good job you had a clean shirt in your locker, though. I thought two of the admin girls were going to faint with excitement when they saw you walk in.'

Gavin rolled his eyes. 'Is her solicitor here?'

'Just arrived.'

'Let's go.'

He held open the door for her and followed her down the stairs, musing about Patricia Wells.

When they had turned up at Kenneth Archerton's house, the carer had answered the door with a glass of water in her hand, and had told them Archerton was at a doctor's appointment, having taken a taxi into town.

When Carys had informed the woman that she was required to answer questions at the police station and that she was expected to accompany them immediately, Gavin had taken the brunt of the woman's reaction.

The water had hit him square in the face.

While he'd stood dripping on the doorstep, Carys had formally cautioned Patricia before marching her to their car.

His colleague had nearly laughed, and spent the entire journey back to the station with her jaw clenched, unable to look at him.

Now, he opened the door to the interview room and noticed that an air of reticence clung to Patricia.

She sat next to her solicitor – a man by the name of Douglas Carter – wearing a meek expression as Gavin and Carys took their seats.

He set out his notes as Carys started the recording and recited the formal caution.

'My client would like to apologise for her earlier actions,' said Carter. 'She overreacted.'

Gavin said nothing, opened the file in front of him and took his time turning to a new page of his notebook. He checked the time on his watch against the clock on the wall, popped his pen, and wrote along the top line before relaxing into the back of his chair.

Finally, he addressed the woman in front of him.

'How long have you worked for Kenneth Archerton?'

Patricia pushed a loose strand of hair from her eyes. 'About five months.'

'How did you get the job?'

'Through an acquaintance. She said she knew a businessman who'd recently been diagnosed with MS and needed some part-time help.'

'Which organisation are you registered with?'

Clearing her throat, Patricia cast a glance at her solicitor, and back to Gavin. 'I'm not. I have all the right qualifications, though.'

He narrowed his eyes at her. 'Are they valid?'

'Yes. Of course they are.'

'Where did you get your qualifications from?' said Carys.

'France.'

Gavin stopped slouching, and rested his hands on the table. 'Whereabouts in France?'

'Laval. It's west of Le Mans. There's a community college there. When I split up with my husband, I moved over there for a while. I wanted a change of scenery. Then the money ran out, and I knew I'd have to find something to do.' She smiled, but it didn't reach her eyes. 'Ageing population, isn't there? At least I had a good chance of not being made redundant.'

'When did you come back to England?'

'About a month before I started working for Mr Archerton.'

'Had you spoken to him before then?'

'No – my friend sorted it all out. I had an interview with him the week before I started, as a formality, but that was it. I suppose you could say we hit it off straight away.'

A sly smile crossed Carys's lips, and then she tugged a copy of an email from the folder beside Gavin and spun it around to face Patricia. 'We've spoken to Annette Victor, who confirmed your story. Unfortunately, the community college in Laval has never heard of you.'

Patricia's eyes widened as she read the email.

'Have you ever seen Kenneth Archerton walking without the aid of his sticks?' said Gavin.

She shook her head. 'No.'

'Who is the friend who put you in touch with him?'

'Why? She's got nothing to do with this.'

'We'll need a name.'

Patricia shoved the email back across the table to him. 'No.'

'If you won't help us, we can't help you,' said

Carys, and left the email where it lay. 'Can Archerton drive?'

'What? I don't know. He always gets me to drive him anywhere, or if I can't or he wants to run some errands, he gets a taxi like he did today.'

Gavin forced himself to stick to the interview plan he and Carys had agreed with Fiona Wilkes, despite his desperation to demand the answers they sought. He took a breath, then pulled out one of the photographs from the crime scene at Tovil and held it up.

Patricia gasped, and rocked back in her seat as she took in the shattered features of Robert Victor.

'Does Ken Archerton own a gun?' he said.

'I-I don't know.'

'Think carefully, Patricia. Do you think Ken is going to protect you when we speak with him?'

The woman's jaw worked, and then she motioned to her solicitor and whispered in his ear.

Carter nodded, and then turned to the two detectives. 'I'd like a word with my client in private.'

'We'll be outside.'

Gavin pushed his chair back, waited for Carys to end the recording, and then gathered up the contents of the file and moved out to the corridor. He spun on his heel as his colleague slammed the door.

'We've got him, haven't we?'

'Almost.' Carys exhaled. 'I wonder how much she knows?'

'Depends how much he trusted her, I suppose. Do

you think Ken simply employed her as part of the ruse that he was sick, or do you think she's more involved?'

'She has to be in on it, doesn't she?'

'Gav!' Debbie appeared at the door through to the stairwell and waved a sheaf of paper at them. 'Andy's sent through the CCTV results from East Farleigh.'

He took the outstretched pages from her and held them so Carys could see at the same time. Each one was a still taken from a security camera on the southern side of the medieval bridge crossing the River Medway.

And in each, a four-door black hatchback with a licence plate matching that registered to Patricia Wells was shown driving over the bridge, then turning left into the car park beside the river.

'Gotcha,' said Carys.

'We can't see who's driving it, though,' said Gavin. 'Are there any more angles, Debs?'

'No, sorry – that's all we've got. Those were clocked at ten-fifteen on Friday night.'

He frowned. 'It was still quite light then.'

'Might've waited in the car park,' said Carys. 'Let it get dark, and then wander along to the boat. There was less chance of being seen by any residents or dog walkers.'

The door to the interview room opened, and Douglas Carter appeared. 'My client wishes to have a word.'

'I'll bet she does,' said Gavin under his breath. 'Thanks, Debbie.'

He followed Carys back into the interview room, closed the door and started the recording once more.

'Before you say anything, you might want to take a look at these,' he said, and placed the photographs in front of Patricia.

She paled, but said nothing.

'We haven't got all day, Patricia,' said Carys. 'Do you have anything to say?'

'I got a phone call at the beginning of April from a woman I'd bumped into in Laval – she approached me one day while I was sitting in a café trying to read the job adverts on my laptop. She latched on to the fact I was English, and I suppose she guessed I needed the money.' Patricia twisted her hands together. 'She told me she worked for a private client who had business interests in France, but that he lived in Kent. She said he had recently been diagnosed with MS, but was still quite independent. He simply wanted someone to be on hand to do the cleaning and washing, but who could help if he took a turn for the worse. I told her I didn't have any qualifications for that, but she just said not to worry about it – that she'd sort it out so if anyone asked, it wouldn't be a problem.'

She leaned over and held her head in her hands. 'I know I was stupid, but I needed the money. My ex-husband and I, we weren't well off or anything, and my savings were starting to run out. Most of our friends were his, and I didn't know what else to do. So, I took the job.'

'Is he sick?' said Gavin.

'No. He said he needed me to help him keep up appearances.'

'Who was the woman who recruited you?' said Carys.

'Beatrice. I don't know her last name. She works for Mr Archerton on the French side of his business.'

'Are we still talking about the wine merchant business, or something else?'

'The other business. The drugs.' Patricia exhaled. 'Look, I only found out by accident a few weeks ago. I overheard him talking on the phone one afternoon – he didn't realise I was outside the study at first. I think he must've smelled the furniture polish I was using, because when he'd finished he called me in. What could I do? He asked me if I'd heard anything, and I said yes but that I'd keep quiet because I didn't want to lose my job. He told me that I could expect to earn a lot more for my loyalty.'

'And you didn't think to report this?'

'I couldn't! I needed the money for a start, and what would have happened to me? He knew I visited my mother in Leicester from time to time – I used her address on the CV I gave to Beatrice because she specifically asked for a UK one. What if he'd harmed her? You've seen what happened to Robert.'

'Tell us about his illness. We have statements here to suggest you were the one who took him to his GP appointments, and to see a specialist he was seeing in Manchester. Who was he really meeting with?'

Patricia's shoulders slumped. 'The GP appointments were real. He has high blood pressure.'

'And Manchester?'

'It's the other end of the drugs business. That's where they're planning to ship them to. Ken likes me to drive there so he can work while we're travelling. He's in the final stages of getting it all set up.'

'Can you describe this Beatrice?'

'About my height. Medium-length black hair. Slim. Not skinny, but not fat, either.'

'What happened on Friday night?' said Gavin.

'Ken told me he was going into town to meet a friend,' Patricia said, her voice barely above a whisper. 'He said he didn't need me to drive, that it was only a short distance and there wasn't much traffic on the road.'

'Had he ever driven your car without you before?'

'Once or twice. Only at night, though. So he wasn't seen, I suppose.'

'What time on Friday?'

'He left at about nine forty-five. He was in a foul temper – I'd heard him shouting on the phone in the study an hour before, and I worried when it went quiet. I knocked and asked if he was okay, and he said he was and that he didn't want to be disturbed.'

'What time did he get back?'

'About eleven-thirty. He went straight upstairs and

showered. When he came back down, he asked me to bring him a light supper. When I took it into the study, he was sitting with a tumbler of brandy staring into space with a fire burning in the grate. He didn't say anything to me, and I didn't want to ask. I put the tray of food on the desk and left.'

FIFTY-ONE

Kay shoved her mobile phone back into her handbag, and then forced a smile as she rejoined Barnes next to the security gate into the prison.

'Have you made your excuses as well?'

'Luckily we were only planning on having a Chinese takeaway tonight,' said Barnes. 'Pia sends her regards.'

'About time we all got together again. I meant to ask you over to ours earlier in the summer, but it's gone past so quickly.'

'That'd be good.' Barnes squinted up at the security camera. 'They do know we're waiting here, right?'

She scuffed her shoe against a stone, sending it flying. 'Probably busy.'

Turning at the sound of the gate opening, she gave him a nudge and then walked through into the prison.

The requisite security checks took twenty minutes

until the guards were satisfied that all the procedures had been followed. Once all their belongings had been confiscated, Kay and Barnes were led to an interview room.

Cameras jutted out from the walls, and a table and fours chairs took up most of the space.

'His solicitor has arrived at the gate, so we'll show him and Victor in presently,' said the guard who had accompanied them.

'Thanks,' said Barnes, and leaned over to familiarise himself with the recording equipment.

Kay hugged her arms around her waist and leaned against the wall while they waited. She wondered if Alice had any idea of the chain of events she'd triggered by dropping the soft toy while on the run with Greg. If she hadn't, would they have ever known?

Robert Victor's murder could have remained unsolved for years, and yet here they were, tantalisingly close to the answers they'd been seeking.

She pushed away from the wall and moved to one of the chairs as the door opened and the guard showed in Greg Victor.

The man had a shrunken appearance, the toll of the past week evident in the lines that knotted his brow, his shoulders slumped as he shuffled across to the seat opposite hers.

His solicitor hovered at the threshold, waited until the guard had advised his client of the process to follow, then nodded his thanks as the man left the room.

'Detectives, I'm Andrew Gillow – senior partner at Blake Arrow. I'm currently representing Mr Victor in the absence of my colleague. It's late in the day, so shall we get on with it?'

Kay handed the solicitor one of her business cards, and then gestured to Barnes to begin.

After making sure the digital recorder was working, he recited the formal caution and turned his attention to Greg.

'Kenneth Archerton hasn't got multiple sclerosis, has he?' he said.

Greg swallowed. 'No comment.'

'We know that the toy rabbit that Alice dropped in the canoe you stole contained a substantial quantity of illegal drugs. Do you have anything to say?'

'No comment.'

'Your brother, prior to his death, suspected his father-in-law of illegal activities that may have endangered his daughter,' said Kay. 'Maybe he thought he could try to gather some evidence before coming to us. Maybe he wanted to confront Kenneth with that evidence in order to get some answers. But he didn't get the chance, did he? Because Kenneth found out he was poking his nose in, and killed him. Why? Why take such a risk?'

'I can't.' Greg closed his eyes. 'I'm sorry, I can't help you.'

'Please, Greg. We're planning to speak with Ken,

but without your help I can't arrest him. Not based on hearsay. I need something I can work with.'

Kay held her breath, unable to think of anything that would change his mind. She knew she was close, but—

'Robert asked me to help him get Alice out of the country. I was scared Ken would harm Sadie if he found out I was involved.' Greg blinked, then ran a hand across his mouth, sweat beading at his temples.

'Your daughter?'

He nodded.

'Has he threatened you or your daughter in any way?'

'He doesn't need to – I know what he's capable of.'

'What do you know about the toy factory in northern France? Did Robert tell you?'

'Yes.' He wiped his palms over his face, and then leaned forward, his arms folded on the table. After a sideways glance at his solicitor, he took a deep breath. 'It was why Robert asked me to move down from Nottingham – so I'd be at the house while he was at work. It's why he asked me to take Alice away that night. I didn't kidnap her. Well, not at that point. Robert was planning to come home to confront Ken. The boat trip was a last-minute decision – he phoned me on Tuesday night to tell me he was travelling up past Le Mans, that he had to go and take a look at something he thought Ken was doing with the business behind the scenes. He wanted to know Alice was safe – he already had his suspicions about what Ken was getting involved in. He just didn't know how he was doing it.'

'What do you know about the payments that Robert received every month since the middle of April?'

'That was Ken, trying to sweeten the deal. He was trying to coerce Robert into taking on more responsibility by showing him what he could get out of it. Robert refused to spend any of it, but the money kept coming in. He told Annette they were performance bonuses, I think. He didn't want to scare her, not until he'd worked out a way to get them to safety.'

'What happened when he got to the boat on Friday night?'

'He told me what he'd found. Obviously he couldn't go into the properties – he didn't want Ken to know he'd been there, but someone must've seen him and reported it. He said he did see that they were toy companies and that was what he'd suspected. He had paperwork, too. Stuff he'd found in Ken's study – some notes, I think – but he was convinced Ken had got involved in something big. Ken had mentioned to him and Annette over the summer that he was thinking of branching out with the business to make sure it became the legacy he wanted to leave behind for Alice. He told Robert that he might have to take on some more work to free up his time. Robert thought that's why Ken employed John five months ago – because he wouldn't have time to run the wine merchants side of things if he was pursuing his other interests.'

'What happened to the paperwork?' said Barnes. 'We found nothing on Robert when he was discovered.'

'Ken must've taken it, then.'

'What about the MS?' said Kay.

'All bullshit,' said Greg. 'Robert worked that one out a while back, but didn't say anything to Annette. He followed him one night from the house. Turns out Ken was meeting someone at a fast food restaurant the other side of Ashford, in the car park. A woman.'

'Did Robert say who she was?'

'He didn't know her name, but he said he'd seen her go into one of the factories in France.'

'Did he describe her?'

Greg leaned back and stared at the floor. 'Black hair, down to her shoulders. Slim. Black jeans and a leather jacket. Sorry, that's all I remember. He said she looked like she belonged on a motorbike, not driving a top of the range SUV.'

'Did he tell you when this was? Did he give you any idea what date he saw this?'

'No, sorry.'

Kay checked her notes. 'Tell me about the boat at Allington lock.'

'Robert hired it. He was paranoid that Ken might find out that I had Alice with me, so the plan was to moor the boat I'd hired next to Allington Castle and then walk up to the lock to pick up the boat in his name. I think he thought it would sow some confusion if Ken found out, because he'd think Robert was still in

France.' He choked out a bitter laugh. 'God, we were so naïve. That's why I didn't use it in the end. I thought they'd figured out the whole plan.'

'Where would you have gone from Allington?'

'Downstream to Thanet, and then switch to a third boat – a larger one. Robert was going to take Alice out of the country, you see. He has contacts through the wine trade in Germany. It was the only thing he could think of doing to keep her safe.'

'Did Annette know?'

'No – he was too afraid Ken would find out and harm her in some way.' His mouth twisted. 'He was going to send for her once he knew Alice was safe.'

'Instead, Ken somehow found out, and knew Robert was back in the country, thanks to his contacts,' said Kay. She leaned forward. 'Do you believe Kenneth Archerton murdered your brother?'

'Yes, of course,' said Greg. 'And you've let Annette take Alice back to him.'

FIFTY-TWO

Sharp appeared from his office as Kay and Barnes entered the incident room, and gestured to the skeleton team that mingled at the far end.

'Carys and Gavin have just finished updating HOLMES2,' he said. 'Grab yourselves something to drink and then join us. I presume your visit to Greg Victor proved worthwhile?'

'I think we're ready for an arrest, guv,' said Kay.

'Good. Two minutes, then.'

The sweet scent of energy drinks underpinned an overwhelming smell of takeaway food as the assembled police officers tried to stay awake by fuelling their tired bodies with fat and sugar.

Kay took a moment to run through her notes, and then once she was satisfied she could provide a succinct account to her colleagues, she pinched a spring roll from

Debbie's desk with a wink as she passed and joined Barnes at the front of the room.

Sharp was already barking orders to the uniformed ranks, planning the details of Ken Archerton's arrest and making sure all the files and documentation were in order for the Crown Prosecution Service.

'Right,' he said, as Kay joined them. 'Carys, let's have you up here to take us through Patricia Wells's interview. Only the relevant points, mind – if anyone's interested in further details, they can read yours and Piper's report on the database.'

'Thanks, guv.' The detective constable stood in front of the whiteboard and cleared her throat. 'Okay, so Patricia has confirmed our suspicions about Kenneth Archerton's illness. She was recruited in France while taking a sabbatical there in a place called Laval – it's west of Le Mans. Archerton told her that her job was to help him keep up appearances. She started working for him five months ago, and met him for the first time a week before her appointment. She maintains that she only found out about the drugs a few weeks back, and that she was afraid for her life so she told Archerton she'd remain silent. He then used her to ferry him back and forth from meetings with an end user organisation in Manchester, under the guise of visiting a specialist about his MS. She scored a pay rise shortly after she found out about the drugs, so no doubt Archerton was ensuring she didn't go back on her word. I think she already suspected what he was capable of if she came to us.'

'What about the night of Robert's murder?' said Kay. 'Could she shed any light on that?'

'Yes – she states that Archerton took a phone call that night. She didn't know from whom, or what it was about, but she said he was in a bad temper afterwards. At nine forty-five, he took her car and left the house. She then went on to say he didn't return until half past eleven.'

'Giving him plenty of time to get to East Farleigh by ten-fifteen when Andy's lot picked up her car on CCTV, wait until it was dark and then walk along to the boat and back,' said Gavin.

'Thanks, Carys,' said Sharp. 'Kay? How does that fit in with what Greg Victor told you?'

Kay smiled. 'I think we've got him, guv. Greg confirms that Archerton doesn't have MS – apparently, Robert suspected as much earlier in the summer, and he also didn't buy into his business expansion. Then, he found some paperwork in Archerton's study that rang alarm bells. Who knows? Perhaps Archerton realised Robert had that – Greg certainly seems to think that Robert had evidence at the time he arrived at the boat on Friday night, but it wasn't in his possession when we found his body.'

'What is interesting is that Greg says Robert saw Archerton meeting with a woman in a fast food restaurant car park the other side of Ashford a few weeks ago,' said Barnes. 'Did Patricia give you a description of the woman who she met in Laval?'

'Black hair, slim, about my height,' said Carys. 'Goes by the name of Beatrice – no surname, unfortunately.'

'Sounds exactly like the woman Robert described to Greg,' said Kay. 'So she's definitely a person of interest in all this.'

'What else have you two got?' said Sharp, updating the notes on the whiteboard.

'Greg said his brother was convinced the toy factory in France had something to do with what Archerton is planning,' said Barnes. 'And we know now that's probably where the rabbit was manufactured.'

'So, Archerton's got a business partner in France who's planning to use his knowledge of importing to bring in toys stuffed with drugs,' said Sharp. He rested his hands on his belt and frowned. 'Why toys though?'

Laura raised her hand. 'Guv?'

'Speak up.'

The police constable rose to her feet. 'When I was at uni, I did a few modules in marketing as part of my degree. So, I just wondered if maybe, using the soft toys, Archerton could get the drugs past customs more easily given they're under pressure with the number of continental goods checks coming through Kent as it is. By splitting up the shipments into smaller quantities of goods he'd reduce his risk and then, if he distributed the toys through a trusted business partner – the Manchester connection – end users could access them under the guise that they were buying the toys for their kids. He could be trying to establish a county lines operation as well by forcing vulnerable kids to move the toys between users, or perhaps sell them on to older kids who are after the drugs, to establish a future customer base. They call that "cradle to grave" in advertising and marketing parlance.'

'If kids got their hands on those drugs by mistake, it could kill them,' said Barnes, his voice little more than a growl.

Sharp sat on the edge of the desk nearest the whiteboard, his face full of wonder. 'Bloody hell, Laura. Good thinking.'

'Yeah,' said Barnes, giving the police constable a light punch on the arm. 'Guess that degree of yours wasn't a waste of time after all.'

FIFTY-THREE

Kay shielded her eyes from the rising sun as Carys turned sharply into Ken Archerton's driveway behind two liveried patrol cars, their lights flashing.

In the door mirror, she saw another car slide to a standstill, blocking the driveway, and then Carys was braking, the manoeuvre pushing Kay into her seatbelt with force.

'Jesus, Carys – that's going to leave a mark.'

'Sorry, guv. I don't want him to get away.' The detective constable loosened her grip on the steering wheel and flexed her fingers. 'Do you still think Alice knew something was wrong?'

'Yes, I do. She may only be five years old, but it was clear from her interview with Bethany that she's incredibly perceptive for her age.'

'I hope she's going to be okay after all this.'

'Me too.'

Kay pushed open the car door and strode towards the front door, her jaw set.

A green four-by-four was parked with its rear facing the house, the engine emitting a ticking noise as it cooled in the morning air.

Before she could raise her hand to knock on the front door, it swung open.

Annette Victor stood on the step, her face wan.

'Where's Patricia? My father isn't here, and he's taken Alice with him – where are they? What's going on?'

'Slow down,' said Kay. 'Patricia's been with us, answering some questions. What do you mean, your father's not here?'

'When I got back from the market in the village fifteen minutes ago, he'd disappeared. There's no sign of him – or Alice. What's happening?'

Kay took a step back. Patricia's black hatchback was parked off to the side of the house, blocking the path leading to the side door. She raised an eyebrow at Carys, then took Annette by the arm.

'Let's go through to the kitchen,' she said. 'Then you can tell me everything your father said to you before you went out.'

As she led the woman along the hallway and into the spacious kitchen, she could hear Carys murmuring orders to the four uniformed police officers to start searching the house to corroborate Annette's assertion that Alice was nowhere to be found.

'What exactly did your father say to you this morning?' she said to Annette, who now leaned against the stovetop, nibbling at a fingernail.

'He said that he wanted some food and things from the market – at this time of year the fruit is better there than the superstore in town. He said he was too tired to go with me, and said he'd keep Alice company while I was gone.'

Lips pursed, Kay turned at the sound of footsteps to see Carys heading towards her. 'Anything?'

'No.'

'Annette, do you know how your father gets around if Patricia isn't here to drive him?'

'No, he's completely dependent upon her. Unless I drive him or he uses a taxi, of course.'

'Does he use a regular taxi firm?'

'Yes – Abbotts Cars.'

'Carys, can you phone them please and ask if they've picked up Ken Archerton and his granddaughter this morning?'

'Guv.'

'What is it you're not telling me?' said Annette. She took a step forward. 'What's going on?'

Kay sidestepped the question. 'Are there any other access routes away from this house, apart from the front driveway?'

'Not that you could use with a car, no. There's a

bridle path that runs along the other side of the stream at the bottom of the garden.'

'Where does that go?'

'Well, if you turn right that'll take you to the farm up the hill. If you turn left, it comes out at the train station on the edge of Headcorn. Why?'

'Hang on, Mrs Victor. I'll be right back.'

Kay brushed past Carys, the detective constable holding her mobile phone to her ear and talking in a low voice, and hurried out to the hallway where the four uniformed officers waited.

'Get yourselves down to the back garden. Mrs Victor says there's a bridle path the other side of the stream. Debbie – there's a farm at the end of the bridle path to the right of the garden. Find out the name of it and give them a call to see if Ken or Alice have been seen there.'

'Will do, guv.'

'The rest of you – apparently, the other direction leads to the railway station at Headcorn. Ken might've boarded a train there, or arranged to collect a car. Hurry, go.'

She turned back to the kitchen, joining Annette at the window as the four officers ran to the bottom of the landscaped garden.

'What are they doing?'

'Mrs Victor – Annette – do you have a note of any of your father's friends? People he might know who he could borrow a car from?'

'Why would he borrow a car? He can't drive.' Annette paced the tiled floor. 'I-I think there's an address book in his study. I don't really know any of his friends. He doesn't have that many – he likes to keep to himself.'

'Guv?'

'What is it?'

Carys raised her phone. 'The taxi company confirms they haven't taken Mr Archerton anywhere this morning.'

'Okay, thanks – can you take a look in his study, see if you can find an address book?'

'It's got a brown leather cover,' said Annette. 'It's usually next to his laptop.'

'Thanks.'

A knock on the kitchen door made Kay spin on her heel, and Annette crossed the room to open it.

Debbie beckoned to Kay. 'We've got two sets of footprints in the dirt on the other side of the stream. One pair is a child's size. There's a similar pair of prints on the other side of the fence on the bridle path and the grass has been trodden down – I think he's gone in the Headcorn direction, guv. They haven't been seen at the farm.'

'Thanks, Debbie. Leave the other two officers here. Take Parker with you and head over to that train station. If there's no sign of Archerton or Alice, then see what security footage there is. Phone me as soon as you've got anything.'

'Guv.'

'Detective Hunter.' Annette tugged on her arm as Debbie closed the door. 'I demand an explanation. What the hell is going on, and where the bloody hell is my daughter?'

Kay sighed. 'You're not going to like this.'

FIFTY-FOUR

Kay ended the phone call and ran a hand over her eyes.

'What did he say?'

Carys stomped on the accelerator and dived over the crossroads in front of a slow-moving tractor, a signpost for Headcorn flashing past the window.

'Sharp's put out an all-ports alert on Kenneth Archerton and Alice. He's been on to British Transport Police and they've alerted all train guards on the stretch of track that runs through Headcorn. If Ken got hold of a car instead of taking a train, they'll put out an Automatic Number Plate Recognition search if Debbie can get a note of a licence plate from security footage at the station, and two of the roads out of Headcorn have had roadblocks set up in the past five minutes. They're posing those as random breath-test stops so as not to alert Archerton.'

'If he's still in the area.'

'Yeah.'

'Christ.'

Kay beat a rhythm against the window with the side of her fist.

'Do you think Annette will be okay?' said Carys.

'I don't know.'

Annette had been disbelieving at first, her jaw dropping open as Kay had informed her of her father's other business activities while two more uniformed patrol cars had arrived at the property. Disbelief had turned to anger soon after, and then she had squared her shoulders.

'What can I do to help?' she said.

Kay's surprise at the woman's comment hadn't gone unnoticed.

'From what you're telling me, he killed my husband and endangered my little girl,' Annette had said. She had pulled her cardigan around her waist, and exhaled. 'I knew there was something going on. Little things, like him not limping on some days if I turned up unexpectedly, or phone calls he hurried to finish if I went into his study. He never did that with the wine merchant stuff – he was always trying to get me involved in the hope I'd change my mind about taking it over. The past five months though, he's been distant, almost rude. Tell me – how do I get my daughter back safe?'

The woman had gone on to tell her where her father had kept all his valuables and private papers, and so before leaving with Carys, Kay had pointed at the safe Annette had shown them hidden behind one of the vineyard photographs and given orders to a police constable to find a locksmith to drill it open.

Now, she sat up in her seat as the train station came into view, and opened the door while Carys was still braking.

Debbie emerged from the ticket office.

'We've got them on camera, guv. He got here forty-five minutes ago and bought two bottles of water from the vending machine, and then waited on the forecourt here. Twenty minutes ago, an SUV turned up. No train tickets were purchased, but a woman got out and frogmarched Alice to the car, and then they all left together, with Alice in the back seat.' Her brow furrowed. 'She put up a fight, guv. She didn't want to get in the car. The woman slapped her at one point.'

'What did the guy on the ticket counter do?'

'He didn't see it happen – there were no passengers waiting, and no trains expected for another forty minutes, so he went back to restocking the leaflets in the information displays. He was as shocked as us when he saw the playback. There's something else – the woman who picked them up matches the description Greg Victor and Patricia Wells gave us.'

'Beatrice. Did you get the licence plate?'

'Yes. I phoned it through to Sharp so they can get the ANPR search started. They went north. Do you think they'll head for the M20?'

'I think so, yes. They'll either try to board a cross-channel train at Folkestone or head to Dover and get on a ferry. We'll head off and get closer to the motorway so we can help with the intercept if needs be. Have Sharp phone through to Folkestone and raise an alert with passport control. We can't let them take Alice to France.'

Kay turned back to the car, then stopped.

'Guv? What's wrong?'

'Do me a favour – ask Sharp to put a watch on the estuary at Rochester, too. Greg Victor mentioned that his brother was planning to use a boat to get Alice out of the country. If Ken was aware of that, he might try the same thing. Greg doesn't know who owned that boat.'

Debbie already had her phone to her ear. 'Get going, guv.'

'Thanks.'

Kay kept a tight grip on her mobile phone as Carys steered the car through narrow lanes, the villages of Langley Heath and Leeds no more than blurs past her window. Soon, they passed the thick privet hedgerow that shielded the castle from the road, then turned left and merged with the flow of traffic entering the junction with the motorway.

Kay closed her eyes.

She had to reach Alice.

She had to save the little girl.

She had to reunite her with her mother.

'Guv?'

She blinked, realising her phone was ringing, then spotted Sharp's name on the display.

'We've had a sighting on the approach into Folkestone,' he said. 'An SUV with French licence plates, and we've spotted the driver on camera – she matches the description we've got for Beatrice.'

'We're joining the M20 now,' said Kay. 'We're probably thirty minutes away.'

'Gavin and Piper are nearly there, and there are four patrol cars in pursuit at a distance as well. We've arranged for our people to be alongside vehicle control entering the international station,' said Sharp. 'They're running it as a standard stop and search, so it'll slow everyone down in the queue for the trains. We've got plainclothes officers in the food court, too. We're working on the basis they're going there rather than Dover, but we've got a similar operation at the port, too.

'Guv? Ken might have a gun. We still haven't located the one used to shoot Robert.'

'I'll alert the officers at the scene and have armed response head over there as well.' He paused. 'Christ, I hope we don't need them, not with a kid involved.'

'Alice put up a fight at Headcorn train station, guv. She might try to make a break for it given half a chance.'

'She's got some guts for her age, that one. All right, I'd best go. Keep in touch.'

Kay relayed Sharp's update to Carys, who

immediately swung the car out into the overtaking lane and accelerated past at over a hundred miles an hour.

'Sod this,' she said through gritted teeth, and honked the horn at a slow-moving sports car.

The driver pulled out of the way when she flashed the headlights, and Kay felt the acceleration push her back into her seat.

Twenty-five minutes later, Carys slowed and exited the motorway at the junction for the international train station.

Kay craned her neck to see over the edge of the road bridge, noting three trains idling and a stream of cars disembarking from a fourth. She checked the timetable on her phone. 'The next one's due to leave in forty minutes.'

'He's been here nearly an hour, guv. So, where is he?'

They both jumped as Kay's phone rang.

'It's Sharp. ANPR lost the SUV after junction ten.'

'What?' Kay's heart missed a beat. 'How?'

'They left the motorway. We've got them on the A20 for a few miles but then they head off cross-country towards Brabourne Lees. After that, we've been unable to trace them.'

Kay swallowed. 'Guv, they could be anywhere by now.'

'I know, but stick to the plan until I can gather more intelligence at this end. They may have switched cars, Kay. Getting the train out of the country is still their quickest option. I've relayed the message to everyone at the scene, along with photographs of Ken and Alice. Patricia Wells has worked with one of the officers here to put together a better description of Beatrice, and that's being circulated as well. I'll message you a copy.'

'Thanks, guv.'

She raised her gaze to the windscreen as Carys steered the car into a parking space behind a maintenance building. Her phone emitted a *ping*, and she turned her attention to the face that appeared on the screen.

Beatrice stared back at her with eyes that were colder than any Kay had seen.

FIFTY-FIVE

'Where are Barnes and Piper?' said Kay, as she fastened a protective stab vest over her blouse.

'On the other side of the food court building, out near the picnic area,' said Sergeant Hughes. He turned down the volume on his radio until the running commentary faded. 'We've got three teams working their way through car park. No sign of them yet. Certainly no sign of the SUV.'

'They must've switched vehicles,' said Kay. 'Have we had any reports of stolen vehicles in the vicinity? Anywhere between junctions ten and eleven?'

He shook his head. 'That doesn't mean they haven't stolen something, of course – there are a lot of places along that stretch of the A20 where they could have found something.'

A rumble of engines filled the air as cars and lorries began to surge towards the departure gates in an attempt to be first in line to drive onto the cross-channel train. Kay cast her eyes over the cars parked around the outer perimeter of the passenger building. 'How the hell did they get through border security?'

'DCI Sharp says word reached the staff on the gates too late to stop them,' said Hughes. 'There's an emergency briefing on at the moment, though – they'll run a search of vehicles while they're queuing to be loaded onto the train.'

She scrunched up her eyelids against a cloud of dust and grit that blew across the asphalt. 'Okay, we'll join the group on the other side of the building. Let me know how you get on.'

'Guv.'

'Carys, with me – we'll cut through the terminal in case we spot them in there.'

Her phone rang as they entered the passenger building through automatic double doors, and she stood to one side to avoid a group of pensioners laden with paper bags full of sandwiches, soft drinks, and chocolate. 'They do know they can get that on the other side, don't they? Hello? Yes, Debbie?'

'Guv, the locksmith has managed to open the safe in Ken Archerton's study,' said the police constable. 'We've found a pistol, and ammunition. I've phoned Harriet with the details and she confirms it's likely the same calibre that killed Robert Victor.'

Kay exhaled. 'Thanks, Debs. Relay that to the incident room, please.'

'Will do.'

'Got a radio, Carys?'

'Yes.'

'Can you let the teams here know that Ken's gun has been located at his house? We'll continue to proceed with caution, but it sounds as if that was the weapon used to kill Robert.'

Carys hurried across to a display of French and English touring maps, and lowered her voice, her eyes taking in the crowd before her. Kay turned her back to her colleague and swept her gaze over the people walking past.

She couldn't see Ken Archerton, but every time she heard a child's excited shriek, she spun around to the location of the sound. Her heart sank as she spotted toddlers and children of Alice's age running between the legs of adults, but she could see no sign of Annette Victor's daughter.

'Message passed on,' said Carys, appearing at her side. 'Do you want to do a walk-through and then head outside?'

'Yes. Uniform will be running regular checks but we may as well while we're here. Can you have a look in the disabled toilets, and I'll do the ladies' ones?'

They split up, and Kay pushed open a door demarcated "Ladies". Two of the stalls were in use, while the rest were empty. She hovered at the sinks, ignoring the haggard face that stared back at her in the mirror above the soap dispensers.

She'd worry about sleep when she knew Alice was safe once more, and Kenneth Archerton was arrested along with his French colleague.

As one woman then another exited the stalls, she hurried to find Carys hovering outside a coffee chain's busy shopfront.

'No luck?' she said.

'No.'

'I asked a bloke to take a look inside the gents' toilets for me as well – I showed him a photo of Archerton, but he confirmed he wasn't in there, either.'

'Okay, let's have a walk past the burger place and then we'll head outside to meet Barnes and Gavin.'

Five minutes later, they had walked back out into bright sunshine, and Kay shielded her eyes against the glare off car windscreens as she stalked towards her two detectives.

'Anything?'

'Not yet.' Barnes rolled up his shirtsleeves. 'The next train's in fifteen minutes, guv. What if we—'

A scream pierced the air.

Kay turned towards the sound, heart racing, in time to see a man duck behind a navy-coloured estate car on the fringes of the car park.

A second scream ended in a strangled cry.

'It's them.'

Kay took off at a sprint, gesturing to Gavin to take up position on the opposite side of her while Carys and Barnes brought up the rear.

Barnes held his radio to his mouth, and Kay hoped the uniformed teams were en route. Slowing as she reached the estate car, she gulped a deep breath, and then called.

'Alice? It's Detective Hunter. Are you okay?'

'Mumeeeeeee…'

'Ken, don't hurt her. Please, don't hurt her. I just want to talk.' She signalled to Barnes to move to the front of the car, then lowered her voice. 'Carys, keep a look out for Beatrice. She'll be close by, somewhere.'

Sudden movement caught her off guard, and she was shoved aside as a blur shot out from behind the car and bolted towards another vehicle further away.

Kay didn't wait, and inched around the rear of the vehicle, while Barnes took off after Beatrice.

Kenneth Archerton sat with his back to the front wheel, his face pale. 'She wouldn't listen. I told her it had gone too far, that I couldn't hurt Alice.'

Lowering herself to the floor, she frowned. 'Are you all right?'

He panted for breath. 'Chest pains.'

'Shit – Carys, get around here and phone for an ambulance. Ken – where is Beatrice taking Alice?'

'France,' he groaned.

'What's her name? What name is she planning to travel on, Ken? It's important.'

'Beatrice Caron. That's what it says on the tickets.'

Kay glanced up as Gavin appeared. 'Stay with him.'

While her detective constable crouched beside

Archerton, and Carys called instructions into her mobile phone as she loosened the man's collar, Kay rose to her feet and peered over the tops of the vehicles parked beyond her position.

Four uniformed officers ran along the periphery of the car park, keeping a wide berth between their position and the unfolding drama.

'Can you see anything, Barnes?'

In response, he pointed across the roof of a dark-green hatchback.

She jogged across to where he stood. 'Is it them?'

'Other side of that white van. I think I heard Alice,' he murmured.

'Okay, with me.' She checked over her shoulder, and then beckoned to the uniformed officers to join them. 'Circle around the van – you take the front end. She can't keep running – there's a perimeter fence beyond the next row of cars. We'll box her in.'

Kay took a deep breath, forced herself to remain calm, and moved around the car.

Crouching on the asphalt, one arm around Alice's waist and a hand across the little girl's mouth, the woman matching Beatrice's description stared up at her with hatred in her eyes.

Alice whimpered, her eyes wide.

'Let her go, Beatrice.'

'Only when I reach France. Then I'll let her go.'

'That's not going to happen. You're not getting on the train.'

The Frenchwoman rose to her feet, keeping a tight grip on Alice's wrist. Her other hand slipped into her pocket.

'Keep your hands where I can see them, Beatrice.'

Shaking her head, her black hair caressing her shoulders, the woman withdrew her hand. She flicked her wrist, exposing a blade.

'Let me go, or I kill her.'

Alice screamed, and tried to pull away from Beatrice, tears puddling over her cheeks.

'You tell Kenneth he owes me. He gets me out of the country, he gets his little girl back.'

'Beatrice, calm down,' said Kay, keeping her voice steady.

The woman tugged Alice's wrist, twisting it backwards, forcing the five-year-old to a standstill.

'Let me go!'

Kay raised her hands. 'You're scaring her. Please, put down the knife and we'll sort this out. This is only making it worse for you.'

'There is nothing to talk about. There is— You bitch!'

Beatrice's grip on Alice loosened as her face contorted with pain. The Frenchwoman dropped the knife, her hands moving to the ankle Alice had kicked.

Alice bolted from her clutches, running towards the waiting police officers before barrelling into Barnes, burying her face into the side of his leg.

Hughes didn't hesitate. He pounced on the

Frenchwoman, swinging her body towards the side of the car to block any escape route.

'Beatrice Caron, you do not have to say anything...'

Kay ran across to where Barnes stood smoothing down Alice's hair, a grim expression etched in his eyes.

'Alice? Are you hurt?'

The little girl shook her head, then turned to face Kay and wiped her nose on the back of her sleeve.

'I want my mummy.'

'We're going to take you to her right now. Do you want to go with Ian?'

Alice nodded.

'All right, let's get you out of here. You were very brave.'

A watery smile crossed the girl's lips.

'Don't listen to her, she's a liar,' said Beatrice, twisting in Hughes's grip to face them. 'Kenneth was stupid to bring her.'

'Not the motherly type, I take it?' said Barnes. He walked away, a hand on Alice's shoulder.

Beatrice glared at them as she was led to a waiting patrol car.

'You can't prove anything,' she said. 'I was only giving Mr Archerton and his granddaughter a lift to the train station.'

'Oh, I think you and I know that's not the case, Mademoiselle Caron,' said Kay. She opened the back door. 'In the meantime, my colleagues can't wait to hear your version of events.'

FIFTY-SIX

Kay flicked the blinds at the window of Sharp's office and watched as Kenneth Archerton was marched across the car park to the cells on the ground floor.

The man appeared defiant despite his predicament, his chin jutting out and his shoulders straight.

'I thought I heard reports he had a heart attack at the scene,' said Sharp as he joined her.

'Self-induced panic attack,' said Kay, and grinned. 'The paramedic saw straight through it and cleared him for questioning.'

'I'll report back to the Chief Super at Headquarters,' said Sharp. 'At least that'll free up you and Barnes to interview Ken. Carys and Piper can handle Beatrice. Have you got everything you need?'

Kay held up the manila folder in her hand. 'Debbie and Gavin have collated everything, and I've made some extra notes.'

Sharp turned his attention back to the car park as Barnes and Carys climbed out of their pool car and hurried towards the building. He smiled.

'Keep an eye on that one,' he said.

'Who? Carys?' Kay frowned. 'What do you mean?'

'I mean, it's only a matter of time before she's going to want to stretch her wings beyond this station. We don't have any roles available in the area for her, Kay – not with our budgets being stripped back the way they have been. She's going to want to start taking on more responsibility after this one.'

'Oh.'

A sadness swept through her as she absorbed Sharp's words. She knew no investigation team could expect to work together for their entire careers, but the thought of losing one of her key people, and a friend and close colleague at that, left her melancholy.

'Don't worry,' said Sharp. 'I'm sure we'll have enough to keep her busy for a while yet. We'll simply have to support her as much as we can when she makes that decision.'

'And stop her getting bored in the meantime,' said Kay. 'Idle hands, and all that.'

'I'll make a manager out of you yet.'

She laughed, and slapped the folder against his arm. 'No, thanks.'

Checking his watch, Sharp moved back to his desk and folded his jacket over his arm. 'Right, I'm off to HQ. Give me a call if you need me.'

'Will do. Oh – before you go, Adam and I are having a barbecue tonight – just a few of us, as a way to wind down after this week. Do you and Rebecca want to come along?'

He winked. 'Wouldn't miss it. Tell Adam I'll bring some beer.'

'Okay, thanks. See you later.'

Barnes appeared at the door, and nodded to the DCI before turning his attention to Kay. 'Are you ready?'

'Yes.' She fell into step beside him once they were in the corridor. 'How is he?'

'Meek, especially once the paramedics told him within earshot of us that he was fit and healthy.'

'Nice try.'

'He isn't the first one, and won't be the last.'

'How was Alice when you got her home?'

'Quiet. Exhausted, I imagine. I had a word with Bethany – she's going to give Annette a call with the details of a child psychologist she works with from time to time, and we've set a time for Bethany to do her formal interview tomorrow morning.'

'Where are they now? You didn't take Alice back to Ken's house, did you?'

'Only briefly, to give Annette time to pack a couple of suitcases. She's going to stay with a friend in Maidenhead for a couple of weeks, to give it time for things to calm down here.' He held up an evidence bag with the toy rabbit inside. 'There is one thing – Ken didn't give Alice this. She admitted that she found this in her grandfather's study the morning Greg took her out on the boat. She isn't meant to go in there, apparently but Greg and Annette were talking in the kitchen about some last minute arrangements and she sneaked inside. When she saw the rabbit, she couldn't resist putting it in her backpack. She assumed Kenneth was going to give it to her as a present anyway.'

'Bloody hell. Right, well shall we see what Mr Archerton has to say for himself?'

Kay pushed open the door to the interview room. She nodded to Archerton's solicitor, then waited until Barnes had started the recording. She didn't waste time.

'Tell us about the toy factories in northern France, Ken. What do they have to do with a successful wine merchant?'

'No idea.'

Kay pushed the bagged toy rabbit across the table. 'Here's what we think, Ken. You got greedy. You wanted more money, and you met Beatrice Caron on one of your excursions to France. Whose idea was it to move into drug smuggling? Yours, or hers?'

When he didn't respond, she shrugged and continued. 'We found a quantity of tablets inside this. This is how you planned to smuggle in the drugs, wasn't it? Except your granddaughter found it in your study and took it, because she thought it was meant for her. Then, when you shot her father and she had to flee with Greg, she dropped it by accident. We weren't meant to find it, were we? Is that when it all started to go wrong?'

She waited, glaring at the man before her.

'We've had officers conducting a search of your property,' said Barnes. 'They've shown a particular interest in the toys labelled "*Fabriqué en France*" in a box under your desk in your study. Four more of them, apparently. What do you think we'll find when we cut them open?

Kenneth ground his teeth, his nostrils flaring.

'Who's in Manchester, Ken? Not a medical specialist, I'll bet.'

'What were you going to do, Ken?' said Kay, not waiting for his answer. 'Distribute them as samples, and then set up a supply chain to channel your drugs through to users? People could buy the toys as if they were for their kids, and instead get hold of the pills, couldn't they?'

Archerton patted his hand against his chest. 'You don't understand, Detective Hunter. It was Robert's idea. He threatened me. He was the one with the gun.'

'Then perhaps you could enlighten us as to what happened that night,' she said. 'Because, as far as I can see, it was Robert who uncovered your plans and tried to stop you.'

'I don't know what got into him. He'd been acting strange the weekend before he went to France, as if something was on his mind.' He closed his eyes, his hand dropping to the table. 'I wonder how I could have been so stupid. It's clear to me now that he wanted me out of the way so he could take over the business.'

'Seems a bit extreme – shooting you,' said Barnes. 'Most people would make a cash offer.'

Archerton glared at the detective sergeant. 'Like I said, he'd been acting strange. That's why I went to the boat. I knew from Annette that Greg had taken Alice away for the night. I thought if his brother was there as well, I could make him see sense.'

'Explain the payments made into his and Annette's bank account,' said Kay. She pushed across copies of the documentation and tapped her finger on the entries. 'Eight thousand pounds in April. Twelve thousand pounds in May. What were they for?'

'They were loyalty payments,' said Ken. 'I didn't want to lose him to a competitor.'

'How did you know Robert had come back to England and gone to the boat last Friday?'

'I can't recall. Annette or Greg must've mentioned it.'

'What went wrong?' said Kay.

'Greg and Alice were nowhere to be seen when I got to the boat. All I wanted to do was talk, but Robert wouldn't have it. He must've hidden the gun on the deck when he saw me approaching. The next thing I knew, he was waving it at me, telling me that I was no good to anyone in my state of health, and that I should've handed over the business to him so he could provide for my daughter and granddaughter.' A ragged breath escaped his lips. 'It happened so fast. I lunged at him, thinking I could knock the gun out of his hand and into the water, but it... it went off. I panicked. I didn't know what to do.'

'What did you do with the gun?'

Archerton swallowed. 'Nothing. It fell in the water.'

Kay leaned back in her chair and drummed her fingers on the table, watching the man in front of her. She stopped, and waited.

For a moment, the only sound in the room was the steady beat of the clock above the door and the scratch of the solicitor's fountain pen across his notebook.

She paused, biding her time in the knowledge that the combined efforts of her team over the past week had come to this. A wave of adrenalin shot through her as she raised her head.

'That's an engaging story, Mr Archerton. But that's all it is – a story, isn't it? Like the multiple sclerosis and the chest pains?'

He frowned, then looked at his solicitor and back to her. 'What do you mean? It's the truth. I didn't mean to kill Robert. It was an accident.'

Pulling out one of the photographs from the post mortem, Kay slid it across the table to Archerton. 'You're a liar, Ken. Robert Victor was shot in the back of the head at close range. You executed him.'

She watched as his solicitor's Adam's apple bobbed in his throat, and then folded her arms on the table. 'The gun didn't go in the water, either. Our underwater search team found nothing, and the current isn't strong enough to carry a weapon downstream. There were no casings either, which tells me you not only shot Robert Victor, you took the time to pick up the casings before leaving the boat.'

'You can't prove anything,' Archerton said, a snarl in his voice.

Kay caught Barnes's sideways glance, and smiled.

'That's where you're wrong, Mr Archerton,' she said, and flipped open the folder. 'My team have been extremely thorough in their work. Shall we try again, starting with the gun we found inside the safe and the remnants of burned clothing in the hearth in your study?'

FIFTY-SEVEN

Adam chopped the last of the tomatoes, fresh from the garden, and tipped them into the bowl of salad leaves and dressing before handing it to Kay.

'Right, that's the last of it. Let Barnes know he might want to put the meat on the barbecue – that breeze is getting chilly out there.'

'Yes, chef.'

She grinned, picked up her wine glass and padded out the back door into the garden, her flip flops slapping against the paving slabs.

Pia, Barnes's partner, stood up as she approached the table and pushed aside napkins and condiments to make room for the salad, and then reached down into a bucket of ice and pulled out a bottle of beer. She passed it to Barnes as he pushed back his chair.

'Cheers,' he said, as Adam joined them. 'Here's to a good result, guv.'

'Team effort,' said Kay. 'As always. Carys – are you joining us? The food will be ready in a minute.'

The detective constable put down the chicken she'd located in the flowerbed, and wandered across the lawn to where they sat. 'She was looking for worms, I think.'

'They're perpetually hungry,' said Adam. He gently nudged a second chicken out from under the table and watched with a smile as it scurried away before stopping to peck at something it found next to the doorstep. 'Needless to say, there's steak and sausages on the menu tonight.'

'Those three are too scrawny, anyway,' said Barnes.

He stabbed at the meat with a set of tongs, the aroma of spices and herbs Adam had used to marinate the food wafting across to the table.

'Did you manage to get the charges you wanted against Kenneth Archerton?' said Pia.

'Yes,' said Kay. 'Once we presented the evidence we had against him, he confessed everything. He'd gone to the boat to try to persuade Robert to see sense, and when he couldn't convince him, he shot him. He viewed him as too much of a risk. That's why the boat was ransacked – Ken was after the rabbit Alice had taken, and any evidence Robert might have hidden in relation to the smuggling operation.'

'What about the Frenchwoman Ian mentioned to me?' said Pia.

'Beatrice decided to talk once we matched her fingerprints to the traces found on the waterproof lining inside the toy rabbit,' said Gavin. 'She's trying to blame Ken, but I have a feeling they were business partners in all this. She was the one who alerted him to the fact Robert had been spotted at the toy factory in Laval, and we think she arranged for him to be followed back to Kent. She drew the line at killing him, though.'

'Ken told us she reckoned Robert was his problem to sort out,' said Kay. 'We'll have to start the process next week to get her extradited to France at some point. Our colleagues over there have wanted to have a chat with her for some time now. Apparently, her real name is Michelle Dubois, which is why her passport was never flagged when she entered the UK – it's fake.'

'Did you find who he was working with in Manchester?' said Adam.

'Yes, and we've passed on details of that aspect of the smuggling operation to our colleagues up there.'

'Poor Alice,' said Barnes. 'I hope she's going to be all right after all this.'

Kay's stomach roared.

'Heard that,' said Sharp.

Rebecca, his wife, rolled her eyes. 'Leave the woman alone – she's been busy.'

'Just a bit,' said Kay. She shaded her eyes against the setting sun. 'Did Debbie sort out the roster for the rest of the weekend?'

'Yes – you're all off until Monday morning,' said Sharp. 'A well-deserved break, I think it's called.'

'Good,' said Gavin, draining his wine glass. 'Hey, this wasn't French by any chance, was it?'

Adam laughed. 'No – it's from New Zealand. Drink up.'

'In that case, can I leave my car here tonight? I'll get a taxi home and pick it up in the morning.'

'Sure,' said Kay. 'Hang on – I'll go and get another bottle out the fridge.'

'I can—'

'No, you're okay. I want to get a sweatshirt to put on anyway. Everyone else warm enough?'

A murmur of voices answered her, and satisfied her guests were comfortable, Kay walked into the kitchen, left her wineglass on the centre worktop and hurried upstairs.

Laughter from the garden floated up through the open window of their bedroom, and she smiled at the sound of Barnes teasing Carys. No doubt the detective constable was making friends with another of the chickens.

Opening a drawer, she pulled out an old favourite sweatshirt, ran her fingers through her hair, and made her way back out to the landing.

She stopped outside the spare room they now used as an office.

A toy bear sat on the corner of her desk, one of its ears lopsided.

She frowned, then walked across the carpet and plucked it up.

Turning it over in her hands, she tried to ignore the ache in her heart. Instead, she peered at the seam on its bottom, and held out the label so she could read it.

Made in Britain.

Kay exhaled.

She put the bear back, patted it on the head, and then hurried downstairs to sort out the wine for Gavin.

When she reached the hallway, a strange sound reached her from the kitchen. She could still hear her colleagues and Adam out in the garden, the sizzle and crack of the meat on the barbecue, but this was different.

'Oh, no…'

She hurried to the door in time to see Mabel, the larger of the two chickens, flutter off the worktop before strutting to the back door.

'If you've crapped in my kitchen, you're going to be in so much trouble.'

She crossed over to the worktop, moved the pile of magazines and cookery books stacked against the knife block, then stopped.

'Adam!'

'Yes?' His voice carried an edge of concern. 'What's up?'

'One of your chickens has laid a bloody egg on the kitchen worktop!'

Raucous laughter filtered through from the garden.

The chicken paused on the doorstep, its beady eyes appraising her.

She glared at it.

Adam appeared at the back door, looking as if he'd at least tried to set a straight face. He picked up the bird and held her to his chest, a smile twitching at the corner of his mouth as he smoothed her feathers, and then winked.

'I don't suppose you fancy an omelette for breakfast tomorrow morning, then?'

THE END

Dear Reader,

Thank you for choosing to read *Cradle to Grave*. I hope you enjoyed the eighth book in the Detective Kay Hunter series.

If you did enjoy it, I'd be grateful if you could write a review. It doesn't have to be long, just a few words, but it really is the best way for me to help new readers discover one of my books for the first time.

If you'd like to stay up to date with my new releases, as well as exclusive competitions and giveaways, you're welcome to join my Reader Group at my website, www.rachelamphlett.com.

You can also contact me via Facebook, Twitter, or by email.

I love hearing from readers – I read every message and will always reply.

Thanks again for your support.

Best wishes,
    Rachel Amphlett

Made in United States
North Haven, CT
10 October 2022

25256477R00221